The Twins of the Golden City

Rachel Drummey

Dear Sarah and Matt,
Happy Reading!
    Rachel Drummey

P R E S S

Blue Mustang Press
Boston, Massachusetts

First printing

Cover Images. Thanks and Credits:
Castle Image - Ruth Whistler
Background Image - Joanna Gait

ISBN 978-0-9759737-8-3
PUBLISHED BY BLUE MUSTANG PRESS
www.BlueMustangPress.com
Boston, Massachusetts

Printed in the United States of America

For my mother, whose limitless love and support have made my dreams seem tangible, and my father, whose advice and affection have guided me through even the roughest waters.

~ RD

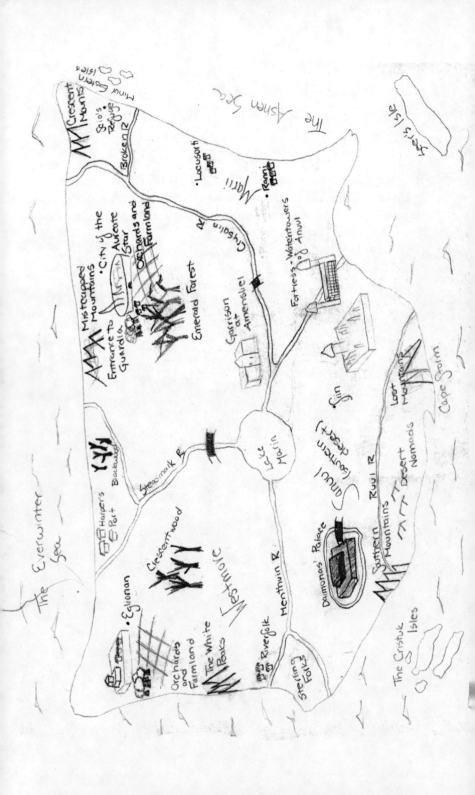

Two infants into bondage born
will from their mother's breast be torn,
one by golden soldier saved,
the other turned to evil's slave.
Into a hero one will grow,
the other bend to serve the shadow.
Cast into dark the world will be,
Until the twain fulfill their destiny.
One will fall, the other reign;
one a monarch, the other slain.
All these things shall come to be:
So says the Oracle of the Ashen Sea.

Chapter One
The Castle in the Desert

Pain…fiery, aching pain…

The girl licked her dry lips with a swollen tongue and opened her fever-rimmed eyes. The rhythmic crunching of approaching footsteps made her lift her head. Though the night sky had dyed the sand a deep azure, the swollen ivory moon cast a glow on the desert plains, and so the girl could see the boots of the man who now stood by her, a svelte bounty hunter wrapped in a black cloak, with a black scarf masking his nose and mouth.

There was an arrow embedded in the flesh of the girl's arm. The bounty hunter bent and brushed his fingers against the shaft, and the girl pulled away with a shuddering gasp. A second crossbow bolt had pierced her calf.

The man's pantherine eyes glittered in the moonlight. He glanced back at his muscular, black charger. The horse stamped and snorted, waiting.

The bounty hunter slid one arm under the wounded girl's legs and the other around her neck, lifting her effortlessly from the sand. Too weak to resist, she only moaned softly in protest as he carried her to his steed and placed her in the saddle. He swung on behind her and wrapped her in an imprisoning embrace, clutching the bridle in callused hands. At a flick of its master's heels, the horse bounded forward, a black blaze beneath a creamy moon.

***

Here in the desert the vast sands stretch for miles, swirling in the wind, whispering to the night. This land has barely known man's interference apart from the footsteps of nomads and the tread of their camels. Their fires dot the desert, their tents pitched like groupings of tiny mountains. Apart from these, this desert country has known the ambition of man in only one other instance.

It stands still in the form of a black-bricked palace, gargantuan, a monstrosity that looms on the very edge of the desert, where the sands run into the mountains. It is forsaken by natives and by the desert creatures, an alien scar on the otherwise pristine landscape.

This palace was the bounty hunter's destination.

His captive had passed from consciousness; she was slumped forward against his horse's thrusting neck, her limp fingers caught in its mane.

A moat of churning, fiery liquid surrounded the black palace, otherworldly in its heat and anger. The charger did not shy at the sight of the fervid moat, but shot across the iron bridge that spanned it, through air that was glassy with heat. Two cloaked and hooded guards waited at the entrance, each bearing a staff with a crescent blade fixed on the end. When the bounty hunter reached the entrance, the guards crossed their weapons, barring his way.

"What business brings you to our master's castle?" rasped one of the guards. He spoke in Histuk, a complex dialect of the South, rich with clicks and hisses.

The bounty hunter grabbed a fistful of his captive's fair hair and wrenched her head to the side so that the guards could see her face. Slowly, they raised their staffs and stepped aside. The dark rider nudged his horse into a walk and entered the antechamber of the palace.

The courser's hooves clicked on the cobbled floor within. The rider dismounted and carefully lifted the unconscious girl from the saddle. They stood before a staircase; already a man had appeared at the top of the steps and begun to descend.

He was tall and very thin, brown-skinned, with pale blue eyes that stood out strangely against his dark skin. His head and face were cleanly shaved in keeping with Sanuulian style; his loose cotton shirt was dyed a deep scarlet, and when he spoke, it was in perfect Sanuulian.

"Excellent work, Mallin." At the sound of his deep vice, the girl stirred and blinked dazedly in the bounty hunter's arms.

"Is she badly injured?" the man inquired.

Mallin did not answer, but allowed his employer to examine the girl's wounds. Only half-conscious, she murmured something inaudible and turned her head. Her cheeks were flushed and warm to the touch.

"Sick, as well as wounded," the man observed, with a nefarious smile. "I see the Keeping Stone is doing its job well." He removed a soft leather boot from the girl's foot to reveal a mutilated ankle. At the center of a web of white scars was a gleaming, red stone, set into the girl's flesh. He licked the tip of his finger and tapped the gem. It sizzled, and the girl arched her back in Mallin's arms with a gasp of pain. The man smiled again.

"I imagine that this experience will discourage any further escape attempts. Thank you Mallin. You have done well, as always." He held out a small pouch.

Mallin set the girl on the ground in a heap and accepted his reward. Coins clinked loudly when the pouch dropped into Mallin's hand, the sound ricocheting off the walls of the antechamber. He weighed the payment in his palm, and then, with only a nod to his employer, Mallin remounted and exited the palace.

The man looked down with contempt at the girl, who, slowly regaining consciousness, was trembling on the floor. With a snapped word in Histuk, he summoned two guards from the shadows. "Lord Pioni," they said, bowing their heads.

"Take her to the first cell. Lock the door, but do not put her in irons; it is not necessary, and we will not risk further injury." Beneath a calm exterior, Pioni was nervous. "See to it that no one but myself enters. Weak and feverish as she is, this is not a true concern, but should she again attempt escape, restrain her, *but see that she comes to no further harm.*"

The guards bowed in unison. One lifted the girl from the floor; the other led the descent down a staircase that wound deep into the bowels of the palace. Watching them go, Pioni, eyes uneasy, placed his hand against one of the black stones in the wall, muttering in a tongue older and icier than Histuk. The instant his hand touched it, the wall flickered, revealing a room beyond it. Pioni cast a furtive glance behind him and stepped through the wall, into the room. After he had entered, the wall shimmered back into solidity, separating the room from the antechamber, and from any prying eyes.

The only object within the hidden room was pedestal made of black marble and a red-veined orb that rested on top of it. Pioni knelt before the pedestal and placed his hand on the globe. At his touch, a swirling, red mist appeared within the orb. Slowly, a pair of silver eyes with black, snake-like slits for pupils, materialized within the mist.

"Is it done?" there were no lips through which the voice could come; it sounded within Pioni's head.

"I've retrieved the girl, Master, and I assure you that this incident will not be repeated."

"No, it will not," the voice agreed ominously. "Remember, Pioni, that I placed her in your keeping because I trusted you to confine her well. Do not betray my trust."

"Never, my lord!" Pioni's fingers quivered on the stone.

"And is she badly injured?"

Lord Pioni hesitated. "There is nothing wrong with her that is beyond my skill to heal. She will recover quickly."

"She had better. She is all we have. Because of your failure seventeen years ago—" Pioni cringed "—she is invaluable to us. You know this."

"Yes, my lord."

"I will arrive to check your progress in three weeks."

"Yes, my lord."

"It would behoove you to see to it that she has returned to full health by that time."

"Yes, my lord."

The eyes faded; empty, crimson fog swirled inside the globe for several seconds, then disappeared.

Pioni got to his feet. "I will heal her," he vowed as he swept across the room. "It will be swift and painful, and she will learn to never do this again."

He stalked back into antechamber and down the staircase, into the dungeons. Two guards stood stiffly on either side of the door. Pioni waved his hand dismissively and they parted. From his belt Pioni drew a ring heavy with many keys; he unlocked the door and shoved it open.

The girl was sitting with her back against the stone wall of the cell, her head on her chest, her shoulders slumped. She raised her head at the sound of the door.

Pioni swept across the cell, curled his fingers around the shaft of the arrow in the girl's arm and wrenched it from her flesh. The skin tore and blood poured in thick rivulets from the wound. The girl shrieked in pain and then slumped, once again unconscious.

Outside, the guards were as still as statues.

Chapter Two
The Prisoner and the Pendant

A hazy, gray light filtered into the cell as dawn broke over the desert. Lena, Pioni's wounded prisoner, stirred on the cell floor. She wore a simple, black tunic, white hose, and boots. These were the clothes of a warrior, not typical garb for a young woman. The tunic itself was unusual in that it bore no mark, as most did, of king or nation; not the golden star of Aurea, or the golden leaf of Westmore, or the silver-crested waves of Marii, or even the scarlet viper of Sanuul, the southern desert country in which Lena now found herself.

She was fair-skinned, with golden curls that fell to her shoulders. Her cheeks were dappled with freckles, her eyes a brilliant shade of green. No stranger to mistreatment, Lena bore scrapes and bruises and several scars. Calluses showed on hands that were accustomed to hard labor. She was thin, not malnourished, but wiry, mostly muscle.

Though her limbs still throbbed where arrows had been rooted in her skin, Lena was aware of the cleansing sting of a salve and saw that her wounds had been bandaged. The dreary, early light revealed a large, stone basin filled with water. A ladle was beside the bowl; Lena pulled herself over to the basin and began to drink.

A shadow shifted in the corner and Lena started, having thought she was alone in the cell. Pioni stepped into the gray light, his blue eyes flashing with anger.

Those strange blue eyes were a sure mark of his heritage; the only Sanuulians with blue eyes were those who had been born of a union between one of the deep desert people, dark-skinned, dark-haired, dark-eyed, and one of a number of Aurean colonists who had once tried to conquer the desert lands but had proved unequal to the heat and hostility of the wasteland. The colonists had not been well liked overall by the Sanuulians, and the generation of mixed children they had left behind were among the most scorned of races, welcomed neither by the Aureans nor the Sanuulians. Tensions stretched thinner by the day between the two countries, and the worse their relations, the more despised the children of their one-time unions became. Many of this hated ancestry sought refuge in the solitude of the desert; many had joined Pioni's service as guards.

"What did I do wrong, Lena?" Pioni asked, his voice dangerously soft. He crouched before her to look her in the eye. "I've always worked so hard to discourage escape attempts."

Lena tried to speak but could only manage an inarticulate mumble.

"You are weak." Pioni stood. "The Keeping Stone has passed your test of its strength, has it not?" He began to pace in front of her. "You have caused quite a bit of trouble, Lena. My master will arrive in three weeks. You will be healthy by then; healthy enough to provide him with an adequate display of your talents. Your little stunt has shunted us both out of his good graces. A demonstration of your skills may be enough to reaffirm his approval." Pioni crouched and grabbed a fistful of Lena's hair, pulling her face close to his. "You will not fail me," he growled.

***

The days passed, and Lena slowly regained her health. Pioni changed her bandages three times a day, cleaning them, applying salve, and watching for infection. Though he did so angrily, he was careful, the necessity of curing her quickly overcoming his desire to see her suffer. He took her outside every day so she could exercise her wounded leg. Gradually, the limp disappeared, and she was able to run again. Pioni monitored her food and water intake, making sure that she ate and drank enough each day. Under his grudgingly attentive care, Lena had returned to full health within three weeks.

In the early morning of the day that Pioni's master was slated to arrive, the door to her cell creaked open, and two of Pioni's cloaked guards hobbled toward her. Though the guards were difficult to tell apart as they typically wore scarves over their mouths and noses to protect them from the elements when they were outside, Lena identified one of them by the scar across his right eye. Lena and this guard shared a mutual hatred for one another. She had felt the back of his hand on dozens of occasions, but had kept the score even with reciprocal bites and scratches.

Now he grabbed Lena's arm and hauled her to her feet, careful to press his fingers most tightly against the tender, pink scar on her arm where the arrow had left its mark. "Up, slave," he growled in Histuk, enjoying Lena's hiss of pain.

Lena swore in the same language and wrenched her arm out of his grasp. The guard snarled and raised his arm. Lena's eyes dared him to let the blow fall, knowing that, today, he had orders not to harm her. He dropped his hand with a grimace, and Lena spat at him. This was too much to bear; he reached out to grab her, but the other guard pushed him away and walked Lena through the door. The other followed, muttering angrily.

They took her down a corridor that stopped at the entrance of a cavernous room. "Take this and wait here," the half-blind guard hissed, viciously thrusting a sheathed sword into Lena's arms. The two swept out, leaving Lena alone.

Despite her earlier bravado, Lena's muscles were taut with nervousness. She drew the sword the guard had given her partway out of the leather scabbard. As she examined the gleaming weapon, she caught sight of her own, frightened reflection in the specular blade.

Footsteps echoed in the corridor outside, and a cloaked man entered, Pioni trailing reverently.

The appearance of the second man cannot be described using the typical terms, because this man could no more be compared to other human beings than a bear could be to an insect. It was not so much that he was a large man as it was that when he entered a room his surroundings seemed to bend around him and lose their proportions. He was similar to a mountain in that everything else was shrunken and insignificant next to him, but *he* was not out of place; everything *else* was the wrong shape. Or perhaps he was more like a volcano, in that he carried himself with a sense of immense power, as well as a sense that he might at any moment erupt.

His physical characteristics were in and of themselves not especially extraordinary—thick and wild black hair, tan skin, broad shoulders—except for his eyes, which were so dark and deep that it was difficult to distinguish the pupil from the iris. In addition to this, if one could bear to meet and hold his gaze, it would have been noted that little silver sparks danced like lightning through his eyes.

At the sight of this man, the blood drained from Lena's face. She dropped to her knees at once and bowed her head. "Master."

"Rise, child, and let me look at you." Like the man himself, his voice was overwhelming; rather than heard it was absorbed to fill the body entirely, leaving the listener trembling, feeling its echoes within.

Lena stood but did not lift her gaze.

The man closed his eyes and began to take slow, deep breaths as if to inhale some part of Lena's aura. Goosebumps rose on her skin as he reached out to touch her cheek.

"She is powerful…very powerful…yes…" the man croaked. A reptilian smile split his sallow face. "I can feel it." His eyes opened. "Let us see how she has progressed since my last visit."

Pioni drew a long, slender sword from its scabbard. Lena unsheathed her own blade with trembling fingers.

Pioni swung first. His blade clashed with Lena's as she brought it upward in a swift block. She spun and cut her sword downwards in an attempt to strike Pioni's thigh. He parried it just in time and countered her with a powerful thrust of his sword.

She leaped away from him; Pioni thrust his hand to his side, and a sparkling globe of scarlet fire grew in his palm. He flung it at Lena, who dove to the floor to avoid it. The sphere hurtled past her and struck the wall, leaving a scorch mark on the stone.

Pioni charged as Lena was getting to her feet; he reached her at full tilt and forced her back, against a wall. "Respond in kind!" he hissed. "I've shown my soulfire, but it is not mine he's come to see. He knows you struggle with it; show him you've progressed!"

Lena pushed him away and darted back a few steps. Pioni raised his sword; Lena met it with her own, and the two blades locked. Pioni placed both hands on the hilt to overpower her; Lena used only one. She felt her muscles quiver under the strain, but it bought her just enough time. She swept her other hand out at Pioni; an invisible blast swept him off his feet. Lena circled, twirling her blade. He rose quickly, forcing her back with a torrent of blows that Lena struggled to keep up with. The last one of these was powerful enough send Lena stumbling. Before she regained her balance, Pioni extended his hand, and his unseen power lifted her up and flung her against the stone wall. The impact brought a cry of pain from Lena; she slid down the wall and landed in a crumpled heap. Pioni came at her swiftly, wielding his sword above her head. She rolled out of the way, struggled to her feet and made a clumsy, one-handed swing at his side. Pioni stepped out of the way and let her momentum carry her into an adjoining corridor. Lena regained her balance and sprinted away down the hall, Pioni following closely. The man in the hooded cloak glided behind the pair.

Slowed by a twinge in her injured leg and sensing Pioni was gaining, Lena stopped at a flight of stairs. She whirled to block Pioni, who was hurtling toward her with gritted teeth. Their blades clashed; the force of the blow knocked Lena down the stairs.

Pioni ran nimbly down the steps. Lena hit the cold floor of the next landing and scrambled away. "Soulfire!" Pioni barked at her. "Now!"

Dazed, Lena tried to obey, but she had never mastered this power, and now was a poor time to try. When she raised her hand, few sparks collected in her palm but died before they amounted to anything. Pioni was striding quickly toward her. She scrambled backward a little more and flicked her fingers. The hem of Pioni's robe rippled, but nothing else happened.

Pioni stopped and brought more sparks to his palm. It grew quickly into another garnet globe. Cursing herself, Lena braced herself for the blow. Pioni raised his palm, about to throw the glowing sphere at Lena, but the man at the top of the stairs spoke. "That is enough."

The bottom of his black cloak trailed behind him as he walked down the steps. Lena got to her feet and wiped a trickle blood from her lip. "Impressive," the robed man conceded. "Although her soulfire still leaves something to be desired."

"Please excuse her, master," Pioni answered, with a glare at Lena. "She has been very ill."

"Ah, yes. The work of your Keeping Stone, was it not? A very impressive piece of work, I must say, Pioni."

"Thank you, Master," Pioni said hesitantly.

"Now, I would like a while alone with her. Leave us, Pioni. And see that we are not interrupted."

Lena's face had flushed with exertion; now the color seeped away again. Pioni, slightly miffed at the dismissal, swept out of the room.

Lena dared not raise her eyes to look at the cloaked man. He took a deep breath and paced in a wide circle around her.

"I can feel that you are afraid," he told her. "Fear is good—you can learn from fear. But you need other attributes to win battles, Lena. You need anger, and you need confidence, and you need a lust for victory."

Lena had fixed her eyes on a spot on the floor and would not raise them from it.

The man continued. "You must learn greed…greed for the blood of your opponent…these emotions, Lena, will help you defeat your adversaries."

Lena's eyes still did not move, but her breathing quickened.

The man stopped and stepped in close to Lena. "You feel it," he whispered. His breath was hot and putrid against her pale face. "You desire it…you know what you are capable of achieving. You know what is in you. Imagine, Lena, punishing Pioni for everything he has done to you…imagine at last reaping revenge on the half-blind guard…"

Lena's skin prickled. He had pulled a memory from her mind.

"Let your passion rule you, Lena," he went on, his voice was as thick and sweet as honey. "Reach for the greatness you could possess. You could be the best, Lena. You could be my champion."

17

Lena was trembling. Her voice came out in a hollow whisper. "No."

The man's eyes narrowed. His voice suddenly lost its guile and became ugly and harsh. "What did you say?"

"No, my lord. I do not possess the traits that you have mentioned. I cannot be your champion." Her voice quivered.

"Fool!" The man struck Lena with a blow that held surprising force. She fell to the ground and scrambled away as he towered before her. The meager light that the room held seemed to drain from its walls; tongues of shadow gathered at his fingertips. He lunged toward her, and all at once he changed. His skin transformed from bronze to black, deep black, like the night sky. His veins were silver, like jagged lightning against his skin. His hair lengthened and fell down his back in long, silver snarls; he curled his lips to show teeth that had become fangs.

"I offer you power! I offer you glory! Such offers from the High Lord Daimonas are rarely given and should never be treated cavalierly!" His voice had changed, too, no more soft or coalescing, but harsh and abusive.

Lena cowered against the wall, trembling, crying from fright."My lord, my master, please! Only hear what I have to say!"

"What reason can you have for refusing my generous proposals? For denying me the rights I won when I placed you, a worthless slave-child, into the care of Lord Pioni? I saved you from a life of servitude and saw to it that you received the highest quality of training. Now you tell me after reaping the benefits of my actions that you will not support me? That you will not defend the one who snatched you from the jaws of doom when you were too weak to save yourself? Without my intervention, you, Lena, would be nothing!"

"Master, listen to me, please!" Lena begged. "I only fear that I— I cannot defend you well enough. As you say you saved—" the word seemed to choke her, but she pushed on "—*saved* me long ago. I could not bear it if you were injured when it was my task to defend you. I do not deserve the honor that you offer me, my lord."

Her pleas appeased him. He slipped fluidly back into human form, and smiled. His voice dropped from an enraged bellow to an enticing hiss. "Why do you say this? Why do you not have pride in your talents? You are gifted. Let me show you the way to greatness."

"Master, tell me what evils you fear. I have no knowledge of the world outside this desert, no knowledge of what lies beyond the confines of the sand dunes. What people wish to harm you?" Lena kept her face impassive, but within, her heart battered against her rib cage. The desert was her prison…the thirst for knowledge of the outside world was almost unbearable.

Daimonas did not answer at once. "Knowledge can be dangerous," he said at last. "But I will tell you what you wish to know. There is a league, far to the north, in the land of Aurea, of people who fear the power that I have spoken of to you. They are weak. They feel that some skills, such as those that you have learned from Lord Pioni, are too dangerous to be meddled with. They will not admit that only people of a certain caliber—a caliber of which they themselves fall short—are capable of achieving what you have achieved, of attaining the skills and glory which can be yours." He gazed at Lena to read her reaction.

She trembled. "But master, if they are so weak, why do you fear them?"

A red tint appeared in Daimonas's cheeks. "I do not fear them! The High Lord fears no one!"

Lena drew closer to the wall, and the angry glow faded. Daimonas smiled. "I forget how naVve you are. Any insurgence that threatens our teachings, no matter how pathetic, must be stopped immediately. Left alone, it could grow into a veritable threat. Besides, the recreants in Aurea spit on all of our beliefs. Allowing their small rebellion to continue would be an insult to our tenets." He crouched so he could look her full in the face. "That is all you need know in order to understand my reasons for desiring a warrior."

"Do they have no powers, master? No training, no skills?"

Daimonas hesitated for the second time. He straightened and began to pace again. "The form of power we study, Lena, in combination with the method of combat training Lord Pioni provides

19

for you, is an ancient art form, but has not been practiced for centuries. There is a lighter side, a *weaker* side, of the same power. It is this feeble side that the Aurean rebels employ in battle. Admittedly, some of them have become strong through their studies, but none of them could ever rival you. Their prospective champion is a boy your own age. The Aureans raised him, just as we have raised you. Had he been brought here at a young age, it might have been possible to train him to be just as powerful as you will become, but because the Aureans got to him first, it is unlikely he will ever reach your level of expertise."

"He is the one you want me to fight," Lena whispered. "You want me to kill him."

"Once he is out of the way, the rest of his kind will crumble. It will be very easy, Lena. Very easy. You are not ready yet, but soon you will be able to defeat him."

"I couldn't Master…" Lena's voice was hoarse. "I couldn't kill anyone."

Daimonas's eyes laughed. "What do you think all your training has been for, Lena? Did you think it was a game?" He seemed to think for a moment. A grin slid across his face. "You think you lack the ability to kill? Perhaps all you need is practice. Guards!"

The two that had escorted Lena from her cell glided into the room.

"Bring in the prisoner from the North!" Daimonas commanded. "And fetch Lord Pioni."

He had turned away from Lena, who was still backed against the wall. She got to her feet and watched with terror in her eyes as the guards returned escorting a man with a shaggy mane of golden hair. His face was haggard and splotched with abrasions. One of his eyes was blackened, and if left unsupported, he had to lean against the wall to remain upright.

Pioni entered the room only moments after the guards brought in their prisoner. He glanced from the wounded man to Daimonas to Lena, who was trembling.

"Ah, Lord Pioni." Daimonas was bloated with satisfaction. "Lena was about to give us another demonstration of her talent." He turned to Lena. "Kill the prisoner."

20

"Master…" Lena looked at the captive.

"Do it!" Daimonas hissed.

"He is unarmed!" Lena protested.

"All the more beneficial to you!" Daimonas snapped. "Do it, or suffer the consequences yourself!" He thrust his hand toward her, and Lena fell to her knees, clutching her stomach. Traces of Daimonas's magic flickered at her waist. He let her writhe for a moment, then released her. "Kill him!" he hissed again. "I will begin the job for you." He turned his hands to the wounded captive. Black fire shot from his fingertips and wrapped around the man, who clutched his throat and began to choke.

Lena watched with tears in her eyes. "No, stop! Please!" she begged.

"You have your sword!" Pioni hissed. "Finish him!"

Lena brushed her fingers against the hilt of the hated weapon. She got to her feet, drew it from its sheath and approached the prisoner. Daimonas stemmed the flow of black fire that flew from his fingertips. The prisoner struggled to his feet.

Daimonas and Pioni watched as Lena crept toward the man. The prisoner took a step back, slipped and fell. Too weak to get up, he lay on the floor and watched Lena approach.

She dropped to her knees before him, the blade in her timorous grasp. Tears fell freely now. Some splashed onto the man's chest, others were caught in his golden beard.

"Do it now," Daimonas urged.

Lena still did not raise her sword. Her breath came in short gasps. Something brushed against her knee and she looked down. The man had pressed his callused fingertips against her leg. She met his gaze but did not find the fear and loathing she had expected; instead there was a calm serenity in his hazel eyes. It was then that Lena heard something that was unlike anything she had ever experienced. There was a sound, a voice inside her head, gentle, confidant, and soothing.

Do not be afraid.

Lena gazed into the face of the prisoner, and miraculously, without even having tried to speak to him in return, she heard her own voice reply, *But I am afraid.*

21

Take this. She looked down. The man clutched a golden chain in his hand.

What is it?

It will guide you. You must get to the City of the Aureate Star.

Where?

The City of the Aureate Star, the capital city of Aurea. The pendant will guide you. There is not time to explain now. Once you have reached the city, go to the Star. The Aureate Guard will tell you everything.

"Lena. Finish him. My patience runs thin." Daimonas stood like a hunched, black vulture behind her.

"Lena!" Pioni's eyes glowed with bloodlust.

How is it that they cannot hear us? Lena asked. Tears still streamed down her cheeks. *How is it that we can talk this way?*

There is no time, the man told her. *You will understand when you reach the city.* He closed his eyes.

"Stupid girl! Kill him!" Daimonas flung a sphere of black fire at Lena. She screamed and arched her back, pain exploding where the fire made contact.

You must do as he says.

No! Lena was sobbing now. *I won't!*

It would be foolish to disobey him. He would kill me, and you would suffer. My time has come. I am not afraid to face the next life. He inhaled deeply. *Rub some of the black dirt on the floor over the golden chain and slip it inside your boot. The dirt will disguise the glow. When you are ready, rub it off, and the pendant will lead you. The prophecy will be countered. Reach the City of the Aureate Star. You will understand.*

"Lena!"

Do it now.

"Kill him!"

Do not be afraid.

Lena raised her sword. *Please forgive me.* She plunged the blade into his chest. The man's eyebrows came together in a furrow of pain, and then the breath left his body and his features relaxed.

Sobbing, Lena pulled the blade out of his body and let it clatter to the floor. With trembling fingers, she took the golden chain from his palm, pressed it to the sooty floor, and brushed the black dirt over it, using her body to block her masters' view of her actions. She slipped the pendant, its glow greatly diminished, into her boot as she stood and turned to face the pair behind her.

Daimonas' chuckle broke the heavy silence. "Good Lena. Good. You have done well." He paused. "And yet, I sense a feeling of…loss, in you. You must learn to detach yourself, Lena, from all of your enemies. You cannot look on those that you must kill as people. You must look on them as threats. Their death is your gain. In destroying this man, you have taken one more step toward the destruction of the rebels in Aurea."

The Aureate Guard, Lena thought. She shuddered.

"Stop crying, Lena. You have pleased me today. Go and rest for the night."

Lena bowed and walked numbly out of the room. The two guards escorted her from the room and led her to her cell. The pendant pulsed inside her boot.

Chapter Three
Escape from the Desert Castle

"You are a disgrace! She is no more prepared to go into battle than she was the day she came to you! Break her spirit, I said. Disrupt her focus, I told you. Do not allow her spirit to flourish. And what have you done? She cowers at the sound of my voice, defies my wishes, weeps over death, sympathizes with the enemy—she is no warrior—she is a pacifist!"

Daimonas paced in front of a prostrate Lord Pioni. "Master, please—" Pioni begged.

"Silence! I ought to kill you where you are for your utter failure. Her wealth of power is all but spent. If she were not unique, if she did not possess an inner strength so potent, I would have nothing left to work with. You have failed me on all accounts. I do not want to see you again. In the morning I will take the girl back with me and finish her training myself."

Lord Pioni was trembling. He stood, bowed, and left the room.

***

The one-eyed guard pushed Lena forward into her cell. She spat a Sanuulian swearword at him as he closed the the door, then fell to the floor in tears. That last gasp of breath, before the man had passed from life, the feel of her own blade, plunging into another's flesh…they would frequent her nightmares.

But Lena managed to bite back the tears. She reached down and tugged off the boot that held the pendant. The necklace spilled out and lay unremarkably on the floor.

Lena looked at it carefully. Bits of gold were beginning to show through the dirt that she had smudged onto the pendant to conceal its glow.

The pendant will guide you, he had said.

But what did that mean? What *was* it? What powers did it have? Hesitantly, Lena reached out a hand and touched the pendant with her fingertips.

Instantly, the room was filled with a burst of white light. Lena quickly shielded her eyes with her hand, but she was still slightly dazzled when the glare finally diminished, and it was a few seconds before she realized what had happened.

The door to her cell had swung open. All that remained of the lock was a piece of twisted, smoldering metal on the floor. The two guards outside her cell had been completely blinded by the unexpected burst of light and were now staggering around the hall, waving their arms and swearing.

Lena's hesitance lasted only one second more. She glanced at the pendant, then back at the guards in the hall before she scooped up the necklace and bolted out of her cell.

With the charm pulsing in her palm, Lena was filled with a confidence she had never known before. She rounded corners, slipped through doorways and ran down steps without hesitation. She hit the wooden door that led to the stables and shoved it with both hands.

So far she had been able to ignore the twinges that had started in her ankle, but when she stepped through this door, the Keeping Stone sent out a shooting pain that turned into a cramp in her calf and made Lena stumble across the stable. She crashed into a stall and spooked a chestnut stallion. It reared and pawed the air with its enormous, iron-shod hooves. Lena managed to duck in time, but another twinge made her lose her balance and sent her careening into the opposite stall. This belonged to an small, ivory mare, small but with muscular flanks and a surprising quietude despite the commotion. Lena pulled herself onto the horse's back, her leg throbbing. She rested the pendant against the horse's neck, and the mare lunged forward. Lena grasped its mane as it bounded toward the door. She raised the pendant, the door burst open, and the mare sprang lightly into the blackness and uncertainty of the desert night.

***

Lord Pioni had designed the Keeping Stone when Lena had first arrived at his desert castle. She had been only eight years old when he had set the burning stone into her flesh, and for nine years it had prevented the execution of any escape plans.

The stone was intended to work in two stages. First, if Lena was plotting a way to leave the castle, the stone sent her enough pain to squander the idea without harming her. If she did succeed in escaping, the stone sent stronger doses. These were not just meant to punish or discourage; these were to render Lena senseless and immobile.

Lord Pioni's plan would have worked, had he not underestimated his prisoner. Lena's training, every lesson that Pioni gave her, forced her to bear pain, taught her to ignore it. Pioni himself showed her how to push pain from her mind, and, in doing so, had taught her how to defeat the mechanism he had designed to keep her captive. However, his pride in his own creation and his contempt for Lena had led him to believe that she could never overcome the stone.

As she grew older, Lena began to test herself. She dwelt deliberately on plans of escape and forced herself to tolerate the pain. This was how her most recent escape attempt had been conceived.

But she had been on foot then, and ill-prepared. Building a stockpile for escape had been no easy task; Lena received little enough food and water as it was, and the small amount of each that she managed to ferret away in the corner of her cell came out of her own meals. She went two weeks with a dry mouth and a hungry stomach, and knew that if she waited much longer, the Keeping Stone would ruin all plans of escape. On foot, with a only a meager supply of food and water and scant knowledge of the desert landscape, she stood no chance against Mallin the bounty hunter and his fleet-footed courser. Now that she had the pendant and a horse from Pioni's stable, the tables had turned.

***

"So, your Keeping Stone has proven useless, and the girl is gone." Every curt and hateful word that fell from Daimonas' lips was to Pioni like a slice from a blade.

"I am sorry, Master. I—" Pioni began, his heart pounding.

"I have no use for the apologies of a groveling dog!" Daimonas spat. "I will give you a handful of hours to correct this error. If you are not back with her by nightfall tomorrow then you have failed me for the last time." Daimonas turned his back to the prostrate man and said no more. Pioni got to his feet and slipped out of the room.

Mallin was waiting just outside the door, with the silence and stillness of stone. His piercing, coal-black eyes glinted when Pioni stepped into the corridor. He gave Pioni a low, stiff bow and waited for instruction.

"We are going to find her," Pioni said. "If she is on foot, it will not take long."

A guard came forward. "My lord," he said. "A horse is missing from the stables."

Pioni gave a roar of frustration and slammed his fist into the wall.

"We may still overtake her," he growled, when he had regained control of himself. "She is not as skilled a rider as either of us, and the Keeping Stone will exhaust her before long. Ready my horse!"

The guards rushed to obey.

***

The pendant had brought Lena not only power, but luck as well. The horse that Lena had chosen possessed a singular patience and tenacity. The Keeping Stone was having the intended effect; Lena was soon unable to offer any direction to the mare; even if she had been alert, she would not have known which way to go, but with the pendant resting against its neck, the mare did.

Horse and rider traveled throughout the night, first over the shifting sands of the Southern Desert, then into the sparse, dry wasteland that separated the desert from the less harsh, more fertile, land beyond it. Finally, as the moon slipped from view and a pale dawn crowded out the night, Lena, slumped over the mare's muscular neck, opened her eyes to see a river just ahead. Her eyes drifted closed again, but she soon heard the clop of the mare's hooves on a cobbled bridge. Had she been aware enough to appreciate that she had just crossed the desert border, she might have felt the beginning of hope. As it was, she was delirious and barely able to notice her surroundings. The pain that radiated from the Keeping Stone had spread up her leg and throughout her body, and now was making her sick. She had vomited twice, and her mouth was dry, her body dangerously dehydrated. She was feverish; little rivulets of sweat trickled from her hairline over her face and down the sides of her cheeks. As black spots appeared in front of her eyes, Lena slipped sideways on the mare's back and finally fell, unconscious, onto the soft grass. The horse whinnied in concern and nuzzled its fallen rider, but Lena didn't stir.

***

The land is different here. The grass grows thick and long, like a plush, emerald carpet. This country is wild and beautiful, lush, rich, and blessed with frequent rains. There is a city and many farmlands to the north, but here, mainly, there is open field, mountains to the west and a thick forest to the east. Hills rise and fall and brooks gurgle. The land is alive, not like the dry and spartan desert of Sanuul, but alive with a twisting, mischievous vivacity. Here woodsmen say that the forests change, that a path through the woods never leads to the same place twice. Some even claim that rivers change direction. It was one of these rivers, in fact, that Lena crossed and unknowingly entered new territory. She still lay unconscious, just beyond the bridge. Two men were now trekking up a hill only a few yards from where she lay, her presence still unknown to them.

***

"A beautiful day." One of the men, blue-eyed and russet-haired, jabbed his walking stick into the ground and gazed around him. "A bit foggy, but that should lift within the hour." There were the beginnings of gray at the roots of the man's hair and a few wrinkles at the corners of his eyes, but he was strong and well-muscled, healthy and in good condition. A tall and handsome young man of seventeen was at his side. He looked strong too, with muscles like ropes and toned, broad shoulders. He had curly, light brown hair that was cropped relatively short, the thick curls hanging just over his ears. He stood a good head taller than the man beside him, but there was a seriousness in his bright green eyes that was inconsistent with his youth. Both men wore simple, brown cloaks made of rough wool and, beneath them, green tunics that bore the golden star of Aurea.

"What's wrong Hadrian?" the older man asked, and turned to face his companion. "You haven't been yourself today."

"Sorry," the boy answered with an apologetic smile. "I just feel strange. Something seems…" he squinted. "What's that?"

The man glanced down the hill in the direction Hadrian was looking. "A horse," he said. "Wild, perhaps."

Hadrian started down the hill. "There are no wild horses in the Copper Fields."

"Escaped, then," the man said but his voice had lost its carefree tone, and he followed Hadrian down the hill with a frown of concern.

"Master Jairdan, there's a girl fallen beside it!" Hadrian was hurrying now, shifting the loose earth and uprooting dead grass. His teacher had also seen the girl and increased his pace. Soon they were both on their knees beside her. Hadrian pressed his fingers to her neck. "She's alive," he said, "but just barely. What's wrong with her?"

"I don't know." Jairdan's eyes were knitted in concentration and concern. "There are no wounds, no signs of struggle."

"Is she ill?" Hadrian asked. "She's certainly warm." He took the back of his hand from her forehead.

"She must be," Jairdan replied, forehead knitted in concern.

29

"Master, what's this?" Hadrian had pulled something golden from the girl's clenched fist.

The older man paled. "We must get her to the Star," he said. He put one hand behind the girl's neck and the other behind her knees and started to lift her, but her body began to jerk with uncontrollable spasms.

"What's happening?" Hadrian cried, dropping the pendant into one of the deep pockets of his cloak. "What's wrong with her?"

"Hadrian, take her horse and get Auxillius down here at once! Tell him it's urgent!"

Wide-eyed at his teacher's concern, Hadrian had already swung onto the horse's back before his master called, "And tell High Master Scio about this as well!"

Soon Hadrian had disappeared on horseback over the crest of the hill, a trail of dust was left in his wake.

Jairdan was left kneeling beside the girl in the open field. He squinted toward the gray horizon line. The fog that had settled on the distant hilltops was rising, but it revealed only ominous clouds. The sky let out a guttural rumble, the beginning of a thunderstorm. Jairdan glared at the heavens. It seemed it would not turn out to be a lovely day after all.

***

"What's wrong with her? Can you tell?" Hadrian was squatted next to the healer that he had brought from the city, a slight, anxious, man named Auxillius. The man did not respond to Hadrian but pulled nervously on his wispy hair as he examined the girl's head and neck.

"Well? What is it?" Hadrian demanded.

"Be patient, Hadrian. He's only just gotten here," Jairdan said.

Another man had arrived with Hadrian and Auxillius. He was small, elderly, and completely bald, with bright, black eyes and a neatly clipped, gray beard. His eyes glittering like jewels, he squinted for a moment at the girl on the ground. He was focused not on her head or neck, as Auxilius was, but on one of the girl's legs, which was twisted at an odd angle. He stooped down and pressed his hand to her calf, then ran it down her leg to her ankle. Auxillius stopped to watch as the old man loosened her boot. When he tried to pry it off, the girl, semi-conscious, stirred and tugged her leg away from him with a moan.

"High Master Scio?" Auxillius' brow was furrowed in concern.

"We must get this off," Scio said, taking the boot in both hands now. "Master Jairdan, hold her leg at the knee. She may struggle. I will guide the boot off as gently as I can."

"What can I do, Master?" Hadrian asked.

Scio looked at him carefully. "Take her hand," he said at last. "If I am right, she will be in much pain."

Without knowing why, Hadrian drew the golden pendant from his pocket and pressed it into the girl's palm when he put her hand in his.

Jairdan put his hands over her knee. Scio gave the boot a swift tug and it came off. The girl arched her back with a gasp of pain, and squeezed Hadrian's hand hard. The pendant, compressed between their palms, expelled a burst of white-golden light. Hadrian lost his grip on her hand and was thrown a yard across the field. He landed on his back with a sickening pain creeping over his leg. His ankle throbbed.

"Hadrian!" Jairdan rushed to the young man's side.

Scio peered at the girl's mangled ankle. He glanced at her face and saw that her eyelids had fluttered open. She seemed to struggle for words, then choked, "Where…?"

"You are in the land of Aurea, in the Copper Fields, and you will be well taken care of," Scio replied promptly. The girl's eyes drooped closed again. Scio frowned.

"What happened?" Jairdan asked. "Hadrian, are you all right?"

Hadrian nodded uncertainly. "I think so," he said. He reached down and massaged his calf. The vicious cramp had subsided, but a faint tingling remained. He looked down at the pendant in his hand. "Master, what is this?" Hadrian asked.

Jairdan looked at the pendant as if it might explode. "Let me have that, Hadrian," he said at last.

31

Hadrian glanced at his tutor and for one of the few times he could remember saw fear in Jairdan's eyes. He dropped the pendant obediently into his teacher's trembling palm. "What is it, Master?" he asked again, voice low.

Before Jairdan could answer, Auxillius bent to look at the girl's leg and shook his head in disbelief. "Merciful Star save us…never in all my years as a healer have I seen…"

Hadrian and Jairdan approached the girl to see what had so disturbed Auxilius. Nausea coiled in Hadrian's stomach when he caught sight of the gem at the center of the knotted scars in the girl's ankle.

"Master Scio, what is that?" Hadrian asked.

Scio leant forward on his staff and closed his eyes. "The end of peace," he murmured.

***

Two horses flew over the sand, dark silhouettes against a stormy sky. Their riders crouched low in the saddle and urged them on, never letting them deviate from their course nor slow their pace. The riders wore dark cloaks that streamed behind them and scarves that guarded their faces from the swirling sand that was risen on the winds of the storm, an anomaly in this part of the world. Clouds like smudges of charcoal stained the smoky dawn, and as Mallin and Pioni rode on, a jagged bolt of lightning crackled through the sky. Rain fell in a slanted sheet, whipped on by a furious wind from the north.

***

"She is too ill to move, and the storm's picking up," Jairdan said. "There's no shelter for miles."

"We can move her beneath those trees for now," Hadrian said, pointing.

"Master Auxillius, you must ride back for supplies," Scio said. "Tell the others at the Star to bring tents, food and water. There is no telling how long we will be out here."

Auxillius looked bewildered for a moment. "We are to stay here, Master?" he asked.

"As Master Jairdan says, she is too weak to be moved," Scio said gravely. "What would you have us do? Leave her to her death?"

"No Master, of course, I only…I apologize. I will go right away."

"Also tell the High Masters that they must come immediately," Scio said.

Auxillius paled. "The High Masters, my lord?" he stammered

"Yes, Auxillius. And please go at once. Much hangs in the balance."

Hadrian's watchful eyes were narrowed. Such commotion was unusual, especially over a matter that seemed so trivial on the surface. To call out the High Masters…Hadrian could never remember a time when they all had left the city at once. There was much more here than met the eye.

As Auxillius' chestnut horse disappeared over the crest of the hill, Hadrian helped Jairdan lift and carry the girl to a cluster of trees. They laid her out on the soft earth, a halo of her golden curls spread out around her head. Hadrian squatted beside her and touched the dusty rose of her cheek with the back of his hand. There was a slight furrow of pain on her brow, but with this small exception she looked as if she were in a deep and peaceful sleep. Hadrian felt a strangely strong compassion for the girl on the ground before him. He looked down again at the horrible stone that was set into her flesh.

A snarl of thunder sounded. The storm was getting closer. The girl's white mare trotted beneath the trees and prodded her unconscious rider with her velvety snout. Rain poured, thunder snarled, and the three figures beneath the trees pulled the hoods of their cloaks up against the storm.

***

The unnatural rain was falling even more heavily than before over the desert dunes. The wind threw vicious clouds of sand up before the two riders and their black chargers. Mallin and Pioni could barely see their way. Bent low over their horses' thrusting necks, their eyes tormented by the flying sand, the inexorable riders pushed forward, toward the desert's edge.

Chapter Four
The Prophecy

A procession of horses, cloaked riders, and torches made its way slowly across the fields. In silence, Jairdan and Hadrian watched the somber cortege proceed. Jairdan had not spoken much since Scio had sent Auxillius back to the city, and Hadrian had had plenty of time to formulate his questions for his teacher.

"Master, what's really going on?" he asked finally, turning his gaze from the procession to his master's face.

Jairdan did not meet his eyes.

"I know there is something," Hadrian persisted. "That pendant—it means something, doesn't it? It's the reason that the High Masters have been called from the city."

"Yes, Hadrian, it is," Jairdan said at last. "The pendant is very important."

"What is it?"

Jairdan sighed. "It is called the Pendant of Light, though most just refer to it as the Pendant, or the Charm."

"*That* is the pendant?" Hadrian asked incredulously. "But I've heard of it; it's legend! I thought it had been lost to us, years ago?"

"We also thought so," Jairdan said. "It was given to one of our best before he embarked on a mission for the Order. He never returned, and we thought both he and the pendant were gone forever."

"The Pendant... I've heard it said that it contains dust from the First Star."

"Legend abounds where the Pendant is concerned," Jairdan said. "It contains *something*, but I doubt it is stardust. More likely it's just sand from where the Great Fathers first broke land for the City."

"But what does the Pendant actually do?" Hadrian asked.

"Many things," Jairdan said wearily. "It is the greatest asset an Aureate Guard could ever carry into battle or on a mission. It is entrusted only to the most honorable men and only when they are embarking on a most dangerous quest." He repeated this mantra in a weary monotone; he had heard it many times before.

"But that girl is not a member of our—"

"No. She does not belong to our Order, and yet she is carrying the pendant."

"How can that be, Master?"

"That is the question, Hadrian, that has drawn the High Masters from the Temple."

The pair looked back at the procession. It had stopped, and Master Scio was hurrying toward it.

"Master, who was the last to have had the pendant in his possession?" Hadrian turned to look at Jairdan again, his forehead creased with confusion and anxiety.

"A man named Emissi," Jairdan replied. "He left five years ago to search for a rumored threat in the South. He never returned." Jairdan glanced again at the girl on the ground. "He was High Master Scio's closest friend."

Hadrian turned to look back at the unconscious girl. Her horse whinnied apprehensively and pawed the earth. The storm raged.

***

The High Masters had been accompanied by a company of Aureate Guardsmen. They were tense; this was an unprecedented situation. Never had all of the High Masters left the City at once. The guardsmen followed orders efficiently and to the letter. It was not long before they had erected several canvas tents and started a large fire. Jairdan and Hadrian were urged into one of these tents and provided with blankets and warm drinks.

Hadrian's good friend, Ince, also an Aureate Guard, had come down from the city with the others. He stepped happily into the tent, glad for the shelter from the rain. His long, straight, strawberry-blonde hair was soaked and plastered to his forehead. He pushed it out of his eyes and greeted Hadrian with a puppyish grin. "Hello Hadrian! I was just helping set up a few tents, and then I asked and heard you were down here so I came to say hello." A year younger and characteristically cheerful, Ince looked up to Hadrian and was always eager to impress his more somber, introspective friend.

"It's good to see you, Ince," Hadrian said. The wrinkle of worry had not left his brow.

Ince cocked his head to look more carefully at his friend. "You all right, Hadrian?"

"I'm worried."

The grin on Ince's face transformed immediately into a look of deep concern. "You were with Master Jairdan, weren't you? When he…when you…Master Auxillius says you found a girl."

Hadrian looked over his shoulder into the gloom where a cluster of healers were examining a prone figure. "She's there."

"Oh." Ince stared with wide eyes into the dusky background in an attempt to get a glimpse of the girl.

"They're here, then?" Hadrian asked. "The High Masters?"

"And a fair few besides," Ince said excitedly. "Practically everyone's here. There's only Lady Magistra back at the Star with the little ones and few Guardsmen. Strange, how they ordered almost all of the Guardsmen out here. It's like they're expecting an attack or something." He laughed, but his easy grin again faded when Hadrian's grave expression did not change.

Jairdan strode through the mud over to the conversing pair. "Sorry to interrupt. Hello Ince. Hadrian, the healers are going to move the girl into the first tent over there. Master Scio requested that you and I come before the High Masters to discuss the matter."

Ince's eyes widened. Hadrian, considered the best pupil the Order had seen in years, was used to attention, but to Ince, clumsy, inexperienced, unappreciated by his teachers and unknown to the High Masters, a summons from the Masters was a thing of unparalleled greatness. He had to swallow hard before he could choke, "I'll let you go then. Good luck. G'bye. Master Jairdan." He bowed and tripped on the hem of his cloak as he took a step away from the pair.

"There are many healers here," Hadrian commented, as he and Jairdan made their way toward the already assembled tent.

"The best from the city," Jairdan replied. "They're going to have a look at her now."

"And what if they don't know what's wrong with her? What that horrible stone is? What then?"

"Try to be patient, Hadrian. Let events unfold and hope for the best. There is little else we can do."

Hadrian fell silent. He and Jairdan stepped gratefully out of the pelting rain into the tent, generously lit by torches and warmed by body heat.

The High Masters sat cross-legged on the ground in simple, white tunics, their wet cloaks spread on the ground to dry. There were only three men, including Scio, who had been sufficiently diligent, patient, skilled, and honorable to achieve the rank of High Master, and they were all assembled inside the tent, looking stern and grave.

Aside from Scio, there was Master Prudentior, who was tall and thin with white hair that reached his shoulders. He was like a statue chiseled from stone; there were no forgiving features, no lines to soften his fierce expressions, no spare inch of flesh on face or body. His eyes were like blue glass; his stare was penetrating and unyielding.

The third man was short and squat. It was difficult to believe that he belonged to the same elite Order as the others; he was chubby and red-faced and typically triply as cheerful as Prudentior. Hadrian was used to seeing High Master Chista with a bright smile on his face. The gravity of the situation hit him heavily and suddenly when he saw that Chista looked as grave as Scio.

Scio was the oldest of the High Masters and the most venerated, unquestioningly acknowledged as the leader of all the Aureate Guard.

Jairdan and Hadrian bowed when they entered the tent. The High Masters nodded in response. Prudentior was the first to speak.

"Master Jairdan. Hadrian." There was a rustle; the tent flap lifted and three healers entered, carrying the injured girl. The healers spoke in concerned whispers as they examined her; seeing their expressions, Hadrian's hopes that they would be able to cure quickly were diminished.

"The two of you found her?" Prudentior asked.

"That's right," Jairdan said. "She was lying unconscious next to the horse."

"And you found the…Pendant?"

"Clenched in her hand," Hadrian offered, stepping forward with a bow.

"Let us see it."

Jairdan reached into the deep pocket of his robe and withdrew the pendant. It lay unremarkably in his hand, but the instant it was visible, the tension in the room heightened.

"Obviously this is a grave matter. You both understand the connotation of the girl's possession of the pendant. The last Aureate Guard to have carried it was Master Emissi, who journeyed to the South and has still not returned. It is possible that this girl has attacked, perhaps killed Master Emissi and stolen the pendant from him."

"Nonsense." Chista snorted. He turned an incredulous eye on Prudentior. "She's a only a child and barely that; the little wisp of thing is more wraith than human."

"She looks strong enough!" Prudentior snapped. "And how else do you explain her having the pendant?"

"Just because you can't think of any other reason for her having the pendant doesn't mean there isn't one," Chista replied coolly. "The idea that this girl, with no training and no assistance, killed Emissi—"

"Is utterly ridiculous." Master Scio had been sitting with his head bowed and his eyes closed. Now he carefully unfolded himself and blinked his clear, black eyes. "If this girl truly has attacked and killed Master Emissi, then she has been instructed in the Arts."

"But High Master, who else practices our craft besides ourselves?" Hadrian asked. "I have never heard of anyone outside of the city who studied it."

The High Masters exchanged glances. Scio took a deep breath. "A few years ago, one of our own, a skilled warrior named Daimonas, broke from our Order and disappeared into the Southern Desert. Daimonas felt that the Aureate Guard could seize more power with the skills that we possessed. He felt that we were not fulfilling our potential. He wanted to take control of the city and eventually the country. I am sure his plans stretched even further, but once he had revealed the beginnings of his plot to other members of our Order, he was turned in, and fled when we attempted to arrest him."

"He wanted to take power from the Queen?" Hadrian asked. "He thought that all the Aureate Guard could rule the city and country better than one Queen? That's ridiculous."

"Daimonas was a very prideful man," Scio replied sternly. "And with pride oftentimes comes greed. He was determined he was right, and he was blessed with an unfortunate and enduring perseverance."

"Does your apprentice know the prophecy, Master Jairdan?" Chista asked quietly.

Jairdan glanced at Hadrian. "I was instructed at a secret council seventeen years ago not to divulge *that* to Hadrian until he was eighteen."

The High Masters exchanged glances.

"What prophecy?" Hadrian asked. "What don't I know?"

No one answered. Scio sighed. "This event changes many things. It is my opinion that Hadrian should be told the prophecy. Immediately."

"I agree," said Prudentior.

"And I." Chista gave Hadrian a firm nod.

Jairdan bowed. "Very well," he said. "Hadrian, follow me."

***

"Master—"

Jairdan held up a hand. "Not here," he said sharply, glancing pointedly at the other Aureate Guardsmen.

The rain had let up significantly and was now reduced to mere drizzle. Jairdan and Hadrian were able to find sufficient shelter under the canopy of a cluster of trees.

Once beneath the protective canopy, Hadrian and Jairdan pushed back their hoods. Jairdan heaved a deep sigh.

"Hadrian, understand that when you were first brought to the City I advocated for this to be revealed to you as soon as you were old enough to comprehend it. The High Masters, however, feared that the knowledge would cause you to become…too sure of yourself."

"Arrogant," Hadrian supplied.

"They ordered me to take an oath never to tell you the prophecy regarding your future until you were eighteen."

"I wasn't even aware there was a prophecy," Hadrian said.

"It is the best kept secret of our Order," Jairdan replied. "And now it is time you heard it. This is the prophecy as it was related to Master Scio several years before I found you." He took a deep breath, closed his eyes, and recited, "Two infants into bondage born will from their mother's breast be torn, one by golden soldier saved, the other turned to evil's slave. One will into a hero grow; the other bend to serve the shadow. Cast into dark the world will be, until the twain fulfill their destiny. One will fall, the other reign; one a monarch, the other slain. All these things shall come to be: So says the Oracle of the Ashen Sea."

The wind whipped across the field, bending the gray-green grass in the storm. Hadrian was pale, his eyes filled with a horrible understanding. "Two infants…from their mother's…do you mean…she's my sister?"

Jairdan barely had the heart to incline his head. "If we are right, she is your twin."

"The Golden Soldier would be an Aureate Guard," Hadrian went on, turning his gaze from Jairdan's solemn face to the tent where his sister was lying unconscious in the hands of the healers. "It was you," he realized, turning back to Jairdan. "When you found me at the slave market in Gnibri…I was the one saved by a Golden Soldier. That would mean…it would mean she was captured by Daimonas?"

"It seems very likely," Jairdan said.

"But how…why could you not save both of us?" Hadrian asked. "Why did you only take me?"

Jairdan sighed. "Hadrian, I am afraid I have not been completely honest with you about your past. I did not find you at a slave market, and it was not chance that brought me to you, as you have been told. High Master Scio, as I said, had heard the prophecy before your birth and suspected the twins from the verse would be born very soon."

"How did he know?" Hadrian asked.

"Daimonas had only recently fled the Order, but we were aware that he was powerful enough to quickly gather a following. As he was so skilled and so corrupt, Scio feared that Daimonas could put into motion the events that would lead to the times described in the prophecy as "cast into dark." He came to believe that Daimonas was the 'evil' destined to capture one of the children. Scio was bent on finding *both* children and countering the prophecy, but at the time we were caught up with the battle against the militants near the Eastern Coast, and it wasn't until very late that we discovered that the twins we were looking for might be close by, in a merchant town a few miles off the coast."

"How did you discover that?"

"On our march to the battlefront near the Eastern Coastline, we stopped to rest and replenish our supplies at the Garrison of Amensliel. While we were there, I heard rumors about twins that had been born in Locusorti, a village a few miles away. We were told that these twins possessed strange powers, were capable of causing small objects to lift off the ground without ever touching them. They never cried, we were told, and seemed to possess a strange intelligence for infants barely out of the womb. I was one of the few to whom High Master Scio had related the prophecy, and I was sure that the twins from Locusorti were the babies the oracle had spoken of. I hurried back to camp before the others and told High Master Scio what I had heard. He was delighted, because the Aureate Guard had excellent relations with the people of Locusorti at the time. Only a few miles lay between us and the village, and I set out early the next day with a small party of men, full of anticipation. However," Jairdan stopped and sighed, "to our bitter dismay, the village had been raided. The men were dead, the houses burned, the women and children gone. Our militant enemies knew how friendly we were with the people of Locusorti, and had destroyed the village to prevent our getting aid from them. High Master Prudentior immediately suspected that any prisoners would be taken as slaves and sold at the nearest market.

"However, we were losing hundreds of men a day at the front, and the stories about the twins were only rumors. Reports came in that the situation grew worse in the battle every day. We were forced to postpone our search. We spent the next week and a half battling for the upper hand on the Eastern Coast. We finally got it; we received reinforcements just in time.

"It was in fact the last day of the battle that we got word from a scout that a slave auction was being held the next day in Gnibri, Marii's capitol city, a day and half's ride from the coast. High Master Scio sent me there in hopes that I would find the children we'd heard about. I set out at once, but I didn't get to the city until most of the auction was already over. I waited for an hour without seeing a child under twelve, and the sickening thought that the captured infants might have been deemed useless as slaves and killed occurred to me. The last slave was sold, and I went away, dejected, to find a place to spend the night.

"On my way, I caught sight of billowing smoke and, when I went to see what it was, discovered an inn in flames. There was a crowd outside, and one of the women was screaming that her sister was still inside, in a room on the second level. I ran in and up a staircase, in the direction of weak calls for help that came from a room on the second floor corridor. When I reached the room, I saw that a woman lay coughing on the floor. A man was bent over her with an infant in his arms. I rushed him with my sword drawn, and he backed away, unable to defend himself while still holding the child. Then, to my shock, he took the baby and held it out of the window, ready to drop it. I froze where I was and lowered my sword. He gestured for me to drop it, and when I did, he kicked it away from me and dashed out of the room with the baby. I turned to follow him, but the woman on the ground moaned for help. I had no choice. I turned back to help her and was astounded to see that she held another baby in her arms. She fainted as I carried her from the house. By the time we were outside, the man that had taken the other baby had disappeared. The woman I had saved from the fire had inhaled too much smoke and knew she did not have much time left. In her last moments, she revealed to me that she had bought the baby that she held, who was, of course, you, and your sister, the baby that had been stolen, from slave-auctioneers for a small price. She was barren, and intended to raise you both as her own. That was all she had time to tell me."

Hadrian swallowed hard and looked away.

"I took you from her and gave her sister a small sum so that I could take you away, then I returned to camp with you. And so it was that the first part of that prophecy was fulfilled."

Hadrian blinked furiously and cleared his throat before he turned to look back at Jairdan. "So the girl inside that tent is my sister," he said. "My twin sister. And she has been a prisoner for seventeen years."

"I know this is hard to take in so quickly," Jairdan said. He put a hand on his apprentice's shoulder. "Are you all right?"

"I don't understand," Hadrian said. "Why did the High Masters think that this information would make me arrogant?"

Jairdan sighed. "Because it made you our champion. If your sister had grown to be Daimonas' hero, instructed in the Dark Powers, you would have been our only hope of rescue."

"I would have had to kill my own sister?"

"It might have been the only choice." Seeing the revolted look in Hadrian's eyes, Jairdan persisted, "But now, if this girl truly is your sister, we have a chance to save her. We can turn her back to the light and crush Daimonas, and maintain peace across the land."

Hadrian nodded, but his eyes were hollow.

"Come." Jairdan put a guiding arm around his apprentice's shoulders. "The High Masters will be waiting."

Chapter Five
The City of the Aureate Star

Hadrian and Jairdan reentered the tent together. The High Masters regarded the pair for a moment, and then Scio spoke.

"Do you understand the prophecy then, Hadrian of Locusorti?"

Chills ran across Hadrian's skin at the haunting addition to his name. "I do, High Master."

"Then you understand that if this girl truly is your twin sister, the infant referred to in the prophecy, her coming could be either a great blessing or a terrible danger. We intend to bring her back to the city for questioning, and we would like you to be present. Do you object to this?"

"No, High Master," Hadrian replied. He glanced over his shoulder at the girl. At his sister.

Chista tilted his head and squinted at Hadrian. "You already feel compassion for this girl, if I am correct, young man."

Hadrian brought his eyes from his supine sister to Chista's piercing stare. "I do, High Master," he replied. "From the moment that I saw her I felt a connection. I cannot explain it, but it's true."

"The deepest emotions tend to transcend explanation," Scio remarked, eying Hadrian carefully.

"When we joined hands in the fields, when you were taking her boot off and pendant compressed between our palms—" Hadrian ventured.

"Yes, it is possible that the Pendant was reacting to an existing bond between the two of you," Scio said. "It is one of many things that made me come to believe that the girl is indeed your sister."

"Nevertheless, perhaps it would be advisable for you to bury any fraternal feelings until we are sure whether the girl is a gift or a threat," Master Prudentior commented.

"Hadrian's compassion is to be commended, not spurned," Master Scio told Prudentior sternly. He addressed Hadrian. "Your capability to feel sympathy toward a girl you have never met speaks well of your character."

Prudentior pursed his lips. "I still think, Master, that until we are certain of the girl's allegiances, we should be sure to proceed with caution."

"Of course. Caution is always wise. But we will not discourage sympathy."

"Discouraging sympathy," Chista mused. "Is practically the same as *encouraging* cruelty."

Prudentior glared.

Scio turned back to Hadrian. "We will camp here until the healers have found a way to safely move the girl back to the city. The stone in her ankle seems to be preventing any such movement at the moment, but we hope to be able to solve that problem by tomorrow. Until then, try to get some sleep."

Jairdan and Hadrian bowed and left the tent, Hadrian with one last glance at his unconscious sister. Together, he and Jairdan stepped back out into the rain and crossed the field to another, smaller tent. Once within the shelter again, Jairdan lit a lamp and took a loaf of bread from a sack that had been left inside the tent by helpful apprentices. He broke it in half and gave one piece to Hadrian.

"You don't look well," Jairdan said. "You're pale."

"It's just...quite a lot to take in," Hadrian responded. He sat on the ground and put a hand to his head.

"I know it is." Jairdan sighed. "Unfortunately, there's nothing we can do now except wait. Much of this mystery will be cleared up when the healers discover a way to revive the girl and bring her back to the city."

Hadrian stood up again. "I think I'll go for a walk," he said.

"In this weather? The storm's picking up again."

"It's not too bad," Hadrian said, lifting the tent flap to peer out. "And I need to clear my head."

Jairdan watched Hadrian step out of the tent. He sat down and took a small bite of his bread, watching the canvas walls of the tent billow and writhe, tormented by wind and rain.

***

"Blessed Star help us." One of the healers stepped away from the girl and put his head in his hands. "I've never seen anything like this before in my life."

"How long have we been here?" another healer asked, wiping his brow. "It feels like it's been hours."

The first healer glanced outside the tent. "It has been. It's getting late," he said. "Almost dark now."

***

Far from the tents now but not too far to still make out the glow of torchlights, Hadrian wrapped his cloak tightly around himself and sat down on the wet ground with his back against the trunk of a massive tree. Slowly, the afternoon began to seep away into darkness. The moon rose behind a distant hill, and the sun disappeared.

Night had fallen.

***

Daimonas strode over the bridge that spanned the fiery moat of Lord Pioni's palace. His ragged, black cloak whipped around him by the vicious wind. Daimonas squinted into the encroaching dusk. "Too long, Pioni," he growled.

He raised his hand, and clenched his fist.

***

Just as the sun had begun to descend in the sky, dread had fallen over Pioni. Clear beads of sweat had formed on his face; he had a white-knuckled grip on the reins. He knew that there was no chance of finding Lena by nightfall, and he knew that Daimonas was good for his word.

Mallin, a few yards behind Pioni, saw the man suddenly stiffen. Pioni fell to the ground and landed in a cloud of dust. His last, guttural choke was lost on the wind.

***

The healers stepped back from the girl sprawled on the ground inside the tent. For hours she had lain completely motionless despite their best efforts to revive her. Now, and for apparently no reason at all, her eyelids began to flicker. She moaned, turned her head. The healers looked at each other in disbelief. She murmured softly and opened her eyes.

Suddenly, she arched her back with a hiss of pain, a line of black smoke rising from her ankle. One of the healers peered at her leg and stared up at the others in shock. "The stone," he whispered. "It's gone."

"Gone? What do you mean?" The others hurried over to look, and indeed, in the place where the stone had been there was now only a shiny, circular burn at the center of a knot of white scars. The group of healers stared at the girl. Frightened, she pulled herself away from them and watched them with wary eyes.

"What's your name, girl?" one healer breathed.

"Lena," she whispered fearfully. "My name is Lena."

***

"Now," Daimonas waved his arms, and a furious wind swept up, swirling the sand into a slanted sheet before him. When he dropped his arms, the wind quieted, the sand fell, and a horse was left pawing the ground, snorting. Its form was perfect, but it was odd. It seemed alive and at the same time unreal. It was the color of sand, but that color was always shifting, always swirling, as if Daimonas had simply caught that wind-whipped sand in a transparent mold.

He smiled as he admired his creation. The horse bowed its neck to its master and opened its eyes.

They were black, with lines of silver.

***

Mallin took his fingers from Pioni's neck; the lack of pulse confirmed what Mallin had already known. He swept two fingers over the dead man's face, bringing the lids down over the terrified eyes. Then he got up and walked back to his horse. He swung up into the saddle, wheeled the charger back the way they had come, and spurred it into a trot.

***

Hadrian's eyes snapped open. He had been sitting pensively against the tree, but now he got to his feet and began to run, an inner sense that he could not explain propelling him toward the tent where his sister lay. He sprinted across the field, slick with the day's downpour. He burst inside the tent of the High Masters, breathless and soaked to the bone.

Jairdan and the High Masters were sitting around Lena, who was huddled cross-legged in the center of the tent, a blanket around her shoulders.

"Hadrian." Jairdan smiled. "This is Lena."

Lena turned to face him. Her eyes were bright green, the exact same shade as Hadrian's, and he recognized the shape of those eyes, the curve of her nose, the light spattering of freckles across her upper cheeks. He knew them from mirrors.

"I'm...very pleased to meet you," Hadrian whispered, and swallowed a lump in his throat.

She gave him a small, nervous smile. "Likewise."

Does she know? Hadrian wondered. He glanced at Jairdan, and as if he had read his pupil's thoughts, his tutor gave an almost imperceptible shake of his head.

Prudentior cleared his throat. "At dawn, we will return to the city," he said. "Lena will come with us. Master Jairdan, Hadrian, when we reach the city, report immediately to the meeting room of the High Council. In the meantime, again, try to take some rest."

***

Sleep did not come easily for either Hadrian or Jairdan, but both finally achieved it. Aside from those on watch, the other Aureate Guardsmen did the same, and soon after Lena had awoken, the fields, which had been bustling by day and dusk, were silent.

There was only one tent that remained well-lit by torches: that of the High Masters.

Scio looked carefully at Lena. "She's asleep," he said at last.

"She may be feigning sleep, to eavesdrop on us," Prudentior said.

"Oh yes. She may also have a crossbow under her tunic that she's planning to wake up and kill us all with," Chista said, examining his fingernails.

"Chista, I believe that you are treating this matter much too cavalierly!" Prudentior said heatedly.

"On the contrary Prudentior, I am treating it with all the severity it *deserves*," Chista replied.

"Then do not begrudge me extra caution!" Prudentior hissed.

"Oh for the sake of the Star, man!" Chista cried. "She's exhausted! She's just missed being killed by that wretched stone, of course she's asleep!"

"If she is associated with Daimonas then she is capable of cunning perhaps beyond our ability to comprehend!"

"She's just a girl!"

"Evil takes many forms!"

"Gentlemen." Scio stopped their argument with a word. "Listen to yourselves."

Prudentior set his jaw and refused to look at Chista. "I believe we are making rash decisions."

Chista grunted.

"You are both correct," Scio said carefully. "Your determination to err on the side of caution, High Master Prudentior, is wise. But High Master Chista is also correct; the stone suggests that this girl has been subject to unspeakable torment at the hands of her captors. She is to be pitied."

"Nothing is for sure. This could all be a plot to enter the City and take us off guard," Prudentior said.

"Nothing is for sure? Did you see the blasted stone?" Chista roared.

"My friends!" Scio seemed agitated for the first time. "Thus far, the only danger her arrival has presented is that of our losing our ability to communicate rationally with each other. If we cannot discuss the matter reasonably, then let us not discuss it at all."

Prudentior took a deep breath. "I feel that our decision to take the girl into the City may be a poor one," he said slowly.

"Aside from believing that the girl poses no threat, I believe that the City is the safest place to question her, not here, where we are vulnerable to ambush, if that is indeed a risk." Chista's voice was strained.

"While I see the merit of that point," Prudentior said rigidly, "I question the advisability of risking the lives of our people rather than ourselves."

"But I believe that, as we can better control the situation within the City than we can out here, there is less overall risk of loss of life."

"And I believe," Scio interposed, "that Chista is correct on this point."

Chista inclined his head toward Scio in thanks.

Prudentior thought hard and at last said, "I also see now that Chista's point is the better, as long as we move the girl to the City carefully, watching for attack."

"That is of course, very wise," Chista said graciously. "And forgive my heated words earlier; my nerves are drawn taut with the severity of the situation."

"As are mine," Prudentior said. The two smiled at each other.

"Good, good," said Scio, pleased. "At all costs, we must maintain brotherhood within the Order. That is our greatest asset; its protection should be our foremost concern."

The other two High Masters nodded. "Agreed."

Scio nodded. "Good. And now, it is late. We will break this conference and resume it later, when we have facts rather than suspicions on which to base our assumptions."

***

The next morning, the horses were laden with supplies and ready to for the return to the city. Hadrian noticed that although Lena was riding her own horse, the white mare, her hands were bound in front of her with a thick rope, and Prudentior was keeping a keen eye on her.

Hadrian wheeled his horse around angrily and rode to Jairdan's side. "Master, why have they bound her hands? And why is Master Prudentior glaring at her like she's a criminal?"

Jairdan glanced at Lena direction. "Hadrian, think for a moment. I told you that I thought this was an excellent opportunity to save your sister and change the prophecy, but that is only my opinion, and it will be very difficult to convince the High Masters to think the same way. I understand that you are in a difficult situation, and believe me, I would like to think that your sister can yet be saved, but you also must realize that there is a chance that she has already been corrupted beyond recall. She may even have been sent here as a spy or assassin. The High Masters are in a very precarious position. Do not begrudge them extra caution."

Barely subdued, Hadrian asked, "What did she say last night, before I came in?"

"She told us that she was from the Southern Desert, but she was hesitant to say more. The High Masters want to question her back in the city, where we are safe from ambush and where they can better control the situation."

Hadrian stared glumly at Lena. "She doesn't know," he murmured. "She doesn't know the prophecy."

"And she must not!" Jairdan said urgently. "She must know nothing until we are sure of her intentions. You must promise me that you will say nothing to her about the secrets I divulged to you last night, Hadrian, nor must you reveal any of the intentions of the High Masters to her. Your own safety could be at risk."

Hadrian glanced at the girl he knew was his sister, bitterly eying her bound hands. Then he looked back at Jairdan, the man who had brought him up from infancy as a surrogate son, who spoke from earnest concern on Hadrian's own behalf, and his features softened. "I promise."

***

Lena twisted her wrists in the thick bonds. Under a deceptively calm exterior, she was terrified. She had thought she was riding towards hope, and was now a captive once again, this time in the hands of an unpredictable enemy. They had revealed nothing to her when she had first awoken, and she had been equally hesitant to unveil her origin. They had been kind to her in some respects, giving her water and some bread, dressing her wounds and allowing her to keep the horse that had borne her out of the desert, but they had bound her hands, and the white-haired man, the High Master, had barely taken his eyes off of her since they left.

And...there was the boy...the boy that looked almost...that seemed so....

Lena shook her head. *The heat must have affected me more than I thought*, she told herself.

***

Jairdan was watching Hadrian with an amused smile as they walked the horses up a grassy hill. The city was in sight now, glowing like a pearl in the early light, but Hadrian was not looking at the steeples or the intricate towers that rose over the city walls. He had not taken his eyes off Lena.

"You know, I didn't forbid you from speaking to her," Jairdan pointed out gently. "I only warned you to use caution."

Hadrian tore his gaze from Lena and glanced at Jairdan inquisitively.

"You're staring at her as if she's got thirteen heads! Go and speak to her before she starts to wonder what on earth is wrong with you."

Hadrian gazed nervously at Lena.

"For goodness' sake Hadrian, she's not going to bite you! Go!" Jairdan gave Hadrian's horse a sharp slap on the rump and sent it trotting toward Lena. Hadrian cast him a dark look over his shoulder. Jairdan laughed and watched his apprentice slow his horse to a walk and ease toward Lena.

***

"Hello."

Lost in thought, Lena was startled when Hadrian approached and greeted her. She started, then gave him a small smile.

Hadrian looked down at her bound wrists and grimaced. "Sorry about that," he said.

Her eyes widened in her astonishment that he should be apologetic. She seemed not to know how to answer. Silent, she blushed and looked away.

"Things will be better when we get to the city," Hadrian promised. "The High Masters are good men, just cautious. In the Aureate City—"

"The Aureate City?" the girl asked eagerly. "The City of the Aureate Star?"

Hadrian blinked in surprise. "Yes," he replied slowly. "You've heard of it?"

Lena quickly cast her eyes downward. "Yes. Stories."

"About?" Hadrian prompted.

Lena hesitated.

"You don't have to be afraid of me, Lena," Hadrian promised her. "You can tell me what you've heard."

54

"I've heard," Lena ventured, "about the Aureate Guard that live there."

Hadrian laughed. "That live there? Lena, that's us. We *are* the Aureate Guard."

Lena's eyes widened. "Y-you're an Aureate Guard? You all are?"

"Well most are—the Masters are considered Aureate Guard—they're the ones on horseback. The ones on foot are apprentices"

Lena had gone pale. She looked as though she was barely listening. Hadrian looked at her with concern. "What is it? What's wrong?"

Pieces began to fall together in Lena's mind. If these men were the Aureate Guard, and they knew she had ridden from South, if they were aware that Daimonas was hiding in the desert, they could have easily drawn the wrong conclusions about her. Now she had been captured as a potential enemy by the very people she had been depending on for safety. What if the prisoner in the desert had been wrong, and the Aureate Guard were not willing to welcome her as he had thought? When she had woken without the pendant she had been sure she had lost it during the ride, but now she began to wonder if one of the Aureate Guard had found it on her while she was unconscious. And if that pendant had belonged to their Order....

"You don't look well," Hadrian said. He clasped Lena's arm. "Are you sick?"

"I-I'm frightened," Lena confessed.

"Frightened? Why? Of us? There's nothing to be afraid of." Hadrian caught her eyes in his. Confused by the sudden anxiety he found there, he furrowed his brow, leveled his gaze, and whispered, "I won't let anything happen to you, Lena. I promise."

Lena felt a sudden, warm relief and a surge of gratitude toward Hadrian. The anxious nausea she had been experiencing slowly subsided. At least she had an ally.

***

The din of horses' hooves on cobbled streets echoed throughout the City of the Aureate Star. Shuttered windows flew open, revealing wide-eyed faces that were eager to watch the procession. A woman outside of her house paused in her sweeping to watch it pass. Children with dirt-smudged faces and hair like duck-fluff stood in awe, staring at the Aureate Guard as they passed. Most of the people were fair, pale-skinned with hair the color of cornsilk. Their clothing was made of wool; the men wore solid-colored tunics, leggings, and leather boots. The women wore simple woolen dresses. Lena was mesmerized by her surroundings. The city's inhabitants and its architecture left her breathless. Pioni's castle had been massive but by no means elegant. Lena was fascinated by the towers of white stone that spiraled into the sky, the tips of some piercing clouds.

"Mostly shops and apartment towers," Hadrian told Lena. He was eager to inform her about his city, and she was content to listen. "You know, no other city has towers like these. Those apartment towers were just developed a few years ago. There are farmlands outside the City, mainly for apple-growers and animal-raisers, but this is the heart of the country. It's the biggest city on the continent, you know. Oh, and that's the Queen's Tower," he pointed to an especially grand structure, the tallest that Lena could see, "it's the tallest building on the Continent. And that's the House of the Aureate Star. That's where we're going."

Lena turned her gaze from the Queen's Tower and followed Hadrian's index finger to a larger building nearby. She looked at it carefully trying to discern what seemed odd about it.

"It's in the shape of a star," Hadrian supplied. "It's hard to see from here, but up on some of the hills, where you can look down on it, it's breathtaking."

The first horse in the procession had reached the stone ramp that led to the entrance of the Star. The apprentices hurried forward to take the reins of their master's horses; Ince was already leading a chestnut stallion but came to take Hadrian's horse from him as well. Lena was about to ask why Hadrian was on horseback if still an apprentice to Master Jairdan, as she had been told, but she bit back the question when she saw who was watching her.

Prudentior, the High Master that seemed to Lena to the sternest of the trio, was waiting for her at the ramp with a scowl on his face.

Hadrian dismounted first and turned his horse over to Ince, who had practically fallen over himself to reach Hadrian in time to gather the reins. Then Hadrian lifted Lena down, mindful of the fact that her hands were still bound. The instant that Hadrian had set her on the ground, Prudentior grasped Lena firmly by the arm and led her up the ramp into the temple. Hadrian followed just behind them, thunder-browed, glaring at Prudentior.

"He's already very attached to her," Jairdan commented to Master Scio. The pair were at the end of the long line of Aureate Guard, walking their chestnut horses up the street.

"It is to be expected," Scio replied. "He has grown up without any true family. It is not surprising that he is intrigued by this girl. Hadrian is a kind boy. It is natural for him to feel compassion and empathy for her. She is his sister."

"It's just…I fear for his sake," Jairdan said. "I can only imagine the life she has been subjected to if she has been raised by one of Daimonas' followers, as we suppose she has. That kind of treatment for seventeen years…it would be almost impossible for her to turn back now. She would have to be an exceptional girl."

"If she is your apprentice's twin, then I think it would be safe for us to assume that she is indeed exceptional." Scio eyed Jairdan severely. "You are one of the few who realizes the amazing chance that we've been granted by her arrival. If we can turn her back to the light, we may not only become strong enough to destroy Daimonas and his followers; we could prevent the most dreaded event of our future."

"'Cast into darkness the world will be'," Jairdan quoted. "The Shadow Age."

"It may not come to pass," Scio said. He glanced up at the sky. "Her deliverance, if she can be saved, is a great blessing."

"But if she can't be," Jairdan said, "then it is a terrible curse indeed."

Chapter Six
At Council with the High Masters

Lena fidgeted under the hot scrutiny of the High Masters. She was uncomfortable with these types of appraising glares, because in her experience, there was usually beating on the other end. She searched for comfort in the kindest pair of eyes: Hadrian's. He had grabbed her arm just before they had stepped into the meeting room of the High Masters and whispered urgently, "Lena, whatever you do, do not lie to them. Be honest, and you will win their trust."

Lena thought about this as she gazed at the other faces in the room. The bald old man, Scio, looked kind, but the intensity of his gaze made Lena nervous.

The other man that drew her attention was middle-aged, with reddish-brown hair. He had been introduced to her as Master Jairdan, to whom Hadrian was apprenticed. She had seen him speaking to Hadrian during the ride to the City and he had appeared kind then, but the look in his eyes now told Lena that he did not completely trust her.

There was another High Master, a man named Chista. Lena found comfort in his eyes as well; he was pudgy and cheerful, and smiled at her when he saw her looking at him.

In sharp contrast to the sympathy in Chista's look, Lena found active dislike smoldering in the eyes of the white-haired High Master, Prudentior, who had escorted her into the meeting room. He was the first to ask her a question.

"You have told us your name is Lena. What is your birthplace?"

A series of convincing lies ran through Lena's mind, but she remembered what Hadrian had said and decided against each one. Aside from Hadrian's advice, there was something about the High Masters that suggested that they would be able to see through a lie.

58

"I- I don't know my birthplace, my lord. I was bought in slave auction as an infant. I never knew my parents."

She was startled by the reaction that this caused in the High Masters. They leaned in and exchanged urgent whispers.

Jairdan spoke. "If I may, High Masters?"

"Of course, Master Jairdan, speak freely," Scio invited.

"Who told you that you were bought at a slave market?" Jairdan asked Lena.

She hesitated. "The man who raised me, my lord."

Prudentior said coldly, "What is the name of this man?"

"Lord Pioni, my lord."

"And you were brought up in the Southern Desert?"

Lena nodded.

"As a slave?" Jairdan asked.

"Yes," Lena said. "But more as an..." she trailed off, chewing on her lip as she to think of the right word.

"Go on," Master Scio urged kindly.

"I was raised as a... a sort of apprentice by Lord Pioni."

"An apprentice? What was your craft?" Prudentior asked.

"I was taught to fight, and to use magic," Lena said meekly. "Lord Pioni's master wanted me to be his champion."

The words fell heavily on the ears of the High Masters. "And what was the name of this Pioni's master?" Prudentior asked.

Again Lena hesitated, sensing that this was the heart of the issue. "It was Lord Daimonas," she whispered at last.

These words caused a veritable uproar. Crushed by a tumult of responses to her statement, Lena glanced desperately at Hadrian.

Don't be frightened.

Lena's eyes widened. Hadrian's words had formed themselves inside her head, just as they had when she had spoken to the prisoner in the desert castle. She held her breath, and without any effort at all, she heard her own voice respond, clear as a bell, the physical voices of the outraged High Masters only a hazy backdrop compared to the clarity of this thought-speak.

But I am afraid. I swear to you, I've done nothing wrong, but I have dangerous secrets. The men who imprisoned me...they are evil.

Tell what you know. You are safe here. You are helping us. You will not be harmed.

How are we speaking like this?

I don't know.

Hadrian's eyes were wide and held the traces of fear, like Lena's own, but his words brought her comfort. She was more confident when she turned back to face the High Masters.

Scio leaned forward to speak to Lena. "How did you escape the desert, child?"

Lena swallowed hard and glanced at Hadrian.

It's all right. Tell them.

"A- a man was taken prisoner. I don't know how long he had been in the dungeons, or why they captured him to begin with, but Lord Daimonas brought him to me and forced me to... demonstrate my abilities." The tears Lena had thus far been just barely able to hold back now sprung from her eyes at the memory.

Scio's face was suddenly stony. "What do you mean?" he asked, his voice low.

"Daimonas was displeased because he told me I would be his champion, but I refused. He wanted me to fight someone... someone of your order... he wanted me to kill him."

Realization dropped like a lead stone in Hadrian's stomach. *Blessed Star*, he thought. *She means me.*

Lena was looking down at her hands, which were still bound with the thick rope. Tears splashed onto her limp fingers as she continued. "I told Daimonas that I didn't want to kill anyone, and he brought this prisoner out and told me to kill him. As a *demonstration*."

"Can you describe this prisoner?" Scio pressed.

"Long, fair hair, middle-aged, hazel eyes." Blinded by tears, Lena looked down at her hands. "Unarmed."

Prudentior asked icily, "And after your master ordered you to kill him?"

"I refused at first," Lena said quickly, "but Daimonas...he started torturing the man. And me. He said if I didn't kill the prisoner, he would. And then, something inexplicable happened."

Every eye in the room was fixed on Lena. She took a deep breath. "The man spoke to me inside my head. He told me that I must get to the City of the Aureate Star, that I must find the Aureate Guard, that they would help me. He said the prophecy would be countered." She raised red-rimmed eyes to meet the gaze of the High Masters. "I don't know what he meant."

Prudentior asked, "What happened after he told you this?"

"He gave me a necklace. He told me to rub it in the soil and hide it in my boot so Lord Daimonas and Lord Pioni wouldn't see it. Then..." another tear dropped and broke on the tightly knotted ropes "...he told me to kill him." Lena was weeping now. "I didn't want to," she sobbed. "I didn't...I didn't want to." She sagged visibly under the emotional weight.

"But you did," Master Prudentior's voice was icy.

"He was unarmed...I begged Daimonas not to make me, but the prisoner said he was not afraid. He said Daimonas would kill him if I did not."

"And so you ran him through."

Hadrian glared daggers at Prudentior.

"It wasn't like that!" Lena burst out. "I had no other choice!"

"Aside from murder?"

Lena shook her head miserably. "You don't understand!"

"Peace, Master Prudentior." Master Scio looked sternly at the High Master on his right. Then, he turned his gaze back to Lena who was wracked by silent sobs, tears running in unending streams down her cheeks. "I realize this is hard for you, child," he said. "But know that you have the protection of the Aureate Guard, and their trust."

"Master Scio?" Master Prudentior looked angrily at the old man.

"The girl is speaking the truth, Master Prudentior," Scio said sharply. "If you are unable to see that, it is because your mind is fogged with the cloud of your distrust."

Master Prudentior snapped his mouth shut and sat back in his seat.

Scio turned back to Lena. "Please, continue your story. Understand that this is hard for us as well, as it seems the prisoner was a man we all knew. His name was Emissi; he was a revered Aureate Guard and a dear friend to everyone here."

Lena put a hand to her mouth in horror. "I'm so sorry," she gasped.

"It is as you say," Jairdan said. "Master Emissi was a very wise man. He would certainly have been killed by Daimonas had you not done it yourself. Given the situation, I see neither wickedness nor dishonor in what you did."

Chista nodded emphatically. "Well said, Master Jairdan."

Hadrian glanced in appreciation at his master. Lena gave Jairdan a grateful smile and wiped her eyes. Addressing Scio, she went on, "Afterward, Daimonas had me sent back to my cell. As I said, I'd concealed the pendant in my boot. I took it out to look at it, and it…did something. The door flew open, a flash of light blinded the guards, I found my way to the stables…I can't explain what happened."

Master Scio interrupted. "I can. The pendant that Emissi gave you is a powerful tool. All the power of the Aureate Guard is invested in it."

"But what about the stone?" Hadrian asked. "Why was that stone embedded in your ankle?"

Lena grimaced at the painful memory. "The stone was a device meant to keep me from running away. If I thought about plans of escape, my leg would start to throb. If I left the palace worse things would happen. I would get sick, feverish, dehydrated. I just don't understand why it suddenly disappeared."

"The sudden lifting of permanent magic such as what you are describing in most cases can only occur if the one who cast the spell is killed," Scio said.

Lena's eyes widened. "Do you mean that Lord Pioni is dead?"

"It is the only explanation that I can think of for the way that the stone suddenly vanished," Scio said.

The revelation of Pioni's death had shocked Lena speechless

He smiled. "You have told us much, Lena of the Southern Desert. Now it is time we revealed some things to you."

Lena's eyes darted around the room. "What things?" she asked.

Master Scio sighed and ran a hand over his bald head. "It is difficult to know where to begin," he said. "Perhaps I should start by telling you about a prophecy."

"A prophecy?" Lena asked.

"Yes. A prophecy that was told to me by an oracle a few years before you were born. You would be seventeen now, wouldn't you, Lena?"

"Yes," Lena said hesitantly. "But how did you know that?"

Chapter Seven
The Aureate Star

Alone with the High Masters, Lena hugged herself, shivering. The sun was setting, and this part of the continent was much colder than her former home. She was frightened, too. She had no idea why Scio had dismissed everyone else in the room, why the High Masters could possibly want a private audience with her.

"Lena." Scio spoke her name gently, and her eyes shot to him, wide and frightened. "We have much to tell you, child," Scio said.

"Perhaps something hot to drink, or a cloak at least, would ease the news?" Chista suggested.

"Yes, that's a good idea. Is there anything else that you need, Lena?"

She shook her head.

Chista smiled and rose. "I'll get that drink," he said, winking at her.

"Thank you," Lena whispered.

"Very good," said Scio. "I suppose I will begin."

***

The sun went down, and the red sunset bled into a night as dark and blue as a sapphire. Hadrian was standing on the balcony that extended grandly from his bedchamber, a warm breeze swirling around him. The night was a mild one, and Hadrian was alone, with only the flickering torchlight for company. He was glad of the solitude; he was still overwhelmed with the weight of the recent discovery and worn by a tumult of emotions; snippets of remembered conversations taunted him.

"He wanted me to fight someone...someone of your order...he wanted me to kill him."

"It made you our champion. If your sister had grown to be Daimonas' hero, instructed in the Dark Powers, you would have been our only hope of rescue."

"I would have had to kill my own sister?"

"It might have been the only choice."

***

Still in the council room with the three High Masters, Lena sat rigidly, staring at nothing. "My- my brother?" she asked. "You're sure?"

Scio inclined his head. "Yes."

Lena was pale. "I never knew..."

"Are you all right?" Chista asked.

"Does he know?" Lena asked, without answering.

"Hadrian? Yes. We told him our suspicions last night."

Lena was on the verge of tears. "I would have killed him," she whispered. "If that man—if Emissi hadn't come, I'd still be there and—Daimonas might have made me..."

"Here, there's no use in that line of thought," Chista said. "He did, you aren't, and he won't."

"Well... now what?" Lena asked.

"What do you mean by that?" Prudentior asked.

"Well, I mean, what do you want me to do now? Do you want me to go away?"

"Go away, Good Star girl, why would we want that?" Chista shook his head furiously.

"Well," Lena hesitated. "I...I was meant to be your enemy... surely you don't want me near?"

"Is that what you would like?" Scio inquired. "To go away?"

"I have nowhere to go," Lena said. "But, if it were what you wanted, I have no claim to a place here."

"On the contrary," Chista said, "it is we who have no right to ask you to stay."

65

"What? I don't understand," Lena said.

Scio sighed. "You were groomed to be a champion of the dark power. Daimonas wanted you as his guardian, and as his hero. If he was willing to trust you with that task, I do not doubt that you possess skills an Aureate Guard twice your age would envy. Because of those talents, and because you have been so close to Daimonas, we must ask you to do something that we have no right to request."

"What do you want me to do?" Lena asked. "You saved me from death in the fields, from a life of captivity and shadow. I will do what you ask."

Chista gave Lena a penetrating stare. "The task that we would give you might claim your life."

Lena's skin prickled. She replied firmly, "My life is yours to use as you will."

Prudentior blinked and looked hard at Lena. There was, for the first time, respect in his eyes.

"You are brave and honorable," Scio said, "and you will need both traits if you are to do what we will ask of you."

"Tell me," Lena said.

"Daimonas is a great threat to the survival of our Order. He will not abandon you as lost. He will come after you. I ask you to defy him again. I ask you to join our Order. Join us in the fight against Daimonas."

"Join you?" Lena breathed. "High Master, that is no request, it is an honor."

Prudentior leaned forward in his chair. "You would be willing to fight him? Daimonas? He held you in captivity—tortured you—and you would not be afraid to face him?"

"His crimes against me would be my principle reasons for joining you." Lena's eyes glittered. "I only hope that I am brave enough, and strong enough, to do what you ask."

"I believe you are," Chista said, rising.

"And I," Scio said.

Prudentior rose slowly. "And I," he said with a stiff nod.

The High Masters smiled. "Welcome to our Order, Lena of Locusorti," Scio said. "There is a small ceremony; we will hold it in two days. In the morning you will be summoned again. We will need to evaluate your skills, before we can teach you anything further. When we have decided your place in the Order, we will induct you properly."

"But for now, please, relax. Go and see your brother; take rest. You are safe here, Lena, and valued." Chista smiled assuringly at her.

Lena left the room, trembling with terror and excitement.

***

Still alone on his balcony, Hadrian turned at the sound of someone knocking at his door. Surprised that anyone would come this late, Hadrian opened the door. Lena stood in the shadows of the outer corridor, tears fresh on her cheeks. Hadrian put one arm around her shoulder and clutched her hand in his own. Gently, he guided her onto the moonlit balcony.

As soon as I saw you, I thought…I knew… The words flowered in Hadrian's head, though Lena's lips had not moved.

Master Jairdan made me promise not to tell you until we were sure you were the right one. But I knew as well.

Lena's lip trembled, and she buried her face in the soft fabric of her brother's tunic. *I never knew I had anyone.*

Hadrian drew a ragged breath. *I was luckier than you*, he said, *I was given this…Jairdan, the High Masters, friends…but I knew…I felt something missing, some hole in me that I couldn't fill.*

For a moment, the twins stood together in silence, clinging to one another. Even when they stepped out of their embrace, they held hands still, reluctant to let that last connection break.

"Master Scio said I might stay in the bedchamber adjoined to yours," Lena ventured. "Would that be all right?"

Hadrian held her tighter, his eyes glassy. "Nothing would make me happier." He led Lena by the hand to the edge of the balcony. "I want to show you something." He pointed to the night sky. "There— do you see it? Just there—the one that looks as if it's resting on the tip of the Queen's tower."

67

A smile of recognition and understanding spread slowly over Lena's face as she looked. There, in the deep and vast blue-dark of night, was a single, golden star that out-shined all the silver ones around it. It burned in the dark sky like the tawny eye of lion. There was a strange feeling of sentience to it; in an odd way, Lena felt that the star was aware of her presence.

"The Aureate Star," she breathed. "I wondered…"

Hadrian smiled and leaned forward onto the white railing that ran along the balcony, his gaze fixed on the golden star. "It's important to this city. We're very proud of it," he said with a smile. "The legend behind is that once, a long time ago, when the continent was still divided among countless tribes, a star fell from the sky and landed in the center of the land that would become the city. The city's founders, the Great Fathers, followed the star and broke ground where it fell. After they had built the City, they saw that a golden star had taken the place of the one that had fallen. The Star is a symbol of the City, you understand, of everything we stand for, and looking at it reminds everyone of that."

Still gazing up at the sky, Lena said, "This feels right…you, the City, the star…it just feels right."

Hadrian nodded. "I think so," he said.

***

The thought of any separation, even one as minimal as goodnight, was too ugly to consider after the past few emotionally taxing hours. Lena sat out on the balcony with Hadrian all night, listening to stories of his training, of the Aureate Guard, and of the Queen Regina, the well-loved leader of Aurea. Lena finally drifted away into a doze, the last sound to touch her ears the soft, pleasing snatches of her brother's tales. She did not even stir when Hadrian lifted her up in his arms, carried her inside, and placed her in a bed in the chamber next to his.

The next morning when Lena awoke and sat up, she was greeted by an unfamiliar sound: the rustle of sheets. She found herself on a down-filled bed, with crisp, white sheets spread over legs. With a contented yawn, Lena flopped back and felt her muscles relax when, accustomed to the cold stone of a cell, they touched the soft mattress. As Lena stared up at the ceiling, she smiled, luxuriating in the novel comfort of a real bed.

There was a knock at the door and a young man that Lena had never seen before poked his head around the doorframe.

"Hadrian?" he looked around the room and noticed Lena. "Oh!" A blush flooded his cheeks. "Begging your pardon. Very sorry." He took a step backward and knocked over a large potted plant that stood on a table just outside the door. It fell to the floor and cracked, and soil spilled across the floor. Lena muffled giggles with her hand. The blush crept all the way up to the tips of the young man's ears as he looked dejectedly at the ruined vase. "Very sorry," he muttered again, and turned.

"Wait!" Lena said. "Don't go! What's your name?"

The young man looked back in surprise. "*My* name?"

Lena nodded.

A nervous grin slipped onto the boy's face. "My name's Ince," he said. He raked his fingers through his strawberry-blond hair, combing it back from his face.

Lena got off the bed. She had spent the night in her dirty, wrinkled tunic, and it was even more rumpled now, but Ince continued to stare as if she were a goddess. "I'm Lena," she said, holding out her hand.

"V-v-very p-pleased to meet you, Miss," Ince said.

"Lena! You've met Ince I see! Excellent, he can come to breakfast with us." Hadrian stepped into the room, barely glancing at the toppled plant. "These are for you," he said, and tipped a stack of folded clothes into Lena's arms. "Get dressed quickly; we'll get something to eat, and then Master Scio wants to see you."

***

Moments later, dressed in a green, woolen tunic similar to Hadrian's and Ince's, Lena was walking through the temple's winding corridors to the dining hall. She nervously smoothed the golden star that was embroidered on the front of the tunic.

When Lena stepped into the dining hall with Ince and Hadrian, she had to blink to be sure what she saw before her was real. Tables lined the enormous hall, and almost every seat was taken; at every table there were people laughing and talking over a breakfast that looked to Lena as if it belonged on the tables of royalty. She took a seat with Ince and Hadrian and for a moment was too overwhelmed by the amount of food to choose anything. She stared as bowls of cut fruit were passed around, watched Hadrian reach for a thick slice of brown bread and slather it generously it with butter, blinked in surprise when Ince held out a pitcher of cold milk to her. "Would you like some?" he asked. "There's juices too—orange, grapefruit—apricot maybe."

"No, milk's fine," Lena said dazedly. Ince obligingly filled the wooden cup in front of her with milk, then poured himself some.

"What are these?" Lena asked. She reached out and picked up a fruit with a thin, pearl-colored skin through which a deep crimson flesh shone through.

"That's an empressa fruit. They grow them in orchards outside the city, all along the border and into Westmore. Try it," Hadrian urged. "They're delicious this time of year."

Lena bit into the fruit. Her teeth broke the pale skin and the flesh and juice exploded into her mouth with a rich, sweet flavor. "It's wonderful!" Lena said, catching a drip of juice at the corner of her mouth with the tip of her finger. "I've never tasted anything like it."

"You like those, try these berries," Ince said, holding out his hand. Cupped in his palm were some plump, purple berries. Ince's teeth were already stained with the juice.

Lena took a few from Ince and sampled them. As she did, she gazed around her at all of the tables, all of the *people*. "There are so many," she said. "So many people."

"Well, The Star's not just home to the Aureate Guard," Hadrian said, his cheeks bulging.

"It's not?" Lena asked.

Hadrian shook his head and swallowed. "No. We're here to defend the Star, and the city of course, but there are all kinds of people here. Orphans, widows, people too poor, or sick, or old, to take care of themselves. Healers and caretakers also train here; they take care of the people who can't take care of themselves. The Star's a safe haven for people who can't make it on their own."

"And the people who live here support the Star themselves; they hunt, cook, and clean for each other," Ince added.

Lena continued to look around her. "It's wonderful," she said.

Ince passed her a thick piece of bread, and Hadrian refilled her glass.

***

Only a short while later, full from the best meal she had ever had, Lena walked with Ince and Hadrian to the door of the meditation center, where Hadrian said she would find the high Masters. "Don't be nervous," Hadrian said, reading his sister's face. "I'll see you soon."

The room was drenched with sunlight let in by glass windows that overlooked the city. There was a semi-circle of six round cushions in the center of the room. The High Masters were seated on these cushions, each the picture of exquisite calm. Their breathing was slow, all their muscles relaxed. Lena was hesitant to intrude; she entered the room silently and waited nervously, not sure whether or not she should speak. Before she had made a decision, Scio opened his eyes with a smile.

"Lena. Come forward, child."

The other two High Masters opened their eyes and inclined their heads in acknowledgment. Lena bowed and stepped into the rich bath of light within the room.

"Please, sit down," Scio offered, and gestured at one of the round cushions in the room.

Lena took a seat, endeavoring unsuccessfully to assume the same relaxed, cross-legged pose of the High Masters. "You wanted to see me, High Masters?"

Scio took a deep breath and surveyed Lena sternly. "Lena, last night when we invited you to join us, we did not explain fully what that entails. You have probably seen that we harbor many here, and you will be offered sanctuary as long as you want it. But if you truly want to join us as an Aureate Guard, we must evaluate your skills. If we are to teach you, we must find what you already know."

"Of course," Lena said. "Whatever you want."

"First, we must know if you speak any languages other than the Shared Tongue," Chista said.

Lena answered, "I picked up a southern dialect that the guards at Pioni's castle spoke. Histuk, it's called. It's derived from the Black Tongue that they speak in Siin, I think."

"Black Language dialects are a very hard to learn," Scio said. "There are very few here in the City that speak them at all, and most that do speak them poorly."

"What about the Old Language?" Prudentior asked. "Have you ever read any of the ancient verses? Ballads, old world prose?"

Lena blushed fiercely. "I—I'm afraid I never learned to read, High Master."

"Ah. I see. Yes." Prudentior turned to the other High Masters for rescue. The inability to read seemed to be both a mark of her poor childhood and a new obstacle in the path of Lena's training. Prudentior was unsure how to react.

"I suppose, then, that you cannot write either?" Chista asked gently.

Lena shook her head shamefully.

"Well, those are two things that you'll need to learn," Scio said. "I can teach you easily; a smart girl like you will pick it up quickly. I'm sure you don't speak the Old Language either, few do, but we'll have to teach you that as well. Most political negotiations are still conducted in that language, for form more than anything, but it is essential that you know it."

Lena's eyes were bright with excitement. "I've always hoped to learn to read!" she said. "I'll study whatever you want; I'll work hard."

"We have no doubt," Scio said, with a smile.

"Now for the more difficult part." Chista reached into the deep folds of his brown cloak and produced a small, white candle. He placed it on the floor. "Can you light it?"

Lena looked up at Chista inquisitively. "Just light it?" When Chista nodded, she waved a hand at the candle, and a flame blossomed on the wick.

Chista nodded. "Put it out." Lena gestured again, and the flame died.

"Can you lift it?" Lena curled her fingers and slowly raised her hand. The candle rose a few inches off of the ground and hovered there.

"Light it while it is in the air," Scio said. With another sweep of Lena's fingers, the candle was lit.

"Extinguish it, and set it down."

Lena did as Scio asked.

"That was very good," Scio said. "It seemed easy for you."

"I've practiced on...larger objects," Lena said carefully.

"How much larger?" Prudentior asked.

Lena cleared her throat. "Boulders, and things."

"Boulders," Prudentior repeated.

"Boulders?" Chista's eyes widened.

"You can levitate boulders?" Scio asked.

"And throw them," Lena said. Anxiously she asked, "Is that bad?"

"No, child, no! It's very good, actually," Chista answered. The High Masters were trading shocked glances.

"You can use a blade, I imagine?" Prudentior asked.

Lena nodded. "Yes."

"Any other weapons?"

"I'm a fair hand with a staff, and I can make do with a mace, if need be, but I much prefer a sword. My soulfire's terrible, but other than that..."

"What was that?" Scio asked sharply.

"I'm sorry?" Lena said.

"What did you say was terrible?"

Hesitantly, Lena replied, "My soulfire."

"Soulfire?" The High Master raised his eyebrows. "So," he brooded softly to himself. "Daimonas has discovered that power. No doubt it was he who first learned the skill and not this Lord Pioni...he must have taught it to him later...no telling how many he's shared the power with"

"High Master?" Lena asked.

"It is not a skill that the Aureate Guard employ," Scio replied. "Hundreds of years ago, we used it quite frequently, but when we learned the results it caused…"

"Forgive me, High Master," Prudentior put in, "but I'm afraid I don't understand. Soulfire? I've never heard of it."

Scio sighed heavily. "You wouldn't have, I'm afraid. It was before our time and has been kept very secret since; I learned of it only through an old friend who was a young man when it was forbidden. Soulfire, you see, is a form of magic so evil and so powerful that, bit by bit, as it is used again and again, it steals part of the conjurer's soul. One who constantly uses soulfire eventually becomes little more than an empty shell, evil intentions encased in a human form. To use it, one needs to have a great source of anger, hatred, bloodlust, and similar emotions to draw on. Without the passion of these feelings, the soulfire cannot exist. You say you never mastered soulfire?"

Lena shook her head. "No."

Chista smiled. "That speaks well of your character."

Lena blushed. "Is there anything else you would have me do, High Masters?"

"Yes." Scio smiled. "Go and get your brother."

***

"Learning to use a sword," Scio said, when Lena had collected Hadrian and the two had met him outside the meditation center, "is at the heart of becoming an Aureate Guard. Practicing the skill teaches discipline, patience, balance, speed—and knowing how to use a blade is of course, essential because the Aureate Guard are, first and foremost, a military force." As he spoke, he led Lena and Hadrian down a sunlit corridor. The twins had to hurry to keep up with the deceptively quick old man.

"Lena, I want you to spar with Hadrian. Seeing what you've been taught in the area of swordplay will help me decide where we should begin your training."

They reached a tall set of white doors with ornate carvings on the front. Scio turned the handle of each door and pushed. They swung open to reveal a grand, cavernous room. Rays of sunlight filtered in through a high window. Scio hobbled across the room to a smaller door. He pulled it open to reveal a tiny storeroom. Blades of all different sizes hung from the back of the door. An experienced eye told Lena that though they were dull for sparring purposes, they were of fine make. She reached out and ran her hands over the weapons. Behind Scio, inside the tiny weapons-room, she could see different types of arms: maces, staffs, and bows. Lena's hungry eyes devoured the sight. She had practiced with all kinds of weapons but had never seen so many fine examples of craftsmanship.

Watching her scrutinize each weapon, Scio smiled. "All in good time," he promised. "But choose a simple blade for now. Hadrian can take you to the armory later to get you decently equipped, but for today all you'll need is a sword."

Lena eventually settled on a light, straight-bladed sword. There were no curved, Southern-made blades like the ones she typically practiced with, but she liked the easy speed and grace of the sword she had chosen. Hadrian selected a broader, heavier sword from the wall.

"Now, go to the center of the floor," Scio instructed. "Slow strokes first, if you please. Concentrate on mechanics."

Lena and Hadrian stepped to the center of the room and began to slowly circle one other, each waiting for the other to make a move. Hadrian swung first, but Lena easily blocked him and brought her blade in slow-motion toward Hadrian's thigh. Hadrian blocked this, and raised his sword again. The sounds of their blades connecting echoed, slow and rhythmic, as they went through a series of simple strikes and parries until Scio ordered, "Faster."

Lena reacted first. She whipped her blade toward Hadrian's chest in a swift uppercut, surprising him with her speed. He blocked her easily enough, but Lena surprised him again by turning her blade and slicing it through the air in a downward curve. It took all of Hadrian's speed and concentration to block her attacks. Hadrian, who had been hailed as the best Aureate Guard of the current Order, potentially of all time, was unused to being consistently on the defensive. He was impressed and pleased with Lena's skill, but slightly frustrated that he was not able to move quickly enough to get in an attack of his own. When he finally did manage a few offensive swings, Lena blocked them easily.

Despite her advantageous speed, however, Lena could not match Hadrian's strength. Hadrian let her tire herself with quick blows and seized the first opportunity he saw, a split-second of hesitation, to thrust his blade at Lena and force her backward with a sudden burst of power. With Lena momentarily off balance, Hadrian took a swing. Lena ducked it and darted away; Hadrian followed.

It was evident that the twins were evenly matched. Neither had managed to get in what would have been a decent blow before Scio finally told them to stop. "You did very well," Scio told Lena. "You will be able to train at Hadrian's level, except for the additional studying with me that we discussed earlier. Hadrian, take Lena down to the armory and let her choose what she needs. Explain to her about the unnamed blades." Hadrian bowed, and Lena quickly followed suit. Hadrian led Lena out of the training room, back into the sunny corridor.

"You fight very well," Hadrian told her, though he was frowning.

"Thank you," Lena said. "So do you. But tell me. What's an unnamed blade?"

A smile broke on Hadrian's face. "You'll see."

Hadrian led Lena outside, across courtyard, and down a small dirt slope that led to a squat, wooden building with a thatch roof. This was the armory; Hadrian took Lena in through a side door and led her down a small, straw-lined corridor, giving a friendly wave to a group of men by the door.

Hadrian stopped and turned into a large room on the left-hand side of the corridor. Lena followed him and gasped.

The room was stocked full of the most beautiful, finely made swords Lena had ever seen. There were countless blades here, glistening golden in the sunlight. Hadrian stopped and leaned against the doorframe, but Lena stepped further into the room, breathless as her fingers brushed the hilt of a blade that rested on a table.

"These are the unnamed blades," Hadrian said softly from behind her. "The Aureate Guard believe that a sword is much more than a weapon, that because it becomes such a part of a solider that it takes on part of his soul. Other weapons are different; they aren't used nearly as much, but swords are used all the time, carried by an Aureate Guard wherever he goes. They believe that a sword should only be used by one person. When an Aureate Guard dies, he is always buried with the sword he carried in life. Because the swords of an Aureate Guard tend to become a part of the soldier, so much more than inanimate steel, every sword is given a name. These are unnamed blades, because they have yet to be chosen by their destined owners."

"This one," Lena breathed. Her fingers whispered over a sword with a crescent blade whose hilt was gilded with a pale gold. "This is the one."

Hadrian nodded. "Then it's yours."

***

Later that evening, Lena sank into the first warm bath of her life. Before, she had always washed with a cloth and a jug of cold water. Tonight, she had drawn her own steaming bath in a wooden tub and now sat in the delicious warmth, scrubbing every inch of skin pink with a soft cloth lathered with a pleasantly scented soap. When she had finished, she tilted her head back against the rim of the wooden tub. Her gaze wandered to her bed, on which were lain out all the weapons she had chosen that day: a staff with barely any weight to it at all, a bow ornately carved with vines and blossoms, a quiver of arrows with phoenix feather fletching, a large, forest green shield emblazoned with the golden star, and the most prized possession of all, the exquisite sword in a brown leather scabbard with a pale, star-like gem set into the leather. Her gaze traveled to her balcony and out into the night, finally coming to rest on the golden star that was the namesake of her new home and that was symbolized on the scabbard of her new sword. For the first time in her life, Lena felt truly blessed.

***

"So she is as good as her brother, then."

There were three candles only lit in the Chamber of Council. Each was held by a High Master; each illuminated the face of its holder, but poorly. The result was that long, blue shadows still obscured the better part of each face, so that each looked drawn and spectral, only just recognizable.

"At least as good," Scio said. "I feel we only tapped the surface of her ability today. I am sure that Hadrian could levitate more weight than we expect at his level, but a boulder? And is that the greatest extent of *her* ability?" Scio sighed. "So much of this is guesswork, I'm afraid we may never be able to say for sure whether they are equally talented or whether one is more gifted than the other."

"Well, we can at least let them train together. They are close enough for that," Chista put in.

"Oh indeed," said Scio, "they'll train well together."

"But Hadrian is an apprentice," Prudentior said. "If we are to raise Lena to the same rank, she will need a master."

"I thought perhaps," Scio said carefully, "as the girl's situation is so unique, she might require a very…experienced trainer."

Chista narrowed his eyes. "You want to train her yourself?"

"What?" Prudentior asked. "A High Master with an apprentice? It's never been done before!"

"We've never had so delicate a situation on our hands," Scio said quietly.

"Exactly. Since there's no precedent, might as well break tradition!" Chista said merrily, looking quite pleased about the idea.

Prudentior was nodding slowly. "Well…I suppose she will require more attention, more *guidance* than a mere master could provide. All right. Perhaps you should train her, Scio."

"I agree," Chista said.

Scio nodded. "I will tell her in the morning."

"She is in quite an extraordinary position," Chista said. "She must be overwhelmed."

"Mm. I imagine so," Scio said. He paused for a moment, and said, "Hadrian must be as well. I did wonder whether he would be at all shaken by her presence. For seventeen years he's believed himself to be the best in our Order. We've made him believe so."

"Oh, I think Hadrian's above petty jealousy," Scio said. "He's too gifted to fall victim to *that*."

***

Alone in the training room, which was lit only by torches, Hadrian was going through a series of complicated stances. He was holding his heavy broadsword, sweating vigorously. He had been practicing alone for an hour already, but still, all he could see was Lena, darting away, just beyond the reach of his sparring blade.

Chapter Eight
Meditation

On the second day of Lena's stay at the Star, there was, as promised, an induction ceremony. The Star's entire military population was called to an assembly in the cavernous amphitheater, the room where all the Star's functions were carried out and the largest room that Lena had ever seen. Lena herself stood before the three High Masters in the pit of the amphitheater in the full dress of an Aureate Guard; she wore a fresh green tunic embroidered with the golden star, white leggings, brown leather boots, and a gray cloak also emblazoned with the star, and wore her new sword on her belt.

Scio came forward holding a large, white candle. "The job of an Aureate Guard," he said loudly and clearly, "is to endeavor always to act with honor on behalf of this our country, the land of the Aureate Star. Do you, Lena of Locusorti, promise always to defend this land, to give whatever is asked of you, to sacrifice your own life if necessary, in the effort to preserve peace in this land?"

Lena bowed. "I do, High Master."

"Do you swear to apply yourself with diligence to the teachings of our craft and to give proper respect to your masters and teachers?"

"I do, High Master."

"And do you, Lena of Locusorti, swear from this day forth, to, as is the duty of a true Aureate Guard, shed light where there is darkness?"

Lena bowed with a flourish of her hand; the candle lit, and she said, for the entire assembly to hear, "I do, High Master."

Immediately the assembled guardsmen rose and applauded. Lena turned to face them and bowed low. This ended the ceremony, and everyone filed slowly out of the amphitheater. In the pit, Scio approached Lena.

"We have decided, Lena, that based on your current skill level, we will induct you into the Order as an apprentice. This means that you will have a master who will tutor you in our craft and whom you will shadow on any missions that he is given." He glanced at the other High Masters then went on, "We have decided that as your situation is…unique…you need the tutelage of someone with more experience than the typical master. You see, to achieve the rank of master, one need only study at the Star for thirteen years; three of those as a novice, five each as an advanced novice and an apprentice. But we think your situation requires someone with a lifetime of experience in the Order."

Lena said nothing. Scio said, "We have decided that *I* should handle your instruction."

"Oh!" said Lena. "I would be honored, High Master," she said, flushed with excitement. "To receive instruction from you…I can't tell you what it would mean to me."

Scio smiled. "Well. You will just have to repay me with a fierce work ethic."

Lena grinned. "I assure you I will, High Master."

And she did. Lena's training progressed better than anyone could have hoped. She was more diligent and disciplined than any other student, except Hadrian. She expressed sincere gratitude at Scio's acceptance of her as his apprentice, and went on to impress him with her skill and determination. She became as strong as she was quick; good meals, proper rest, and general happiness made her healthier than she had been when she arrived in the City. She would have soon been able to defeat Hadrian in any sparring match had her fervor for training not kindled a renewed passion in her brother. Hadrian worked alongside his sister every day, observing her cat-like quickness, learning from her ways to become more efficient. The two became better conditioned together and soon could have sparred in an endless stalemate, neither tiring but neither overcoming the other.

Lena also progressed quickly in her study of the written word; she had been honest about her desire to learn to read and write, and her eagerness, as well as a natural penchant for languages, made the lessons easy. She had an exceptional grasp of both the Shared tongue and the Southern dialect she knew from the desert; teaching her letters and their sounds was easy, and it soon became no trouble for her to meld them together to make words and sentences. At the end of Lena's first week of training, even the skeptical Prudentior a had to admire her prowess with a blade, the magnitude of her power, and her thirst to learn more.

There was, however, one area of Lena's training in which she did not excel, in which she could not even have been considered to succeed. Meditation, as foreign an area of study as reading and writing, posed a constant problem for Lena. The skill, Scio said, enabled an Aureate Guard to clear his mind and approach negotiations without bias and battles without fear. It was mastered through careful practice and extreme mental focus. Each meditation session was a nightmare for Lena. Opening her mind lowered her defenses against memories of her past; she was tormented by gripping, painful memories in each session. To Lena, the peace that Hadrian experienced during a meditation session was unattainable; she was unable to let her mind go, and therefore unable to achieve the internal quietude Scio insisted was the key to a Aureate Guard's inner focus. She grew continually frustrated as her best efforts to master the skill failed.

"Breathe deeply," Scio said patiently late one evening as he, Hadrian and Lena sat in the meditation room. Though Hadrian had long ago mastered meditation, he often stayed for late sessions with Lena for moral support.

Lena sighed and shifted on the round cushion. "I can't," she said in frustration. "I can't do it."

"If you give up, you have already failed," Scio said gently. "Don't think about it so much. Just sit here in the quiet. Don't try to meditate. Just relax your body, and your mind will follow."

Hadrian bowed his head and closed is eyes in tandem with his sister. *It's all right,* he told her through thought speak. *You can do it.*

82

Lena wrapped herself deeper in the folds of her brown cloak. She didn't hear the door when Jairdan, familiar with the trouble she was having with meditation, stepped into the room to check her progress. She concentrated on her own breathing, felt her muscles slowly relax with each exhalation.

Hadrian could feel her sliding into the peace of meditation. *You're doing it,* he voiced. *You're doing well.*

*Well...well...*the word reverberated in Lena's drifting mind. *You're doing well...you're doing....you're doing...*

Terribly! What on earth is wrong with you? Focus! Pay attention to what you're doing! Concentrate!

Hadrian was shocked at the abrasive voice that had suddenly invaded his mind.

I-I'm trying! That was Lena's voice, trembling with timidity. *I really am trying—*

Hadrian felt the slap across his own cheek, heard the smack as the blow in Lena's memory connected with her skin. *Don't speak back to me! Just do as you're told!*

Hadrian could not only hear voices now; he could see out of Lena's eyes as the memory became clearer. Her vision was blurred by tears and her fingers trembled as she glanced down and drew a deep, quivering breath. A curtain of darkness descended on the memory as Lena closed her eyes in concentration; when she opened them again, her gaze was fixed on a large, black brick. She put out her hand, took a deep breath, and raised her arm, her fingers quivering with exertion. The rock wobbled, lifted slightly, then fell back to the floor. Lena glanced up hopefully, and for the first time Hadrian saw the face of her old master, Lord Pioni, a dark skinned, blonde-haired man with hard, cold eyes.

What are you looking up for? That's the best you can do?

Lena turned back to the brick and tried again to levitate it, droplets of sweat running down her forehead and catching on her eyelashes. Hadrian's own eyes stung as the salty perspiration dripped into Lena's eyes, already hot with held-back tears.

The brick rocked from side to side but did not lift off the ground.

Lena dropped her hands, breathing hard. *Please Master,* she whispered, *I'm so tired…if I could just rest I'm sure I could do it tomorrow…*

Have I taught you nothing? Do you even listen when I speak to you? You should be able to do this with a flick of your fingers!

Pioni levitated the rock with barely any effort and hurled it against the wall behind Lena. It broke on contact and Lena cried out, covering her head as the pieces rained down on her. Pioni clenched his hand into a fist and suddenly Hadrian was struggling to breathe. Lena's hand was at her throat, prying desperately at fingers that were not there. Pioni lifted Lena off the ground and pinned her to the wall.

Perhaps you do not want to do what I ask of you, Pioni speculated, walking slowly toward Lena. *Perhaps you are reluctant to strive to become stronger? Or is this a rebellion against me?*

Lena shook her head fervently, robbed of the ability to speak.

Pioni clenched his fist tighter. *We will try again tomorrow.*

A veil of darkness carried the memory into unconsciousness.

Hadrian opened his eyes and gasped for air, his lungs burning, blood pounding in his ears.

"Hadrian." Jairdan was bent over him, his hands on Hadrian's shoulders. "Are you all right?"

Hadrian looked around the room; he and Jairdan were the only ones there. "Where's Lena?"

"She just ran out in tears," Jairdan said. "High Master Scio went after her. What happened?"

"She…we were trapped in a memory," Hadrian said. "Pioni wanted her to levitate a stone. She couldn't do it and…he was punishing her." Hadrian stumbled over the words, nauseous from the memory.

Jairdan surveyed him in silence.

Hadrian shook his head. "It could just as easily have been me," he whispered, his eyes vacant. "If Pioni had just taken me rather than her…I would have been in her place." He looked up at Jairdan.

"You cannot dwell on what might have been," Jairdan said firmly, looking away. "It will drive you mad."

"I want to see Daimonas dead," Hadrian said through gritted teeth. "I hate him."

Jairdan frowned. "Daimonas is an evil man, Hadrian, and one who must be destroyed in order to preserve peace. But be careful of your anger. A man who lets his passions rule him is easily manipulated."

"Maybe," Hadrian said. "But nonetheless…"

***

Lena had fled to a courtyard near the center of the temple, outdistancing Scio and losing him by weaving through the maze of hallways and rooms that made up the Star. Now she sat alone in the dark courtyard on a stone bench beneath a pink-blossomed tree, crying quietly to herself, barely aware of the hazy droplets falling around her.

Ince was on his way to dinner after a late training session with his own master. The sound of someone crying in the courtyard made him pause to investigate.

"Are you all right?" Lena started when Ince put his hand on her shoulder and sat down beside her on the bench. "What is it?"

Lena wiped her eyes and shook her head. "It's nothing Ince, don't worry…"

"Oh all right. I understand. Me, I always come out into the courtyard alone for a good cry when I'm feeling my best."

Lena looked up at his honest eyes and good-natured smile and laughed through her tears. "It's just, I've been having such a hard time with meditation. I can't do it properly. Every time I try to relax, I start remembering…things."

She put her face in her hands. "Everyone wants me to do well," she said, "and I want to make Scio know how grateful I am to be his apprentice. But sometimes I feel like I'll never be good enough!" Her shoulders shook as she broke down into sobs again.

"Are you joking?" Ince asked, in earnest astonishment. "Lena, you're one of the best fighters this order has ever seen! All the little ones want to be like you; my youngest cousin trains here as well and she's constantly pestering me about you, wanting to know when you're going to be training so she and her pals can go down to watch you and pick up a few tips. So you haven't quite got the art of meditation down, so what? There are plenty of great Aureate Guards who struggle with certain things. You've never meditated before. You can't expect to excel at something you've never done."

A smile broke on Lena's face again. A gentle breeze tousled her curls, and Ince was struck by how lovely she looked, her eyes still bright with tears, the soft roses of her cheeks dusted with freckles, her golden curls lifted on the breeze. She put a hand on his knee. "You're a good friend, Ince," she said. "You've made me feel much better. Now." She stood up and wiped the last few tears away from her face. "Maybe you'll help me find Hadrian and join us for dinner?"

Ince stood up so fast that he bumped his head hard on a bough that jutted out above the bench. "Of course," he said, rubbing his head, while Lena muffled good-natured giggles. "I'd be delighted."

Chapter Nine
Wolf's Bane

Daimonas rode deep into the desert, into the very heart of Sanuul, to the capital city of Siin. He dismounted at the outskirts and raised his arms. A fierce wind rose up and caused his cloak to whip so furiously about him that his face was completely obscured by the black cloth. Suddenly, the cloth crumpled into a heap, and the wind died as quickly as it had come. A black Sanuulian viper, the deadliest creature on the Great Continent by far, feared by most but, as Daimonas knew, revered as near-gods by the people of Sanuul, poked its head out of the folds of the cloak and made its way into Siin, toward the palace.

Daimonas, the snake, slithered into the palace, sensing that he would find Queen Rhea in the gardens. He passed over tiled floors and into the lush, tropical gardens, the smell of soil and hot moisture nearly overpowering his heightened sense of smell.

Rhea was there, as a he had known she would be, and was mesmerized to see the great, black snake winding its way toward her. She bent and put her hand in front of it; Daimonas slithered onto her arm and coiled himself around it. Rhea stared, fascinated, at the snake and into its blood-red eyes.

It was there, in the depths of those ruby eyes, that the scene unfolded. Rhea gasped as a scene, no reflection but a vision, revealed itself to her in the gleam of the viper's eyes. Her husband Lord Raul appeared there, with Regina, the queen of Aurea. Raul had gone to Aurea recently, to discuss a new trade agreement; now, Rhea saw Regina offer her husband a glass of wine, saw the exchange of a smile, and saw a treacherously passionate kiss.

For centuries, many in Sanuul had believed the vipers to be

harborers of terrible truths that they could reveal to chosen few; Rhea had no trouble believing that she was one of those select people. With a shriek, she mounted the stairs to her bed chamber, pulled a dagger from her boot, and pierced her husband's heart. Raul choked and died with a gasp of shock and pain, his final glance resting on his beloved murderess. Rhea pulled the dagger out of her husband and continued to scream with rage, waking the entire household with her promise of revenge.

His work in the Southern Palace completed, Daimonas returned to his human form and to his horse, which was waiting just where he had left it. The horse that Daimonas had crafted from sand and smoke possessed an unnatural speed, and it bore him to the Western Lands, ruled by King Bruteaus, shortly after night had fallen. He again stopped his horse along the outskirts of the capital, Eglionan, and again raised his arms and disappeared behind the veil of his black cloak, but this time it was a gigantic, black crow that stepped forward from the cloak when the transformation was complete. The great bird flapped its enormous wings and rose into the sky, flying directly toward the castle of Bruteaus.

Daimonas perched on the sill of the window in Bruteaus' bedchamber. The night was warm, and the window was open. Daimonas poked his head inside and checked for guards. Finding none, he stepped into the room and glided silently to the bed where Bruteaus and his wife Elixa lay asleep. Daimonas beat his great wings, and from them poured forth a thick and evil fog. Unsuspecting, the couple in the bed inhaled that fog, and within moments began to toss feverishly in what had become a troubled sleep.

For with the smoke Daimonas had sent the slumbering king and queen a vision each, a terrible vision, a dream more real than any other, a dream that would grip to them like tar, poisoning their minds, muddying their ability to distinguish truth from reality. It was a dream about the Golden Soldiers of the northern country of Aurea. To Bruteaus Daimonas gave a vision of his wife and daughters viciously murdered at the hands of an Aureate Guard. To Elixa, it was a vision seen through the window of a room where she had sought safety with her daughters; through that window she saw her husband and three sons fall to the Aureate Guard, and heard banging at the door of her sanctuary. She knew the paralyzing sense of fear as the realization came that she and her two little daughters were cornered and had no hope of escape.

Bruteaus gritted his teeth and tossed in his sleep. Elixa moaned in sorrow and terror.

Daimonas kept his crow's form as he swept North, to the tower where the fair queen Regina slept, her short, ginger curls spread out on her pillow like copper corkscrews. Her window, too, was thrown open in the heat, and through it Daimonas was granted entry. He hovered above her dormant form and beat his wings, issuing another dark, filthy smog which was inhaled by the unsuspecting queen. Before his eyes Regina began to sweat; she tossed in the bed and shook with fever-chills.

Daimonas' final destination made was the Emerald Wood, home of the black wolves, located in the westernmost part of Aurea. Still in the form of a crow, he flew into the wolves' lair, screeching a warning decipherable only to birds and beasts. He said that Aureate Guard planned to destroy the wolf pack, that they lived in fear of the wolves and wanted them all killed. He flew among the pack and found the alpha, a strong, grizzled wolf, and beat his wings again. The wolf nipped nervously at the smoke that this produced, and the black fog caught on its teeth like char. The alpha's eyes spun madly, and it threw back its head and howled. The other wolves took up the cry, and within moments, Daimonas was alone in the forest.

The pack was on the move.

***

Hadrian let his sword fall to his side, a sheen of sweat covering his face. He grinned at Lena, who was also perspiring in the humidity of the training room. "Well fought."

Lena returned the grin. "Thank you. Well opposed." She wiped her forehead with her sleeve.

89

Hadrian bowed with a smile in reception of the compliment.

"Thanks." He put his arm around his sister's shoulders. "Hungry? Shall we go have something to eat?"

Lena laced her fingers through her brother's and looked out the window at the pale yellow daylight. It was still very early; there were few people awake, and the day was promising to be a blissfully bright and lovely one. "Let's go riding instead," Lena suggested. "It looks like a beautiful morning."

"I'd love to," Hadrian said. "Captain hasn't been out for a good trot in a long time."

"And Lady would love to get out and stretch her legs," Lena said.

So in ten minutes' time the twins were leaving the stables, Hadrian leading his black stallion, Captain, and Lena following with Lady, the white mare that had borne her out of Pioni's clutches. They mounted, and the horses, wild with pleasure at the day's beauty and the endless stretch of fields, bolted down the small hill that led to the open plains and streaked across the grass, their riders laughing, reveling in their freedom and in each other's company.

They had not been riding very long when they reached the crest of a hill and saw, spread below them and getting closer at every moment, a sea of black figures.

"What's that?" Lena asked pulling up sharply, causing Lady to rear.

"I don't know." Hadrian's hand went to the hilt of his sword.

"Wolves." Lena looked down at the encroaching wave of now identifiable figures. "It's a wolf pack. Let's go back to the Star." Lena glanced at her brother. Hadrian was staring, transfixed, at the approaching surge of wolves. "Hadrian, let's go back."

"The black wolves never leave the forest," Hadrian said. "And there's something unnatural about their speed, they shouldn't be—"

"Hadrian, the farmers on the outskirts will have no warning! Hurry, we have to go back and warn them to get indoors!"

Lena's urges finally convinced Hadrian to wheel Captain back in the direction of the city, but this decision came too late. Soon Lena, just ahead of Hadrian, could hear the snap of jaws at Lady's hooves. The mare whinnied in a frenzy, neck thrusting as she strained to outdistance the pursuers. Lena could see Hadrian out of the corner of her eye; suddenly, he was torn from her view. She heard Captain shriek with pain and looked over her shoulder to see what had happened. One of the wolves had sunk its jaws into Captain's leg, and the horse had fallen. As the wolves converged on him, Hadrian slashed at them with his sword. "Go!" he shouted to Lena. "Go back!"

She did not listen. She turned Lady back toward the pack that surrounded her brother, managing to keep her seat in the saddle as the horse rose up on her hind legs and pawed the air in terror. Taking advantage of her higher position in the saddle, Lena stabbed at the wolves as they rushed Lady and, snarling, leaped up to bite at Lena's legs. One of the wolves, the largest of the pack, the fur on its back bristled, crouched and then sprang toward Lena. The wolf hit her in the chest and knocked her off of Lady's back. Lena's elbow smashed against the ground, causing her to fling her sword several feet across the field. As she scrambled to reach it, she caught sight of Hadrian, still slashing madly at the circle of wolves around him. A thin wolf approached her brother from behind, snapping its teeth.

"No!" Lena's hand found the hilt of her blade; she slashed at the alpha, which was rushing toward her. The wolf yipped and dashed away from Lena, who quickly pulled herself to her feet. She slashed down two of the wolves, then heard Hadrian cry out in pain. The alpha wolf had Hadrian by the leg and despite its captive's kicking would not let go. In desperation, Lena pulled her dagger from her boot and threw it at the alpha. The dagger hit the wolf in its shoulder; it howled in pain and released Hadrian to advance on Lena. Two more of the pack jumped at her; she struck them down with her blade and scrambled to her brother's side. Hadrian was bleeding profusely from his leg. he was clutching the wound and writhing in pain. "Hadrian! Hadrian, get up!" Lena begged. "Hadrian!"

One of the wolves sank its teeth into the back of Lena's leg. Lena screamed, turned, and knocked the butt of her sword against the brute's head. It stumbled back, dazed, and Lena pushed herself closer to Hadrian, her sword raised. The wolf pack was closing in on them.

"Lady!" The wolves followed the scarred, muscular alpha with glittering, green eyes, the wolf responsible for the torn flesh on her brother's leg. "Lady!" Lena cried again. Lady heeded Lena's call, approaching Lena from behind, the only path unblocked by the encroaching semi-circle of wolves. Lena put her hands under Hadrian's arms and tried to haul him to his feet. Hadrian managed to raise himself up on his uninjured leg, and Lena put his hands on the reins. "Come on, Hadrian. Get on Lady's back. Come on, Hadrian!" Lena swung the sword to keep the wolves at bay. They continued to approach with hungry eyes, licking their chops, crazed by the taste and smell of blood. Hadrian lifted his foot toward the stirrup; it slipped, and his foot hit the ground again. Lena beat back two wolves that had crouched to leap at Lady, shouting, "Hadrian, hurry!"

Hadrian managed to fit his foot into the stirrup; Lena gave him an upward push, and he swung his leg over Lady's back. Lena started to climb up after him, but a large wolf sprang and locked its jaws around Lena's boot. Its teeth did not penetrate the thick Aurean leather, but the wolf pulled so hard that Lena lost her grip on the reins and fell backward onto the ground. She raised her sword to protect herself, but a second wolf lunged itself at her arm and knocked the blade from her hand. The wolf that still had its teeth around her foot dragged Lena a few more feet, out of reach of her blade.

Lena swept her hand across the grass, feeling desperately for anything she could use as a weapon. The green-eyed alpha approached her lazily and, when it reached her, put its forepaws on her chest, pinning her to the ground. To Lena's shock, when the alpha bared its teeth, a deep, gravelly voice sounded in her mind. *I am Luprir, golden scum. Memorize my features, before I kill you. All your kind will perish by my fangs.*

Lena's searching hand closed around a sharp rock. With all her strength, she drove into Luprir's eye just as he thrust his neck forward, teeth bared. Howling, blood spurting from its mangled eye, the wolf stumbled away. Lena pushed herself up onto her feet and limped to back to Lady. The grass under the mare's feet was stained with blood, and Hadrian was slumped in the saddle. Lady was neighing and shrieking; the rest of the pack were trying to pull Hadrian from her back. Lena cut three down when she reached her horse's side. She swung onto Lady's back, and clutched a now-unconscious Hadrian so he would not fall as Lady tore away across the open plains. Looking back, Lena realized there was no hope for Captain. All she could see of the horse was his legs; wolves stood around him in a hungry circle, their muzzles red.

***

Lena rode Lady harder than she ever had before; some wolves pursued them still. She reached the farmers closest to the gates yelling at the top of her voice. "Get indoors! Get your children and get inside! Quickly, there are wolves at my heels!"

As she flew by astride Lady, clutching Hadrian to her, farmers stopped their work and wives plucked children from their play to hurry inside. One farmwife brained a wolf with a shovel as it lunged toward her infant; the woman snatched the child up and ran with it inside as her husband pulled an alarm bugle from their door and blew a blast that echoed throughout the valley. Lena heard the warning taken up by distant farms; the sound was repeated from all sides. Lena charged forward, a wave of wolves still behind her.

The city gates came into view, and Lena was crying, "Close the gates! Close them, there are wolves following just behind me!"

The gates began to close before she reached them; Lady's speed delivered her riders safely into the city and into the central square. Three wolves managed to dash inside the walls before the gate was closed; they were dealt with quickly by the Aureate Guard that kept watch over the gates.

Lena slid from the saddle. Crimson drops of Hadrian's blood fell and broke on the white cobbles as she tried to lift him from the saddle herself. "A healer! A healer, quickly, he's hurt, my brother's hurt! Please!" Lena wept in pain and fear as two more Guardsmen sprinted from the temple and lifted Hadrian from the saddle. He was pale and unconscious. Jairdan was among the Aureate Guard issuing from the Star in response to the commotion; he watched the others carry Hadrian inside, then rushed to Lena. She clutched him desperately, barely able to stand. "We were attacked,"she sobbed. Her leg finally gave out; she slipped and had to double her grip on Jairdan's arms.

"It's all right! It's all right!" Jairdan repeated the words over and over, but they became less reassuring as his face drained of its color from his shock at the severity of Hadrian's wounds. He lifted Lena easily and carried her inside, feeling the blood from her leg soak through the sleeve of his tunic.

***

Having returned to his human form, Daimonas was now making use of the seeing orb that Pioni had kept in the hidden room of his palace. He watched the wolf attack unfold, and had seen the alpha sink its teeth into Hadrian's leg. Aside from that, only two others had been killed, farmers, a mother and a son; but Daimonas barely cared that the attack had been so bloodless. It had turned out to be better than he had hoped.

Aside from that success, he saw too that King Bruteaus had been seized by a fury that, though incomprehensible to his children, was supported by his wife, who was pale with terror as she explained that their allies, the Aureans, were plotting to betray them, and to take Westmore for themselves, though the allegiance between the two countries had stood from more than a century.

As for Rhea, she had dropped all pretenses of peace with the North; relations between South and North had been unstable since the Second Great War, but a recent trade agreement had relaxed tensions. That peace had evaporated with Rhea's visions the night before.

Daimonas was very pleased.

***

Hours later, with her leg wounds cleansed, treated, and bandaged, Lena sat in a chair beside Hadrian's cot. She had fared much better than her brother. Lena had managed to beat off the wolf that had bitten her calf relatively quickly. She was left only with a series of puncture wounds in the pattern of a jaw; they were small, and not very deep. Hadrian's flesh had been torn; his leg was mangled. There were bones broken, and he had lost a lot of blood. His head and side injuries, the lesser of his wounds were bandaged, and seemed better, but his leg, where the alpha had bitten him, seemed somehow to have gotten worse. The area around the wound was swollen and tender, crimson, and hot to the touch. Hadrian slipped in and out of consciousness, sweaty and feverish.

The door creaked open; Lena turned. Scio entered the room and put his hands on Lena's shoulders.

"I'm sorry, High Master," Lena whispered hoarsely. "I couldn't get to him in time."

"Lena, you have no fault in what happened today," Scio said firmly. "You are the reason you and Hadrian are still alive, not the reason Hadrian is injured."

She shook her head. "If I had just gotten to him sooner, I could have pulled the big one off—"

"Stop," Scio said, squeezing her shoulders. "You'll drive yourself mad."

Jairdan entered the room with a warm drink for Lena. "That leg should be up," he scolded gently, and dragged over another chair so Lena could prop up her wounded leg.

Lena obliged silently, without taking her eyes off of her brother.

"Quite an adventure," Jairdan said gravely, his gaze on his apprentice's face. He glanced at Lena and said, "It doesn't help to worry, you know."

A haggard smile broke on Lena's face. "You're right, I suppose," she said. She seemed to consider something, then said, "Well, at least now I have a name for my sword."

Jairdan looked at her quizzically. "What's that?"

Lena's fingers brushed the hilt of the blade. "Wolf's bane."

Chapter Ten
The Queen's Illness

The night that fell after the wolf attack was a fog-laden and drizzly one. At midnight, when the moon hung as a giant, ivory orb at its zenith at the sky, a solitary messenger hurried over the cobbles toward the Aureate Temple. His cloak bore the golden star, but it was not gray like those of the Aureate Guard; it was white, signifying that he was an imperial servant. When the reached the heavy, wooden door of the temple, he raised the iron knocker and hammered it against the door three times. Within moments, an Aureate Guard opened the door and admitted the queen's messenger.

***

Lena, who had refused to leave Hadrian's bedside, dozed now in the chair beside his bed. She did not see her brother's face suddenly tighten, as though he was in pain. Hadrian did not wake but tossed his head on his pillow. A dream floated before his subconscious mind, more alive and real than any other dream he had even had.

He was cold, and it was dark. He could see nothing of his surroundings, but he could hear someone speaking. The voice held an icy power. It was repeating words that Hadrian knew well, and in this voice the words beat through his veins and pounded in his ears.

Two infants into bondage born will from their mother's breast be torn, one by golden soldier saved, the other turned to evil's slave...but who is the real slave, Hadrian of Aurea? In her home in the desert, Lena was allowed to explore all her powers. You are imprisoned within the strict yet simple dogmas of the Aureate Guard. There are powers that they do not tell you about...powers that they know you could achieve. Do you know why they do not reveal them to you? Because they are afraid of what you could become. They know you could be great...you could be the greatest, Hadrian, and they fear and envy your power...fear and envy, fear and envy...

It became a singsong taunt, and Hadrian tossed feverishly from side to side on the bed. *Cast into dark the world will be, until the twain fulfill their destiny...destiny? Hadrian, fate is what you make it. Lena sees that. Can you not? One will fall, the other reign, one a monarch, the other slain. You are meant to be the monarch, Hadrian. For seventeen years you have dedicated yourself to this order, given everything to it...and now your sister seeks to take your place! She wants you to fail, because she fears that she will fall. She desires the greatness that is rightfully yours. One of you is to succeed, and it is to be you, Hadrian, you, who have worked for years to become the best. Who knows what dark powers Lena learned in the desert...perhaps she summoned the wolves herself knowing you would get injured. She wants you to fail, Hadrian...she wants you to fail...*

"No...no..." Hadrian moaned, suddenly released from the grips of the chilling voice.

Lena stirred in her chair, saw her brother looking at her, and jerked upright in her seat. "Hadrian? You're awake? How do you feel?"

"I...I don't..." the words failed on Hadrian's lips. He felt exhausted.

"Rest," Lena said, sweeping her cool fingertips over her brother's forehead. "Everything's all right."

Hadrian's eyes drifted closed again.

Two infants into bondage born...

***

Someone at the door cleared his throat pointedly, and Lena turned. Ince was staring with concern at his wounded friend. "How is he?" he asked softly.

Lena shook her head. "He woke a few minutes ago but he didn't say anything much; I think he was only half-awake." She pressed a hand to his forehead. "He's so warm..." she dropped her hand. "The healers say there's something strange about the wound on his leg, something unnatural. Some kind of magic, they think. It must have come off of the wolf's teeth...the alpha. He bit Hadrian, but not me." She sighed and wound her hair nervously around her finger.

"But he'll be all right?" Ince asked anxiously.

"The healers don't recognize the magic. They say it's very dark. I don't know, Ince."

Ince forced a reassuring smile onto his clouded face. "He'll be all right. I know it."

Lena looked up at him and smiled. "You always look on the bright side of things, Ince."

"It doesn't help to worry. He *will* be all right, Lena."

To Ince's surprise, Lena took a shuddering breath, buried her face in her hands, and burst into tears.

"Don't cry," Ince said, crouching down next to her. He put his hand on her shoulder, and to his shock, Lena turned and pressed her face into his chest. Ince went as stiff as an oak tree and felt his palms start to sweat, but Lena was too upset to notice. She mumbled something inaudible, and Ince had just bent his head to hear, dizzied by the flowery scent of her hair, when Master Jairdan swept into the room.

"Both of you, with me," he ordered breathlessly. "Something's happened to the queen. The High Masters have called a special assembly for all Aureate Guard."

Lena and Ince both rose immediately. "What is it?" Lena asked, wiping away tears. "What's wrong with her?"

Jairdan sighed, his face haggard. "No one knows," Jairdan sighed. "The healers are flummoxed once again."

***

Minutes later Ince and Lena filed into a row of seats in the amphitheater. The three High Masters stood at the center of the room looking grave. Shortly after Lena and Ince sat down, the assembly began.

"We have received news that Queen Regina has taken ill," Scio said. There was no need to raise his voice; the room was utterly silent. "The best healers our city has to offer are tending to her even as we speak, but they have thus far been unable to cure or even diagnose her."

"There are no coincidences," Prudentior put in, "and the Queen's illness coinciding with the unprecedented and violent attack of the black wolves on our own apprentices Lena and Hadrian can hardly be counted as an exception. The High Masters and I agree that something very serious is beginning, and we would warn all of you to be on your guard in the coming weeks. What exactly is occurring we cannot divine, but we sense a storm is brewing. A small group of Aureate Guard will attend the queen tomorrow to discuss the matter. We will inform you of the outcome of this meeting tomorrow evening. Thank you."

Lena squeezed Ince's hand and said, "I ought to go down and speak to High Master Scio. Thank you, for earlier. You're a great comfort to me."

Before Ince could sputter out a reply, she was weaving her way down the steps, into the pit of the amphitheater, where Scio was waiting with Jairdan and the other two High Masters.

"Lena." Scio addressed her gravely. "Has there been any progress with Hadrian?"

"He woke for a moment but didn't speak, High Master. He's still very sick. The healers aren't sure why." Lena forced herself to keep her voice from shaking.

Jairdan shook his head. "First the healers can't find out what's wrong with Hadrian, now it's the Queen they can't diagnose. They're the best on the Continent, everyone knows that; why can't they do something?"

"If I may, High Master?" Lena said, addressing Scio, who nodded encouragingly. "There was another time, recently, when the healers were lost for answers. It was when Hadrian and you, Master Jairdan, first found me."

Jairdan nodded. "The stone. They didn't even recognize it."

Lena took a deep breath. "It was Pioni's magic; he developed the stone himself, but almost all of what he knew came from Daimonas."

"You fear that these incidents, the wolf attack, your brother's strange reaction to the bite, the Queen's illness…you are afraid they might have been caused by Daimonas?" Chista asked, trading glancing with the other two High Masters.

Lena nodded.

"It is a concern that has been weighing on the minds of the High Masters as well," Scio said.

Lena shivered. "But, what can we do? If it is him…how can we fight him?"

Scio sighed. "The other High Masters and I intend to examine the Queen and your brother ourselves, with the hope of discovering the secret power in their wounds."

"We *must* discover something. The Queen is deathly ill—"

"Chista!" Prudentior snapped. "That is information best kept between the High Masters."

"I won't repeat it," Lena promised quickly.

Prudentior pursed his lips. "Nevertheless," he said.

Jairdan cleared his throat. "Then perhaps we should tell Lena what we were discussing earlier."

"Yes, of course," Scio said. "Lena, you know that as an apprentice, your responsibilities include joining me on any missions that I carry out."

"Yes, of course," Lena said.

"Tomorrow, High Masters Chista and Prudentior and I have an audience with the Queen. You will be attending as well."

"Yes, High Master," Lena said, flushed with the importance of the task.

"It will be early in the morning. See that you are ready shortly after breakfast."

"Yes, High Master." Lena bowed.

Scio smiled affectionately at her. "Go and get some sleep then."

Lena bowed and turned to go.

"I need some rest as well," Jairdan said. "I'll accompany you, Lena."

Together, he and Lena mounted the steps that led out of the amphitheater. Lena glanced back over her shoulder and saw Prudentior speaking furiously to the other two High Masters.

"I don't suppose he'll ever trust me," she said dryly.

Jairdan looked back as well and shrugged. "Prudentior is an overly cautious man, but his heart is in the right place."

The two had just left the amphitheater when Jairdan clutched Lena's arm suddenly and drew her aside. "Lena, listen to me," he hissed urgently. "You are in a very precarious position. What has been happening—these strange incidents—Lena, if Daimonas truly is behind them, then you are in grave danger. You must be ever on your guard. Do you understand me?"

"Yes, of course, Master but I—"

"*Ever on your guard!*" Jairdan repeated fiercely. "Promise me!"

"Of course," Lena said.

Jairdan nodded, and seeing that Lena was slightly surprised by the intensity of his warning, he said, "Hadrian is like a son to me, Lena, and it has not taken long for you to become like a daughter. Seeing Hadrian hurt like that...I couldn't bear it if something like that happened to you, too, Lena."

Lena blushed, deeply touched. "I'll be careful," she promised.

***

In the pit of the amphitheater, the High Masters were having yet another flurried conversation.

"Do you really intend to allow the girl to come with us to see the queen?" Prudentior asked.

Scio sighed. "Prudentior, your constant distrust of Lena wears on my patience. Has she given you any reason for it? Have you any real reason to think that she is dishonest?"

"I grant you that she has been trustworthy so far, but for all we know, she may have been biding her time for just such an opportunity.

How are we to know that she is not somehow behind all this? The wolf attack, the queen's sickness…she could be a part of it. This could be what she has been planning!"

"Lena has been a part of our order for weeks, and she has excelled in every way. Do not create shadows where there are none," Scio cautioned sternly.

Prudentior scowled.

***

Lena's room was unusually quiet that night. It was odd to not hear Hadrian in the next room. Lena felt uncomfortably separated from her brother as she fixed her candle in its sconce in the wall and prepared for bed.

Not long after she had fallen asleep, Lena tossed in bed, a frantic memory passing as a dream before her eyes.

Do you listen to nothing I say? On your feet! Raise your sword! On your feet, I say! Get up, you wretched girl!

There was the hum of steel through air, the initial twinge of the blade on her skin and then…as Lena looked and saw the blood seeping out of the wound on her shoulder, there was the searing pain as her mind caught up with her body…

Lena sat bolt upright upright in bed, sweating and gasping. She slid her nightgown partway down her shoulder and ran her finger over a thick, white scar, which was throbbing slightly with remembered pain. Sleep seemed impossible. Lena got out of bed and left her room, stepping into the cool corridor just outside.

The cool stones of the hallway felt good under Lena's bare feet. She walked out onto the stone bridge that spanned one of the temple's many courtyards and leaned against the rail, enjoying the feel of the breeze against her face.

She had thought she was alone and started when she heard the click of a wooden staff on the stones behind her. When she turned, she saw that Scio was walking toward her through the darkness.

"Lena," he greeted her with a smile. "Having trouble sleeping?"

Lena nodded. "Yes, High Master."

"The dreams again?" Scio asked quietly.

Lena looked away, picking absently at a loose thread on her sleeve, and nodded again. "Some things are difficult to forget."

Scio regarded her carefully. "It is not always better to forget things. Sometimes it is important to remember ugly parts of our past. It keeps us humble, and grateful."

Lena smiled. "I am certainly very thankful for what I have now."

After a moment's silence, Lena asked, "High Master, may I speak freely?"

Scio smiled. "Always, child."

"High Master Prudentior doubts my loyalty."

Scio hesitated for only a moment. "I cannot deny that."

"I wish there was something I could do…I want for him to trust me," Lena said.

Scio reached out and put his hand on her arm. "Lena, listen to me. You have done wonderfully here. High Master Prudentior's mistrust is…it is not to do with you."

"How can you say that?" Lena asked. "It has everything to do with me."

"No. Listen now, Lena, because this is important. High Master Prudentior's mistrust concerns not you but the sickness that is descending over the Great Continent. His caution was at first not surprising; he is a cautious, methodical man, and I expected that he more than anyone would have trouble welcoming you into our Order. Yet his fixation on the idea of your disloyalty has escalated to a point beyond reason. I have no doubt that is due to the recent events; the Queen's sickness, the wolf attacks…they suggest that all is not well, and men like High Master Prudentior have a singular difficulty in dealing with a foe that they cannot see. Caution is important, Lena, but trust is even more so. Brotherhood is what has made this Order great, and it is my job, and High Master Chista's, to see that High Master Prudentior remembers it. Do not blame yourself; you are not the cause of his mistrust. Rather, you may be instrumental in destroying its cause."

Lena smiled.

Scio patted her arm. "I am very proud of you, Lena."

In the darkness, Lena blushed at the compliment. "Thank you," she whispered.

"Now, do try and get some rest," Scio said. "One should not greet a queen with sleepy eyes." He winked, and Lena bowed with a smile.

Scio strode back down the hall, the clicking of his staff fading slowly and eventually becoming inaudible.

Lena returned to her room shortly after he left her lay down to go to sleep. A violent memory nipped at her subconscious as she began to doze off, but she thought of Scio's compliment and was able to slip into a sleep untroubled by dreams.

***

She felt that no sooner had the veil of sleep fallen over her eyes than Jairdan was gently shaking her shoulder to rouse her. Lena was coherent immediately. "Has Hadrian—"

"He's awake," Jairdan said with a smile.

Lena's face lit up. She swung her legs over the bed, grabbed a shawl from her bedpost, and ran barefoot out of the room toward the infirmary.

"The queen expects you within the hour!" Jairdan called after her. He shook his head with a smile as the corner of her white nightgown disappeared around the doorframe.

***

"Lena." Hadrian smiled weakly at his sister and pushed himself into a sitting position on the bed.

Lena seated herself next to her brother on the bed and kissed him gingerly on the cheek. She took his hand in hers and asked, "Are you all right?"

"I'm fine." Hadrian winced as his leg twinged. "Well, I'm better, anyway. Listen. Master Jairdan told me what happened, about the queen and that you're going to see her."

104

You should be going as well.

Hadrian cleared his throat and blinked.

"I'm so nervous," Lena said. "I won't know what to say." She smiled. "I'd rather you were going."

She lies. This is what she wants.

Hadrian put a hand to his temple. When he spoke, it seemed strained. "Don't worry. The queen is very kind. But I want you to be careful. The wolves' attacking us, the venom in their bite, the queen's illness—"

"Not coincidences," Lena finished for him. "I know."

Knows because she plotted them!

"Just be careful." Hadrian's voice was definitely strained this time.

Lena bent and kissed his cheek. "I will. And you rest. I'd better go, but I'll come to see you the moment I return." She squeezed his hand, stood, and left the room.

"Give the queen my regards!"

This was her intention all along. She knew the wolves would attack you, and now she is taking advantage of your injury to surpass you. Normally, you would follow Jairdan to the queen. But how could she outshine you if you were present?

"Stop it!" Hadrian shouted aloud, pinching the bridge of his nose. "Stop it, stop it!"

She wants you to fail.

"No she doesn't!" Hadrian gripped fistfuls of his own hair and squeezed his eyes shut.

She has been planning this since she arrived here.

"No! No, no no!" Hadrian slammed his fist into his pillow. When he stopped, he was breathing hard. He looked down at his hands. They were shaking. Slowly, he lay back down on the bed. "What is wrong with me?"

Chapter Eleven
An Audience with the Queen

When Lena returned to her room, she was shocked to find a lovely, brown dress on her bed. Puzzled, she trailed her fingers over the beautiful garment.

"Oh!" There was a crash, and Ince stuck his head into her room, his face heated with embarrassment. "Sorry. Walked into the bedside table and knocked some books off the top. Anyway, Master Jairdan left that. He said you were to wear it to see the queen today."

"This is for me?" Lena gasped, paling. "I-I've never worn anything like this before! I have no idea what to...how to...I mean I..." she stopped, glanced at Ince, and whispered, "I'm a little nervous."

"You'll be fine," Ince said comfortingly. He backed out of her room. "I'll let you get changed."

Lena sank down onto her bed and pulled the dress onto her lap. There was also a pair of delicate, brown dress shoes on the bed. With an enormous sigh, Lena slipped out of the comfort of her nightdress and into the stiff, unfamiliar territory of formal attire. The dress had a wide, square-cut neckline, a golden star on the skirt, and lacing in the back. After several futile attempts to do up the laces herself, Lena threw one of the shoes at the door in frustration and sat down heavily on the bed.

A moment later the door cracked open and Ince's face appeared again. "Everything all right?" he asked.

Lena laughed and shook her head. "I can't tie up the back," she said. "I'm ready to hang myself by the laces."

Ince grinned. "I'll help you."

Lena rose, lifted her hair off her shoulders, and turned her back to Ince. "Thanks."

A tremor coursed Ince's fingers as he reached out for the laces. He did the dress up quickly and then stepped away, as if he had gotten too close.

Lena released her curls, letting them cascade down her back and frame her lovely face. "Well?" she asked nervously, smoothing the dress' skirt in the mirror. "What do you think?"

Ince was lost for words. Her loveliness choked him.

"Is it all right?" Lena, concerned by his silence, spun to face him. "It feels so strange, Ince. I've never worn anything like this before."

"It suits you," Ince said, finally capable of a more natural tone.

Lena smiled. "You're sweet," she said. "And a great friend. Thank you for the help. I could never have managed on my own. I'm afraid I've bored you with my fussing."

"No," Ince blurted. "I mean, not at all."

Lena laughed at what she thought was polite denial. She stepped into the pair of brown shoes, and lifted the skirt of the dress to her ankles so she could hurry across the room. "I can't be late!" she said, pausing to raise herself up on her toes and kiss Ince's cheek. "Save me a place with you at dinner! I'll tell you everything!"

Her footsteps dwindled, but still Ince stood where she had left him, touching the place on his cheek where her lips had brushed his skin.

***

Lena's palms were already sweaty with nervousness by the time she reached the entrance of the Star where the three High Masters, Chista, Scio, and Prudentior, waited for her. They too had changed into formal attire; forest green tunics that bore the star. Lena greeted them awkwardly with something between a bow and a curtsy.

"Let's go then," Prudentior said grumpily, "We do not want to be late for an audience with the queen."

***

Hadrian had led Lena on tours through the city until she knew it inside and out. Now she could have walked the cobbled road to the gate of the queen's palace blindfolded. When the four Aureate Guard reached the gate, they were admitted immediately and led to the doors of the queen's bedchamber by an attendant. The attendant requested a moment to announce them to the queen and slipped silently inside the room.

Lena was fascinated by the carvings on the walls outside the queen's bedchamber; they had been sculpted directly into the white stone and depicted famous battles and the faces of warriors and monarchs. Lena had just leaned into look more closely at the face of one of the warriors when the doors to the queen's room opened and the attendant reappeared. "The queen will see you now," he said, and pushed open the door.

Lena did not know exactly what to expect when she stepped into the queen's bedchamber, but what she saw was something quite beyond the borders of her imagination. Lying on the grand, four-poster bed inside the room was not a figure of majesty, not a tall, proud, or commanding woman, but a girl who looked barely older than Lena herself, with tight curls the color of russet chrysanthemums and cheeks as pale as the white sheets on which she lay. When she pushed herself into a sitting position to greet them with a smile, Lena saw that the muscles in her arms quivered with weakness. Nevertheless, her sapphire eyes were bright when the Aureate Guard entered.

The attendant announced, "The Three High Masters of the Aureate Star, your majesty, and High Master's Scio's apprentice, Lena, of Locusorti."

All four bowed in tandem, Lena having abandoned the curtsy. The Aurean custom of attaching a birthplace to a formal name wore on Lena; she felt no attachment whatever to her Mariian birthplace, and the title felt strange no matter how many times she heard it.

"Your Highness." Scio's eyes were soft with pity.

The queen seemed unused to her weakness; Lena caught a pained expression of embarrassment on Regina's face as she struggled to sit up. "Master Scio. I hope you are well?"

"Better than yourself it seems, my lady," Scio replied.

Regina's smiled faded. "The healers exaggerate," she said, sinking back onto the pillows. "I'll be better in no time at all."

"I certainly hope so, your highness, but my concern for your health seems to be greater than your own."

"Only because I know better how I feel," Regina said firmly. "I will not have these healers planting stories about my condition. Please believe that I am fine. There—" here she broke off into a coughing fit. Lena winced in sympathy as the deep, rattling cough wracked the queen's body.

"Excuse me," Regina said, when the coughing finally ceased. "Now. There are several matters I must speak to you about. First, Lena, I have heard much about you. I am delighted to meet you at last." The Queen gave Lena a genuine smile, and asked, "I believe it was your brother, Hadrian, who was injured in the recent wolf attack? How is he? The wolf attack may not have claimed many lives, but the damage it did, the fear it caused, and the lives that it *did* take— it is horrible to see my people so aggrieved, so afraid."

"Hadrian would be glad to know you asked for him, Your Majesty," Lena said, "for he is equally concerned for your welfare. He is much better this morning and bade me send his best wishes for your quick recovery."

"That is good news," Regina said, looking carefully at Lena. "I have met your brother, and I can see his face in yours. Please forgive my absence at your induction into the Order; I typically do come to see the ceremonies, but I was negotiating a new trade agreement with the South, and could not get away."

"Your Majesty, your presence would have been an unexpected honor," Lena said, flustered. "I am merely glad of the chance to meet you now."

"Well, allow me now to bid you a much belated welcome to the City of the Aureate Star."

Lena bowed. "Thank you, Your Majesty." She retreated back to her former place beside Chista.

"And now I am afraid I must address some graver issues," Regina said, addressing Master Scio now. "My avian scouts recently reported strange activity in the west and in the south."

"Avian scouts?" Lena whispered questioningly to Chista.

"Giant-birds," Chista murmured. "Hawks mostly, and some eagles. They use thought-speak to communicate with Aureate Guard assigned to live in the queen's palace for just that purpose. They're extremely useful; able to cover large amounts of ground in practically no time at all."

Thought-speak? Is that what Hadrian and I can do? Can all Aureate Guard do it? Can all animals do it? Lena's mind buzzed with questions, but, eager to hear the rest of what the queen had to say, she decided to save them for later.

"It seems," Regina went on, "that the Bruteaus and Rhea are both preparing for war."

"War?" Prudentior asked, his eyes popping.

"We have heard nothing from either about any conflict," Regina said. "But what is more disturbing is that their hostility seems to be directed not towards each other, but toward us."

Lena's mind raced. Scio had had her read passages from a thick, dusty volume that detailed the entire history of Aurea's relations with the other Great Continent countries. The passages were long and difficult to read, but Lena had struggled through them with help from Scio. She thought hard now to recall what she had read. She had learned that the Aureans had always had poor relations with Sanuul, despite a few attempts at peace, all of which had ended badly. Scio had told her, though, that recently relations with Sanuul were the best they had ever been. Lena had also learned from her reading that Westmore had ever been the amicable ally of Aurea. So why would Sanuul choose now to attack Aurea? And what could cause such a sudden change in sentiment from Westmore?

Chista seemed to share her incredulity. "But Bruteaus has been our ally since he took the crown, nearly two decades ago!"

"I am as confounded by the news as you are, High Master," the Queen said.

"If the two are preparing for war, combined they will make a formidable enemy," Scio said. "We have two hundred elite Aureate Guard and hundreds more of lower rank, but together Sanuul and Westmore will have over a thousand troops."

"We must discover what has angered them," Prudentior said.

Lena frowned. "I—if I may?" she asked tentatively.

All eyes shifted to her. "Please," the Queen said, with an encouraging smile.

"Yes," Prudentior said sarcastically. "Let us hear what Lena has to offer."

Lena reddened, but pushed on shakily, "It seems to me that Daimonas must behind Sanuul and Westmore's sudden preparations for war."

"Daimonas? The man who broke from the Aureate Guard several years ago? I heard about his connection to you, Lena. We have long known that he harbored hatred toward Aurea, and it seems he has grown powerful in his absence. Yes, it would make sense." Regina looked concerned.

"After all, what easier way to destroy us than by beginning war?" Lena asked. "He hates and fears our country, and by inciting our allies against us, he both weakens us and gains forces."

Scio sighed. "We have begun to fear that Daimonas may be behind the wolf attack, your majesty. It seems more and more likely that he is becoming active in his attempt to bring us down. He has hidden in the shadows of the desert for seventeen long years; no more. He is beginning the second wave of his campaign against us."

"My scouts are out even now, scanning the South and West for clues as to what could have stirred this conflict. If Daimonas is behind it, they will know."

"Perhaps they will not," Jairdan said. "With all due respect, Your Majesty, Daimonas eluded the best members of the Aureate Guard for seventeen years. He is meticulous; he will leave no evidence of his involvement, if he is indeed behind the sudden hostility of our former allies."

"Well what can we do then?" Regina asked, with mounting frustration. She grew flushed as she ranted, "The wolf attacks, the sudden change in sentiment from the West and South, my own infuriating illness—no one can find me a cause, or a solution! I requested an audience with you, High Masters, because you are the best that I have, my last hope."

111

The Queen was breathing hard. Lena saw some of the sparkle drain from her eyes as the burst of emotion passed and exhaustion took over. "Forgive my emotion," she said, "but I have nowhere else to turn."

"Your Majesty, we will devote ourselves to discovering the answers to these riddles," Scio promised. "Your own illness is, although you would minimize its severity, at the forefront of our concerns. We have sent you our best healers; would you now permit, in light of their failures, my presence as they tend to you?"

Regina smiled. "High Master, if anyone can help me, it is you. But promise me that you will not sacrifice time better spent dealing with the questions of Westmore and Sanuul for my sake."

"I will apply myself to those problems after I have seen to you, majesty, and I promise that I will dedicate myself entirely to finding both the cause and the solution."

Chapter Twelve
A New Tutor for the Little Ones

The walk home was drizzly and cold. Thoughts and questions paraded themselves across Lena's mind. Things that had seemed confusing before were even more so now, and there was a new, threatening kind of feeling that Lena had never experienced before in Aurea. She looked around her at the people in the streets, the people who did not yet know of the danger. How long would it be before they found out that there was the possibility of an attack?

One of the questions that had been bothering Lena was one she had to ask. As she walked beside Scio on the way back to the Star, she said, "High Master, there is something that I don't understand."

"What is that?" Scio asked.

"I know that Daimonas is very skilled. I understand how clever he is. But you and the other High Masters must be his equals. Why is everything so different, so much more difficult because it is Daimonas that is behind it all?"

Scio nodded. "It has to do, Lena, with the fact that Daimonas has begun to invent his own way of doing things. There is an old way of handling power like ours that has been handed down for centuries. There are certain things that the Aureate Guard does, and certain things that we do not do. To any Aureate Guard, recognizing or undoing another Guard's work would be simple. It is different with Daimonas because he has never adhered to the old ways, and still does not. He has found new ways to channel his powers, new, more dangerous ways. As a result, his powers have changed. They are no longer those of an Aureate Guard; they are unrecognizable. Imagine, Lena, that instead of first teaching you the letters and their sounds, I had given you the Third Ancient Ballad of Taippanas and asked you to read it. Trying to understand and undo Daimonas' work is like trying to read without knowing the language."

113

"Oh." Lena looked crestfallen. If that was the case, how could the High Masters hope to help Hadrian?

"But there is hope yet," Scio said. "Don't ever lose hope."

***

Mallin the bounty hunter reached the desert castle of Lord Pioni just as Daimonas was returning. From the crest of a tall sand dune, Mallin watched as, unseen, Daimonas rode his other-worldly stallion across the bridge that spanned the fiery moat of Pioni's castle.

After Daimonas had entered the castle, Mallin walked back across the dune to where his horse stood pawing the sand, waiting for him. Mallin took the charger's reins in his hand and led the horse down the dune. He remounted and rode toward the castle, crossing the black bridge with the two familiar guards, their bladed staffs barring the entrance to the castle. Mallin dismounted, his dislike for the guards visible in his scowl.

"What business brings you here?" one asked, its voice a low growl.

"My own," Mallin growled. He took a step toward the entrance. The guards snarled in anger, and one rammed the butt of its staff into Mallin's gut. The bounty hunter doubled over and for a moment was dizzied by the sight of the moat beneath him.

"Our master admits no one," the guards seethed.

"Your master is a cold corpse under the sand," Mallin snapped, straightening. "Whom do you serve now that Pioni is dead?"

"We serve the one true lord, a master capable of crushing all the armies of the world in one fist."

"There is no such man," Mallin said. "But if you speak of Daimonas, it is he who I have come to see."

"You will not enter here, bounty-hunting scum. Our master has no use for the likes of you."

"He has had use for me before, and if he seeks the girl that escaped his grasp and fled to the golden city, than he will have use for me again."

For several throbbing moments, the guards did not react. Then, one of them hissed something to the other and entered the castle. It returned moments later, and bowed to Mallin. "Forgive our insolence. If you know of the golden slave's whereabouts, then our master will see you."

Mallin stepped past them, leading his horse under the familiar archway, into the dark castle. Two more guards stepped forward from the shadows. "I will take your horse," one said.

"And I will lead you to our master," said the other. His horse's reins were slid out of Mallin's unresisting fingers. The other guard led him forward into the darkness. Mallin's eyes narrowed as they approached the room in which the orb stood, its ghostly light paling the walls around it.

Mallin had not often seen Daimonas, but he was no fool. He was well aware that Daimonas had always controlled Pioni and was therefore Mallin's true employer. There was nothing like the chill of power that clung to Daimonas, the intensity of that dark stare, the tension in the air around him. Mallin considered himself the inferior of no man, but having seen firsthand Daimonas' power, he did not believe that the being before him was in fact a man. Mallin bowed deeply to Daimonas, demonstrating respect he rarely gave.

"Ah. Mallin. I did wonder if you would return. You are loyal to a fault they say, one of your best qualities."

"Loyal to those whom I respect," Mallin replied carefully.

"Admirable," Daimonas said. "A trait, no doubt, that Pioni treasured."

"Pioni is—"

"Dead. I know. I killed him myself. It is why I questioned whether you would return. I am pleased you have. One in my position needs certain...*agents* to accomplish what one needs done."

Mallin stiffened. Daimonas' lips had said *agent*, but the tone, and his body language, had said *slave*.

"I need someone with your talents," Daimonas continued, a small smile of amusement flickering at his lips when Mallin tensed. "I believe you are the man I need." Daimonas gestured to a corner of the room, where a large sack spilled over with gold.

115

Mallin relaxed slightly and bowed again. "I am at your service, my lord."

***

Hadrian was sitting up when Lena returned to the infirmary. His head was bowed, his eyes closed. His deep, slow breaths told Lena that he was meditating. To her surprise, his entire body jerked when she entered the room. He opened his eyes, and for a moment seemed to look at her in terror.

Lena smiled. "It's only me. Did I startle you?"

Hadrian shook himself. "No. I mean, yes, a little. How is the queen?"

"Very ill," Lena said, "though she won't acknowledge it."

"She's very brave," Hadrian said with a nod.

"Here." Lena got up and filled a cup with water from a glass pitcher. She held it out to Hadrian.

Her brother paled, looked blankly at the offered cup. He swallowed hard. "You first," he rasped, "you must be thirsty, after all. It's a good walk from the palace."

Lena's brow furrowed, but she took a sip from the cup before holding back out to her brother. "Thank you."

Hadrian's features relaxed, and he took the cup. He watched Lena for a moment, then took a deep gulp.

Lena studied her brother sternly. Finally she asked, in their shared and secret language, *What's wrong? Something is bothering you.*

It's nothing. I'm just tired. Hadrian tried to avoid her gaze.

Stung, Lena persisted, *Hadrian, I know you better than that.*

Hadrian looked into her eyes, eyes that glittered with concern and sorrow for him. His suspicion, for the moment, dissolved, *I'm sorry,* he whispered, and even in their secret thought-speak, Lena could hear his voice tremble with emotion. *I don't know what's wrong with me.*

You're ill, Lena said sympathetically. *You're hurt, and frustrated.*

Hadrian shook his head, irritated. *It's more than that.*

Lena looked quizzically at him. *What? What else is bothering you?*

Biting his lip, Hadrian hesitated, then asked, his eyes locked on his sister's face, *Why do you think I'm sick like this and you're not? You were bitten too.*

It was the alpha. That big one that attacked you. There was something...different about it. Something wrong, unnatural. Her eyes glassy, she whispered, *I wish it had bitten me instead of you!*

LIES!

Neither of the twins had said it. Lena reeled from the power, the anger of the voice. It pounded in her head, making her wince with pain. She looked in horror at Hadrian.

Did you say that?

Her brother answered only with a look of fear.

Hadrian, did you say that? Lena asked again, her voice trembling. Still, she got no reply.

"Excuse me, Lena?" A young, apprentice healer appeared in the doorway. "Master Jairdan wishes to you."

Lena looked back at her brother.

Go, Hadrian said, *I'm tired anyway.*

We need to talk about this, Lena urged.

Later we will. Leave me now. I'm tired.

Lena turned to go. Just before she left the room, the voice again pierced through her mind.

Liar. Betrayer. Manipulator!

Lena let out a gasp and had to catch herself on the door frame.

"Are you all right?" The apprentice healer put his hand at Lena's elbow to steady her. Lena turned back and stared at Hadrian. Her brother shifted uncomfortably under her gaze, then turned on the bed so he was no longer facing her.

Lena drew a shuddering breath and forced a smile at the apprentice. "I'm all right. Thank you."

The apprentice nodded and let go of her arm.

Lena looked back once more at Hadrian. *We* will *talk about this.*

She got no reply.

***

"You wanted to see me, Master?"

Lena was anxious, her face clouded, her eyes still filled with shock and pain. Immediately, Jairdan sensed it. "Lena," he said. He stepped closer to her and touched her elbow. "What's the matter?"

Lena shook her head, and Jairdan saw she was close to tears. "What is it?" he asked.

"It's...Hadrian," Lena said. "There was a voice, something awful...I can't describe..." she trailed off nervously.

"Come with me," Jairdan said, taking her by the arm. "We'll see High Master Scio."

"But, you wanted to see me...there was something else," Lena mumbled distractedly.

"I've just decided it can wait," Jairdan said.

***

They found Scio in the Great Library, speaking with two apprentice Guard that Lena recognized from meals.

"High Master," Jairdan said, "I apologize for the interruption, but we must speak to you." Jairdan looked back at Lena, who was still pale. "It's urgent."

"Master Jairdan, of course," Scio turned to address the apprentices, "If you'll excuse me." The two apprentices bowed low to Scio, and left.

Lena was picking nervously at the hem of her tunic, greatly disturbed.

"Somewhere private, I think," Scio said, eying her carefully.

***

Moments later, they were in Scio's chamber.

"Please, Lena, sit down. You don't look well. A drink, perhaps?" Scio was looking concernedly at his apprentice.

Lena shook her head.

"Can you tell us now?" Jairdan asked. "It will be all right, Lena, just tell us what happened. You said something about a voice?"

Lena nodded numbly. When she spoke, her voice was gravelly and strained with emotion.

"Hadrian and I can communicate by…speaking to each other in our minds."

"Thought-speak? Yes, it's not uncommon in Aureate Guards that are as close as the two of you."

"Well, I was just speaking that way with him now."

"And?" Jairdan prompted.

"I heard another voice."

Scio frowned. "Another? What voice?"

"I don't know but—terrible. It was so *angry*. It…it was awful, it was like…like nothing I've ever heard."

"What did it say?" Jairdan asked.

"It…called me a liar," Lena whispered hollowly.

"A liar?"

"We were talking about the day with the wolves, and I said that I wish it were me who had been bitten, rather than Hadrian. And then this awful voice it…it screamed that I was a liar…I…it went on…liar, betrayer, manipulator…" Lena shook her head.

"Have you ever heard the voice before?" Jairdan pressed.

Lena put her head in her hands. "I don't know…I…the only time I've ever felt that kind of power…that kind of anger…"

"Was when you were with Daimonas," Scio completed for her.

Lena nodded, silent horror welling within her.

"But, well that's, that's impossible," Jairdan said. "I mean, it wasn't really Daimonas…inside Hadrian's head…it, it's impossible. It's impossible." He muttered it again, looking desperately at Scio for consolation.

Scio sighed. "I have never heard of this Lena but, if it is true, you were right to come to me. A second voice…what it could mean I do not know but it has possibilities that are…very dangerous."

"What can we do?" Lena asked. "If it's Daimonas…what can we do?"

Scio hesitated.

"I mean that's just it, isn't it?" Lena said. "We haven't been able to fix his leg, we haven't been able to cure the Queen…it…it's useless."

"No!" Scio's voice was harsh now. "Do not say that, Lena. Do not!"

"We will do something. We will fix it," Jairdan said, and Lena felt a surge of sympathy toward him. Jairdan, who had been a father to Hadrian, and to her, and who believed with concrete resolution in the power of the Aureate Guard.

"I will speak to Hadrian," Jairdan said.

"No, Master Jairdan, you must not," Scio said. "He will sense that Lena has spoken to you. You are too close to him to guard your feelings. I will go; I will speak to him."

Jairdan nodded. "I understand, High Master. Lena, we will go together to where we met earlier; I still need to speak to you."

Lena nodded, though it was evident that her thoughts were elsewhere.

"Go with Master Jairdan," Scio said. "I will see what I can learn from your brother."

***

"The High Masters and I have a task for you," Jairdan said, as he and Lena strode through the corridors, back the way they had come. "It's not an obligation, but we would appreciate it greatly if you consider it."

"Of course," Lena said absently. "Whatever you ask."

"The numbers of little ones whose parents want them to study our teachings are growing so quickly that Lady Magistra cannot possibly train all of them. Master Scio suggested that you might take charge of a small number of them."

"Me? Train little ones?" The pure shock drew Lena's mind momentarily from her worries for Hadrian. "I wouldn't know how!"

"Lena, all you would have to do is teach them patience and show them how to hold a sword. The things they need to learn are things you already knew for years before you came to us. Besides, you're no doubt already on first name terms with the lot of them; they follow you around like you're a goddess."

Lena laughed. "I do love them. They're adorable, with their little sparring swords practically as long as they are tall." She smiled. "You're sure it's only simple things I'd need to show them? Things I already know?"

"You could teach them in your sleep," Jairdan assured her.

Lena bit her lip. "I *would* love to work with them, but I'd be afraid of making a mistake."

"Well, I know you don't have to worry about that, if even you are doubtful of it. The experience will do wonders for your confidence. Come with me. I'll introduce you to your group."

Jairdan led Lena to the gymnasium where the children trained. Five of them were assembled in one corner of the gym, blinking, wide, adorable eyes at Lena as she and Jairdan entered the room.

"Hello everyone," Jairdan said.

"Hello Master Jairdan," the children chorused. They bowed, their tiny hands clasped behind their backs, a few of them fidgeting nervously. Lena recognized some of them; Ince's cousin Willow and her best friend Kiara; and a cherubic, blond-haired boy named Crispin she had occasionally seen trailing some of the older boys.

"This is Lena," Jairdan said. "She is going to be your new teacher."

"Hello Mistress Lena," the children said. Again, they bowed in tandem.

Mistress Lena. She fidgeted inwardly at the discomfort of the new name. "Hello little ones," she said. "I know a few of you, but not all." She crouched down in front of a tiny girl, no older than six, whose face was all but hidden behind tousled brown curls, and who was sucking nervously on her index finger. "What's your name?" Lena asked kindly. The girl took her finger out of her mouth long enough to whisper, "Elissa."

Jairdan waited at the door long enough to see the children transformed from shy children to eager pupils, approaching Lena to offer their names. As a delighted, giggling clamor rose in the room, Jairdan slipped outside room and left Lena to her students.

Chapter Thirteen
The Eternal Paradox

Scio sensed the darkness immediately. It hit him like the cold current in a stream; the medical ward was filled with it. Hadrian was asleep on the bed, and Scio could feel the cold deepen as he approached the boy. Even Scio was surprised by its strength.

He saw that Hadrian slept fitfully; his face was drawn, and he was sweating profusely, even mumbling inaudibly under his breath.

Scio closed his eyes and drew a deep breath. Gently, he focused his power on Hadrian…

…and saw it at once. There it was, coiled like a thick, black serpent at the back of the boy's consciousness…

The serpent rose its head and struck furiously. Scio was jolted from his meditation, and Hadrian woke.

"High Master?" he said dazedly. "I'm sorry, I didn't hear you come in." He pulled himself into a sitting position.

"Have you been sleeping well, Hadrian?" Scio asked.

You must not trust him.

Scio forced himself not to react.

Hadrian's face went taut. "Yes. Yes, of course, High Master."

Scio said, "Your sleep did not seem restful."

Hadrian forced a shrug. "A bad dream, perhaps. I cannot remember now."

Scio smiled. "Well, rest is important. I came merely to check on you. Please, go back to sleep."

You cannot turn your back on him for one moment.

"Th-thank you, High Master," Hadrian said. He lay back down on the bed, and closed his eyes.

Scio extended a gentle, calming energy that quickly put Hadrian back to sleep. Again, Scio closed his eyes and focused on the boy.

The snake was roused now. It narrowed its blood-red eyes at Scio and hissed at him.

Creature of the Shadow...you have no claim on this boy.

The snake did not move.

Scio concentrated harder. *You have no claim! Leave the boy!*

The snake uncoiled itself slowly, and Scio steeled himself for the strike. None came. Slowly, the snake turned and wound away into the shadows, beyond the borderlands of consciousness.

Scio opened his eyes. He was breathing hard with exertion. He looked at Hadrian, who seemed to be sleeping peacefully now.

***

It was early. The sand dunes were a pale gray under the pre-dawn sky. As Mallin checked his horse's saddle, the first sliver of orange light split sand from horizon, creeping over a dune in the distance. Mallin's horse snorted and pawed the ground nervously. Mallin patted the charger's neck, his eyes fixed on the horizon. He reached up and clasped a black, silken kerchief to the base of his helmet to mask his mouth and nose from the swirling sand. His eyes glittered in the fresh light. He turned his gaze to Pioni's palace and felt Daimonas' eyes on him. He looked again at the gold coins that filled his horse's saddlebags and ran his tongue over parched lips. The light spilled across the dunes closer to him, and Mallin reached for a flask of water. He took a swallow, glanced at the approaching rays of light, and swung onto his horse. With a flick of his heels, Mallin urged his horse away from the flooding light. The charger's heels kicked up the still-shadowed sand as Mallin left the light behind him, outrunning the stretching rays in the east as he coaxed his horse into a canter toward the north.

***

"But did you vanquish it? Is it gone? Or is it hiding?"

Lena, Jairdan, and the three High Masters were gathered in Scio's chambers. Scio was still pale and fatigued. Lena had never seen him so before, and found it disconcerting. Worse was what he had described; the snake in Hadrian's mind…Chista's question echoed Lena's own. Was it gone for good, or might it come back?

"I don't know," Scio said, in answer to Chista. "I had no way to tell."

"But if Daimonas can do this to Hadrian…he can do it to anyone," Jairdan said.

"No," Lena spoke up. "It was the wolf bite. Somehow, it must have created a connection. That's the only possibility."

"This is power beyond what we have ever encountered before," Prudentior said. "What should be done with the boy?"

"He must be watched with extreme care," Scio said. "We must see if the voice returns. While it lies dormant, he is safe from its poisonings."

"I won't leave his side," Lena said.

Scio nodded. "That is good. Lena, be kind to him. Show no distrust. This darkness is no fault of his own."

***

Lena's students prospered under the instruction of their new teacher. Jairdan observed them making enormous strides, quickly progressing to talents beyond their years. Lena's confidence grew with her students' capabilities, as Jairdan had expected it would. It took Lena no time at all to learn her students' names and ages along with their skills, weaknesses, and histories. Elissa, for example, had been orphaned as an infant and was normally afraid of her own shadow, but with a staff in her hands, Lena found the six-year-old was capable of the focus and ferocity of a practiced warrior three times her age. Eight-year olds Kiara and Willow were attached at the hip, and Lena suspected them of being able to communicate through thought-speak. Crispin, blond with eyes like blue glass, was the youngest but the most daring, claimed not to be afraid of anything but had secretly confided to Lena that he was terrified of the dark. Roland was nine, dark and serious, the oldest and most focused member of the group. Lena immediately noticed his tendency to take care of the younger ones. His skill at settling their disputes was enviable; all the children loved him as a brother and looked to him for leadership. Lena adored her students and watched with increasing pride as they mastered every skill she taught them.

Lena's new assignment, however, was the only thing that was going right for the Aureate Guard. Bruteaus had been kind; the Aurean messengers sent to his kingdom had simply disappeared. Rhea had the heads of the messengers that entered her domain sent back to Regina in a bloodied basket. There were more reports of wolf attacks from farmers that lived outside the city. People grew afraid to go out after dark. Mistrust crept over the city like a fog, turning friends into strangers and strangers into enemies. Avian scouts brought more reports of the preparations for war in the West and South every day. Regina's health worsened, and Hadrian's improved much more slowly than anyone had anticipated.

Lena spent every extra moment she had with her brother. She did not mention the voice, and Hadrian seemed, for the moment, to be improved, in spirits at least. His leg grew no better, and even without the taunting voice, Hadrian grew increasingly frustrated. The healers were at a loss to find a cure or even a real cause for the glacial pace of his healing. Hadrian could walk on the leg for short periods at a time, but could not run and had to rest every few minutes. Lena could see that he gritted his teeth against the pain as they walked through the gardens and courtyards of the Star together. Once, he stumbled and broke down in anger and frustration.

"This is ridiculous!" Hadrian hurled his cane across the courtyard. "I can't stand it!"

Lena hung back, not sure how to react. Hadrian glanced at her expression and sank down on a bench with a dejected sigh. "I'm sorry," he said. "It's just…I don't know how much longer I can take this, Lena."

She sat down next to him and put a hand on his shoulder. "I know," she said. "It will be all right, though. You'll see. I promise." She leaned in and kissed his cheek, looking into his eyes as if to seal the earnestness of her words.

A small smile flickered on Hadrian's face. He took his sister's hand in his and squeezed it tightly.

***

A few days later, Lena came upon Hadrian in the training room. His sword was drawn; he was going through the motions of a complex and deadly dance, whipping his sword through the air as he swept across the room, his bad leg dragging clumsily. Suddenly, he dropped his sword and fell to the floor, clutching his bad leg. He gave a roar of rage and slammed his fist against the floor.

"Hadrian!" Lena ran into the room and dropped to her knees at her brother's side. "Are you all right?"

Hadrian did not answer. He was panting and still grasping his wound.

"Hadrian, you can't push yourself like that. You're not strong enough."

"Do not tell me what I can and cannot do, Lena!" Hadrian snapped. "You are my sister, not my mother!"

Lena's expression changed as though Hadrian had slapped her across the face. Numbly, silently, she got up and began to walk across the room.

"Lena," Hadrian said, "Lena, wait. I'm sorry. Lena!"

The door swung shut behind her, and Hadrian was alone. He dropped to the floor, exhausted, his leg aching, the sweat on his face mingling with tears.

You are right not to trust her.

The voice! He had thought it gone, but now it returned, as vehement and treacherous as ever. Hadrian tried to deny it, speaking aloud to the empty room. "No. No, you're wrong. She loves me. I love her. Would die for her."

Your trust and love is admirable but naïve. You are beginning to realize it now, are you not? You have incredible talent, an unending wealth of power. All around you are jealous of it. They covet it, they envy it...they hate you for it. All of them...your tutor Jairdan, your friend Ince...even your sister.

"No! That isn't right! You're wrong, you're wrong!"
Everything you have been taught is a lie.
"No! I won't listen to this anymore!"
You don't have to listen to know that it is true.
"What are you? Some demon? Some lying snake?"
No Hadrian. I am the Truth.

***

Lena went immediately to see Scio, and found him with Prudentior and Chista. She launched into an explanation of what had happened, and as she spoke, Scio's face darkened.

"The voice is back," Lena said. "It has to be. He wouldn't talk to me like that unless it was back."

Scio was silent, and Lena's shoulders sagged. "You disagree."

He contemplated what she had said for a moment more, and said at last, "If it was Daimonas who was speaking to your brother…Lena, you know firsthand the power of his words. Even if I managed to expel the voice, it is possible that its darkness lingers. Lena, when you came here, you trusted no one. Daimonas poisoned you against trust. If the voice had been with Hadrian since the wolf attack…that is a long time. Time enough for Daimonas, I think."

"But he will recover," Lena said. "He will recover."

"Of course he will," Prudentior said. "He is the best. He will overcome it."

Scio remained silent.

"Still, we must try to discover if the voice has returned," Chista said. "We must know."

"It cannot have," Prudentior said. "A high master is Daimonas' equal; Scio conquered the snake."

"You are too sure, Prudentior!" Scio snapped. "We cannot be so confident. You take great leaps on faith alone."

Prudentior looked stricken. Lena lowered her eyes and froze; she felt a shame and a terrible fear at this show of disunity. The High Masters were the great harmony of the Star; to see them disagree felt foreign and utterly wrong.

127

"I will speak to the boy," Scio said. "We must know if the voice has returned."

***

Moments later, Lena found herself in the training room, beginning another lesson with her students.

"And can anyone tell me what makes our city special? Different from other cities in Aurea?" she asked her attentive group of little ones. "Yes—Willow?"

"It's the capital city," the dark-haired girl replied. "It's the most important city in the country"

"Very good!" Lena said. "That's excellent Willow." The girl tossed her head proudly, and Kiara giggled.

"Now," Lena went on, "does anyone know the name of the Queen of our city?"

"Queen Regina," Elissa offered shyly.

"That's right—"

"She's sick," Crispin put in.

"They say she's going to die," Elissa mumbled.

"Is she going to die, Mistress Lena?" Roland asked solemnly.

"And I heard other countries are going to attack us!" another voice cried. Before Lena could tie this comment to an owner, she was overwhelmed by a chorus of concerns from her students.

"Hush, little ones, hush," she told them, raising a hand. She sighed, crouched to be at their eye-level. "I can see that you are too wise to be fooled by lies. The Queen is very ill, but I have seen her, and she is hopeful that she will soon be well. As for your other worries, it does indeed seem that the country may soon be at war." She chewed on her lip, nervous about the effect that this would have on her students, but firm in her decision to present them with the truth.

Elissa's lip lower trembled. "I'm scared, Mistress Lena," she mumbled. The eyes of the rest of her students held the same fear.

"It is frightening, Elissa, I know. But you must all have faith. We fight on the side of good, little ones, and no evil, no matter how

128

strong, can ever overcome true good. You must be brave little soldiers. And all of you, no matter what the cost, have the promise of my protection. Always."

Silence fell, interrupted only by the occasional sniffle. Lena held back the tears that threatened to spill down her own cheeks. "Can you be strong, my little ones?" she asked. "Can you have faith in me?"

"Yes, Mistress Lena," they chorused.

Lena smiled, struggling harder than ever to hold back tears. "Then you are Aureate Guards already. Let's practice with the staffs now, yes?"

Outside the glass walls of the training room where Lena held her lessons Jairdan and Scio stopped to watch on passing.

"She is good a teacher," Scio observed. "She will make a noble soldier."

"Yes," Jairdan agreed. But his brow was furrowed; he was clearly deep in thought.

"What troubles you?"

"I worry that...you don't think that Hadrian will be hurt by any of this? By Lena's progress?"

Scio studied Jairdan's face gravely. "You suggest the eternal paradox," he said. "That by saving one twin we've condemned the other."

"It's just that the prophecy...one twin is to fall into shadow...the other to avoid it...how can we be sure..." Jairdan trailed off hopelessly.

"Prophecies are not always fulfilled, Master Jairdan."

"I know that," Jairdan said, pinching the bridge of his nose. "I know. But still...a strange feeling of foreboding descends on me."

"Perhaps your anxiety is founded in the Queen's illness and the growing tensity of our relations with the Western and Southern kingdoms."

"Perhaps."

"I am going to speak to Hadrian now," Scio said. He put a reassuring hand on Jairdan's elbow. "He has many people watching over him."

Jairdan nodded, but looked worried nonetheless.

***

Scio entered Hadrian's room. It was empty. He searched the dining hall and courtyards and could not find him. He stopped passing Guardsmen to ask if they had seen Hadrian; no one had. Frustrated, Scio hurried through the halls as the shadows lengthened with the approach of nightfall.

***

"Lena." Alone in the training room, her pupils departed, Lena turned at the sound of her name and saw Hadrian standing in the doorway, his face clouded. She went to him and put her hand on his shoulder. "Don't apologize. I know you're frustrated, I understand your anger. I just—"

"I want to spar with you."

Lena blinked. "What?"

"I want to spar with you now."

Lena's hand dropped from Hadrian's shoulder. "Hadrian, did High Master Scio find you? He was looking for you."

Hadrian was silent.

"You're not well enough to spar," Lena said, unnerved. "You'll make the injury worse and double your recovery time, not to mention that—"

"Do you enjoy this?" Hadrian spat. "Do you see this as a way to surpass me, training when you know that I'm not able to?"

"Hadrian, I have never put myself in competition with you!" Lena said, stung. She took a step away from him. "What's wrong with you?"

"Don't pretend!" Hadrian snapped. "I've seen you. Practicing twice as hard since I was hurt. Taking over all my duties."

"Hadrian—"

"I want to spar with you."

130

Lena set her jaw. "Fine."

She took off her cloak and tossed it aside. Hadrian's sword slid from its scabbard, and he raised his dark eyes to meet his sister's. Lena drew her own sword, and Hadrian immediately stepped forward, swinging. Lena had intended to go slowly, but Hadrian attacked with such force that it took all Lena's speed to keep up with him. Despite his injury, Hadrian was sparring with a ferocity Lena had never seen before. Their blades locked; for a moment the two struggled, each trying to gain the upper hand. Hadrian finally prevailed, putting all his strength into a shove that sent Lena to the ground.

"What is wrong with you?" Lena cried.

Hadrian said nothing. The moment Lena got to her feet, Hadrian swung again. Lena parried the swing and took a step away from him. Hadrian lunged forward, forcing all of his weight onto his bad leg. With a gasp of pain, he dropped his sword and had to steady himself by putting one hand on the wall.

Lena paled and dropped her own sword, hurrying to his side. "What is it?" she asked, putting her hand on his arm.

"Don't touch me!" Hadrian roared, shaking her off. "You did this to me! You wanted me to injure myself again! This is what you intended all along!" He took his fingers away from his leg, and Lena saw blood on his fingers.

"You've split the wound open," she said numbly, blinking away tears. "I'm going to get Master Jairdan."

"Yes, that's right, go get help, Lena! Pretend this isn't what you wanted!" Hadrian hissed, clamping his fingers back over his bleeding leg.

"How can you say that?" Lena cried, whirling to face him. Tears that she was unable to hold back rolled freely down her cheeks. "How can you?"

Hadrian glared back at her with red-rimmed eyes.

Lena shook her head and ran out of the room.

***

Later that evening, Lena stood in the corridor outside the infirmary and watched the burning sun sink behind the golden hills. Her eyes were swollen with spent grief. She hugged her arms around herself and leaned against the wall. *You did this to me!* her brother's accusing voice scorched her memory. *You wanted this to happen!*

Lena rested her head against the cool glass of the windowpane. *This isn't what I wanted,* she assured herself. But a treacherous part of her questioned, *Are you certain?*

Lena felt her palms begin to sweat. This voice…*was* it a part of her? Or was it something else?

Are you certain? the voice asked again.

Of course, Lena retorted. *I love Hadrian, more than anything.*

But you could gain from this, the voice returned. *You could become the champion. Let Hadrian's fame wither; let his name die on the winds of time. You could be the Champion of the Golden City. You could have fame. You could have glory.*

A sudden surge of fierce emotion gripped Lena. *I do not want fame!* she shrieked in silence. *I love my brother, and I want only him! I would give anything to have him back as he was. I do not want to be a champion—I only want to be myself!*

The potency of her emotion left Lena trembling. *Leave me alone, I will not bend to you!*

…miles away, in the desert, Daimonas was struck to the floor by a blaze of pure, golden light. He was alone, and had deserted his human form. He was now as Lena had once seen him; black-skinned, lightning-veined, his hair like molten silver. He shifted onto all fours and paced, beast-like, across the floor, snarling with rage.

The girl then, was lost.

But the boy…

Daimonas bared his teeth in a mirthless grin.

There was still the boy.

***

The hateful voice was silent. Lena stood alone, breathing heavily in the empty corridor.

"Lena?" Jairdan came around the corner, and saw that Lena was shaking. "Are you all right? You're trembling!"

"I—I heard it," Lena said, her eyes wide.

"What?"

"The voice," Lena said. "I heard it."

"What!" Jairdan guided Lena a bench and sat her down. "Tell me everything."

"I was thinking about Hadrian," Lena said, "and it was just there, speaking to me. It tempted me with power. With glory."

Jairdan was clutching her arm. "What did you—"

"Something in me thrust out at it," Lena said. "Something surged up in me and I was shrieking in thought-speak at something I couldn't see. I've never felt the like of it."

"And the voice?"

"It's gone," Lena said hollowly.

"How can you be sure?"

"I don't know," she responded, "but I am. I feel…empty. When it had me, when it was speaking to me, I felt…pressure, like I was sharing my skull with someone else."

"We must tell the High Masters," Jairdan said.

Lena nodded. "As soon as I have the chance. But first—Hadrian. Is he…all right?"

"His leg is no worse than before. They stopped the bleeding."

"Is he all right?" Lena repeated.

Jairdan raised his eyes toward the heavens. "No," he said with a sigh. "I have never seen him like this. He rants like a madman."

"He says that I did this to him," Lena guessed sullenly. "That I wanted this to happen, for my own gain."

"He is not himself," Jairdan said solemnly, putting his arm on Lena's shoulder. "That is not what he believes."

"It is what he says," Lena whispered.

"Listen to me," Jairdan said levelly. "This was not your doing."

"He wanted me to spar with him," Lena breathed. "I knew he was too weak. I knew he wasn't ready. But he angered me." Tears caught on her eyelashes; she brushed them off and looked at the floor ashamedly. "If I had ruled my emotion, this would not have happened."

"Lena. Look at me."

Lena raised her glassy eyes to Jairdan's face.

"All Aureate Guard share a common flaw. *We are human.* We anger, as humans do. You hold no blame in what happened today. Hadrian is the one who was at fault. He wrongly accused you of taking advantage of his injury. You, who have sat at his bedside all these long days, who have loved him with a patience that very few possess. I know you, Lena," Jairdan said, gripping her shoulder tighter. "And I will never doubt your loyalty to this Order, to this city, and to your brother, even if you lose faith in it yourself."

Lena swallowed hard.

"Lena?" A healer stepped out of the infirmary. "Your brother is asleep. Would you like to see him?"

Lena stepped wordlessly toward the door, past the healer, and into the infirmary. Hadrian lay supine on the bed, his eyes closed, looking completely at peace. Lena touched her brother's shoulder and kissed his forehead. His skin was warm beneath her lips. *Hadrian?* she whispered. She got not reply, and shivered. *Hadrian!* This whisper was harsher, more desperate.

Asleep this way, calm and seemingly untroubled, Hadrian looked to Lena as he always had. The Hadrian she saw now was the one who was ready to love, comfort, or laugh, ready to take her in his arms or the by the hand. A sick fear gripped Lena. She felt a terrible sense of foreboding that that Hadrian was falling away, and that a new one that she did not know was rising up to take his place.

Lena dropped to her knees at her brother's bedside, buried her face in his chest, and began to weep.

She felt a kind hand on her shoulder and turned to see Scio looking on her with pained sympathy in his eyes. "Lena, child. Wipe your eyes."

Lena brushed away her tears and took a deep breath to steady herself. "Excuse me," she said. She rose and gave Scio a bow.

"I was speaking with Master Jairdan," Scio said.

"He must have told you." Lena nodded. "I was going to come to you immediately. I just wanted to see to Hadrian first."

"I understand, Lena. But this incident is serious. Tell me what happened."

Lena carefully recounted what she had experienced in the corridor. "I truly feel that the voice is gone, High Master," Lena said. "I can't explain why, but I'm sure of it."

"Close your eyes, Lena, and relax your mind," Scio instructed. A look of mild panic passed spasmodically across Lena's face. "I know you struggle still with meditation," Scio said, "but it will be for only a moment."

Lena obediently closed her eyes and tried to think of nothing. She let go of her concern for Hadrian, tried to release the memory of the haunting voice.

Scio closed his eyes as well, and, when he sensed that Lena was calm, gently concentrated his energy on her.

Lena felt Scio enter her mind; it was a slightly uncomfortable feeling, not unlike a head cold. She shifted her position and focused on keeping her mind blank.

What Scio saw within Lena was quite different than what he had seen within Hadrian. Lena's mind was like a golden-walled room with black scores like burn marks along the sides. The scorches, Scio decided, must be the remnants of her time with Pioni. But Scio could see that the scars were fading, their shadow being expelled by a glowing flame of white light at the center of Lena's mind. As the flames licked at the walls, the burn marks were slowly growing fainter; some were barely visible.

There was no sign of a serpent, or any creature of shadow.

Lena shifted again, uncomfortable with the scrutiny, and Scio withdrew.

Lena felt him leave her, and opened her eyes.

"There is no shadow in you, Lena," Scio said. "You were right."

Lena breathed a sigh of relief. "Thank the Star." She put a hand to her forehead, still feeling the effects of Scio's presence. "High Master, how do you think the voice came into me?"

135

Scio's brow furrowed in thought. "My only guess is that it must have been able to transfer itself through your thought-speak. Your mind and Hadrian's are joined when the two of you are conversing in that way; that bridge must have been a way for the voice to cross from Hadrian's mind to yours."

"So it will not affect anyone else?" Lena asked.

"I don't think so," Scio replied. "For one thing Lena, I don't think Daimonas would have much interest in another mind. You and Hadrian are young, malleable." He smiled. "We old men are set in our ways. Daimonas would know better than to think he could turn one of us to his cause. He chose you and Hadrian as prey because he believed he could turn you both."

"He will fail," Lena said. "He cannot turn us, not either one."

Scio nodded. "You showed remarkable resistance, Lena. I am proud of you."

"I am tired," Lena said wearily, letting her hand drop.

"Yes," said Scio. "As am I. You should go and get some rest."

Lena rose and bowed to Scio before leaving the room. Scio turned to Hadrian, who lay, still sleeping, on the bed. He extended what energy he had left to the boy. In his mind, Scio could find no lurking shadow, but there was not the light that had been present within Lena, and Scio was not assured that his inability to find a snake meant that there was not one hiding there.

Chapter Fourteen
War Declared

"Hadrian, get up. This is serious. You must come."

Hadrian blinked open his eyes to see Jairdan standing over him. "What is it?" he asked, pushing himself up onto his elbows. "What's happened?"

"You must come," Jairdan said, and Hadrian caught a tinge of anxiety in his teacher's voice.

"My leg—" he began.

"Your cane's here," Jairdan said quickly, and this time the solicitude was obvious. He held the cane out to his apprentice.

Sensing the urgency, Hadrian got out of bed and took the cane. Leaning dependently on it, he accompanied Jairdan to the amphitheater.

When the pair entered the room, it was filled with other Aureate Guard whispering anxiously to each other. Hadrian spotted Lena sitting with Ince a few rows from where he and Jairdan took their seats. Lena gave him a nervous smile, and Hadrian responded with a bright grin and a wave. He was feeling better this morning; despite a dull headache he felt like some of his pain had been neutralized.

Lena's smile widened when Hadrian acknowledged her; he gave her a final nod and sat down to face the pit, where the three High Masters stood, looking grave.

Also in the pit was a large, magnificent falcon. Lena was fascinated by it; the bird had captured her attention the moment she stepped into the room. It stood as tall as her waist; its beak was curved and polished; its feathers, a tawny, golden color, gleamed in the sunlight that streamed in through the glass windows. This, Lena realized, must be one of the avian scouts that Jairdan had mentioned. Its black eyes darted around the room, coming to rest on Hadrian's face when he entered.

You are touched by shadow. The voice echoed within Hadrian's head, but this was not the voice that he had heard before. The falcon was speaking to him. Its piercing stare cut Hadrian to the bone. *You are sick with darkness.*

Hadrian jerked his head to the side, breaking eye contact. The bird surveyed him a moment longer, then turned its attention to Lena.

Child of Light, it addressed her. The bird spread its wings, and Lena saw that their span was much longer than she was tall. It inclined its head, and Lena realized that it was bowing to her. *I have waited many moons to make your acquaintance. I am Aquilus, Captain of the Queen's Cavalry of the Sky. It is a great honor to meet you at last.*

The honor is mine, Lena responded silently. *My only regret is that we meet in such uncertain times.*

I am afraid that the certainty that my message bears only worsens the situation, Aquilus said.

What message is that? Lena asked, afraid to hear the answer.

"War has been declared," Prudentior said, over the din of the combined murmurs of the crowd in the assembly room, "by both Westmore and Sanuul. There can no longer any doubt that the two are united in this battle against us. Aquilus brings even graver news. He tells us that the west and south are already nearly prepared for battle."

"We won't be able to defeat them alone," said Jairdan. "Their forces, combined against our own…Bruteaus was our most powerful alley. Who can we turn to for help now?"

"We have heard that there may be some Westmorian troops still loyal to our alliance that are willing to help us. But their pledge is too fragile to rely solely upon it." Prudentior shook his head gravely, his eyes tired with worry.

"You see the problem that presents itself," Master Scio said. "Our nearest remaining allies are the warriors that reside along the eastern coast."

"Less warriors than hunters," Jairdan put in. "And disorganized."

"But trainable, and, unfortunately, our last remaining ally," Scio replied.

"The problem," Prudentior put forth, "is that Bruteaus is also aware of our relations with the Easterners, and he will taken every precaution to see to it that we do not receive any help from them. He has taken control of the Easterners' fort along the Misty River, and his troops have formed a blockade across the Silver Bridge. Help that would ordinarily be a few days' ride away is now almost impossible to reach. Aquilus estimates that we will be under siege within the month. We have only one choice."

"That is?" Jairdan asked.

"We must send two of our best to elicit the help of the Easterners. Messengers alone are not up to the task; with enemy troops stirring it would be too dangerous. We need skill for this endeavor. The ones who go may well determine the outcome of a battle that is now inevitable, though it would certainly be a dangerous mission."

"If you wish it Master," Jairdan said, "I will go."

"Yes, Master Jairdan has seniority amongst the Masters; you are the logical choice," Scio replied. "But there must be another, to help you. Neither Master Prudentior nor myself can accompany you; we will be detained here, trying to delay the war for as long as possible."

"I hold next seniority," said a tall, broad-shouldered, red-haired man, standing. "I will accompany Master Jairdan."

"Your offer is appreciated, Master Ruben, but we are hesitant to expend two of our highest ranking members; besides, as Master Archer, you are needed in the event that we come siege earlier than predicted and require the use of your forces."

"I will go," Hadrian said. "I'm Master Jairdan's apprentice, it makes sense. Apprentices always accompany masters on missions."

"We considered this as well," Scio replied gently, "but we do not believe that you are strong enough, Hadrian."

"I can ignore the pain," Hadrian said. "I will not let it affect me."

"Your injury is too great to ignore," Scio said. "You are not up to the task. We propose another."

"You want me," Lena realized. "You want me to go."

"Yes, Lena," Scio said. "I, your master, cannot go. Hadrian, Jairdan's apprentice, is also unable to make the journey. You seem to fit."

Lena's eyes met Hadrian's. He gave a minute shake of his head, his eyes desperate. Lena looked away. "I will go," she told the masters. "I do not know if my skill is equal to the task, but I will muster the courage to find out, if it is the will of the High Masters."

"No!" Hadrian shouted. "The task is too dangerous. Lena is not ready for that. Please, let me go in her place."

"You are too weak, Hadrian," Jairdan said."You are not strong enough."

They want you to lose your power here. She *wants you to.*

Hadrian jerked his head, trying to shake it of the voice. "I am strong enough!" he cried. "Let me go!" He looked in fury at the rest of the assembly. "It's too dangerous for Lena to go! Are you all out of your minds?"

"That's enough, Hadrian," Prudentior growled. "This is not your decision."

"She is my sister!" Hadrian snapped. Again, his eyes searched the room for an ally. His eyes fell on Ince, who stood beside Lena. Shocked by Hadrian's outburst, Ince looked away, unwilling to meet Hadrian's eyes. Hadrian gave a snarl of disgust and stormed out of the room, his cloak billowing angrily behind him. The urge to go after him and the responsible compulsion to stay nearly tore Lena apart.

"Our minds would be at rest if you agree to this, Lena" Scio said.

"Then be at peace," Lena replied, her face like stone. "I will go with Master Jairdan."

***

Prudentior shook his head. "I still do not think it is for the best."

"The girl is the logical choice!" Chista said, in the aggravated tones of someone who has been arguing the same point over and over.

"After she has heard this shadow voice, you are willing to trust her?"

"The voice was gone from her," Scio said.

"You thought it was gone from her brother as well, when clearly it was not!"

Chista rounded on Prudentior. "He's already told us it was different! The girl's mind was different!"

"I trust in our decision to send Lena," Scio said. "She will have Master Jairdan to look after her, and she may well be the key to reaching Marii. She has great skill."

Prudentior shook his head. "I defer to your decision, but it was not one I would have made myself."

***

"It's ridiculous! It's humiliating! I will not stand for it!"

"The choice is not ours," Lena replied numbly, as she rolled up a white tunic and stuffed it into a satchel.

"It *is* ours! We each made our choice and the High Masters ignored us! I wanted to go, and you did not, yet you are going and I am staying here!"

"Hadrian!" Lena whirled to face her brother. Hadrian was taken aback when he saw tears in her eyes. "I am sorry we have to part, but I see no other way to—"

"Well perhaps they would have listened to me if you took part in the discussion!" Hadrian snapped. "Instead you just stood there and let me make a fool of myself for you! Anyway, they would have let me go if you hadn't made me injure myself again yesterday afternoon!"

Stung by his anger and even more by the injustice of the remark, Lena retorted, "I am doing what I have to do! I know I'm not as good as you Hadrian, I know that, but it's the only way!"

"The only way? You've barely been here a month and you think you can handle a task of this magnitude? I was trying to protect you, but you are being too stubborn and arrogant even to protect yourself!"

"Protect me? Is that what you were doing? Because lately it feels more like you're attacking me!"

Momentarily lost for words, Hadrian was silent.

Lena stalked across the room toward the door. She had her hand on the doorknob when she paused. "I'm sorry they didn't ask you to go."

Anger burst as Lena left the room. "That's what you think this is about?" Hadrian roared at the door that was closing behind his sister. "That's what you think?"

The door clicked shut.

Hadrian sank weakly onto the bed and grasped with both hands his throbbing leg. Lena's words ran through his mind.

She thought I was...attacking her...I was *attacking her.*

You were defending yourself. She was the one who attacked you.

No. Hadrian shook his head, gritted his teeth. *She's right. I've been...I've been so cruel to her. How could I?*

You were simply—

No!

Silence.

Hadrian was breathing hard. His hand clenched around his cane and he rose. He hobbled quickly across the room and flung open the door. "Lena!"

***

"Lena?" Ince stepped into the courtyard. Lena was sitting on a stone bench, staring despondently at the ground, her fingers picking idly at a loose thread on the hem of her tunic.

Ince took a seat beside her on the bench, and for a moment said nothing. Finally, he said, "It's very brave, what you're doing."

Lena let out a short, incredulous laugh. "I wish Hadrian thought so."

"Well..." Ince struggled to compose a comforting word. "I'm sure he does, really."

Lena shook her head. "He's angry."

"With you?" Ince asked, disbelieving.

"With me, with the High Masters, with himself..."

"He's worried for you. That's all."

Lena sighed. "It's more than that."

Ince shook his head. "It's not. Trust me. I know Hadrian."

Again she shook her head. "There's something…wrong with him. Since he hurt his leg…something's changed."

Ince hesitated for a moment, then reached out and put his hand over hers. To his shock, Lena let out a heart-wrenching sob and buried her face in his chest. For a moment Ince was too stunned to react. Then, he wrapped a trembling arm around her shoulders. "It's all right," he murmured. "Everything will be all right."

"I'm not like Hadrian, Ince," Lena sobbed. "I'm not brave. I'm terrified to leave this place."

"Courage isn't not being afraid of a hundred men with swords," Ince said. "That's stupidity."

This drew a small, strangled laugh from Lena. Ince went on, "Courage is being terrified of something and doing it anyway. You *are* like Hadrian, Lena, and you *do* have courage."

Lena sat up and rubbed her eyes. "I'm sorry," she said. She smiled through her tears. "I've cried all over you." She reached out and rubbed at a dark stain on Ince's tunic. She let her hand drop, but to her surprise, Ince caught it and clutched it in his own. Lena looked at him and saw something in his eyes, something she had never seen there, something hard and fierce and burning. "Ince?"

"Lena, I—" Ince glanced at her face and faltered. "I want to tell you that…that…" Again he looked at her, and again he stumbled over the words. His mouth worked spasmodically for a moment, and then he stopped and seemed to droop resignedly. "That I have faith in you," he said. His grip on her hand relaxed, and he released.

"Oh," Lena said, puzzled. "Thank you, Ince."

***

Hadrian stood alone in a hallway, gazing bitterly out at the city, bathed in the deep orange light of a descending sun. Shadows played against the walls as dusk settled over the city. Hadrian did not turn when Jairdan approached him, seemed not to notice when his master leaned against the railing and scanned his pupil's face. After some moments of silence, Jairdan turned to look out at the city as well. "You've been fighting with your sister."

143

Hadrian still did not look at him. "I was trying to protect her."

"By that display in the assembly room? That looked more like jealousy or anger than fraternal concern."

"I was angry at the High Masters for insisting that she go with you."

"Insisting that she go? Hadrian, she volunteered!"

"They pushed her to it," Hadrian snapped, but it sounded forced, as if he had been saying it to himself over and over but had still not been able to make himself believe it.

"Hadrian," Jairdan said, "you have been my apprentice for seventeen years, and I have never known you to be this irrational. You haven't been yourself for weeks. What's wrong?"

Hadrian turned from the window and ran his hand through his hair. "I don't know," he said, sinking onto the floor.

Jairdan sat down next to his apprentice.

"I'm so angry," Hadrian said, "and I don't know why. I'm suspicious of everyone…I get enraged at things that mean nothing. But the emotion is so powerful…I feel like I'm drowning."

Jairdan looked with pained concern at his apprentice. "Hadrian, there is nothing to fear here, nothing to hate. This is your home, and Lena is your sister. She is sick with worry for you."

Hadrian put his head in his hands. "I know," he choked. "But how can I go to her now? How can she forgive me?"

Jairdan put a hand on Hadrian's shoulder. "She will," he promised. "Go to her, and she will forgive you."

Chapter Fifteen
A Nocturnal Meeting

After parting with Ince, Lena walked slowly down to the training room. She was supposed to begin to teach her little ones how to use daggers, but she did not feel up to it. When she reached the training room and saw them gathered in a circle in the center of the room, she sighed sadly. She entered the room and gave them all the strongest smile she could muster. "Hello children," she whispered.

"Hello Mistress Lena," they chorused in response.

"I need to tell you all something, my little ones," Lena said. She crouched down in front of the group. "I need to go away for a little while. The High Masters need me for a mission in the east. High Master Scio will see to your training while I am gone."

"Why do you have to leave?" Crispin's duck-fluff eyebrows came together in a furrow of concern.

"The High Masters have asked me to help them with a very important mission," Lena said. "They need me to go to the east and ask the warriors there for help."

"Because we're at war," Roland said.

Lena nodded. "That's right," she said softly.

"But why do you have to go, Mistress Lena?" Willow asked. "Can't they send someone else?"

"They asked me to go," Lena said, "and it is a great honor to do this duty for the city. Master Scio is the wisest Aureate Guard alive. You are lucky to have him teach you while I am away."

"But we want *you* to teach us!" Elissa cried pitifully, throwing herself into Lena's arms.

Lena stroked the little girl's hair and blinked furiously. "I want to teach you, too, Elissa. But we can't always have what we want." She stood up and said, "Roland will take care of you while I am gone. Listen to him."

Roland's dark eyes reflected his gratitude at her choosing him as the leader.

"Now," Lena said, her voice quivering only slightly. "Let's have one last lesson, shall we?"

***

Hadrian, who had been looking for Lena, caught sight of her just as she was finishing her lesson with her students. The students bowed to Lena, and she returned the bow. Then, Elissa burst into tears and locked her arms around Lena's waist in a final embrace. Lena smiled and patted the girl's head. Elissa detached herself from her teacher, and Roland led the the little girl by her hand out of the room. Hadrian saw tears shining in Lena's eyes as she watched the children leave, and his feeling of guilt tripled. *It's killing her to leave this place,* he thought, and no voice answered.

Within the training room, Lena sank onto the floor and put a hand to her head. Hadrian entered the room and crossed quickly to where she sat, crumpled and broken by emotion.

"Lena," he said, dropping to his knees beside her. "I'm sorry. I'm so sorry."

A pained smile broke on Lena's face. "It's all right. It doesn't matter."

Hadrian encircled her in his arms, and Lena leant wearily against her brother, allowing herself once more to absorb the comfort that she found in his embrace.

***

Lena tossed in bed. The night was cool, and Lena's body was tired enough, but her mind whirled. Finally, she swung her legs over the edge of her bed and reached for the candle in a sconce on the wall. Barefoot and with nothing more than a light shawl for warmth, she slipped out of her room and down a winding staircase, out into the central courtyard of the temple. She inhaled the night air and relaxed into a stroll in the winding maze of greenery that grew in the courtyard. She was startled when she stepped around a flowering tree to find Aquilus perched on the hedge, his eyes closed, breathing slow. Lena turned to go so she would not disturb him, but his falcon eyes blinked open and his deep voice said in her mind, *Do not go on my account, Child of the Golden Warriors.*

I do not wish to disturb you, Lena replied politely.

I enjoy the company of an Aureate Soldier.

You address me through epithets. Why? Lena asked.

Because they are more meaningful than names.

Lena sighed and wrapped her arm around the trunk of a tree.

You are troubled, young one.

I am frightened, Lena replied. *And...*

And?

Lena sighed again. *Somehow I feel that this, all of this, the war, the problems with my brother, must be my fault somehow.*

Why do you feel this way?

There was no trouble here before I arrived, and there has been nothing but since I came.

Aquilus shifted his position on his perch. *You are not the cause of a storm. You are a creature caught in one.*

I will not bend to it. I will fight for this city to the end.

Aquilus cocked his head appraisingly. *Yes. You are not a like a tree that bows in a storm. You may be the ray of the light that pierces the cloud. Just remember that even clouds too thick to be pierced by the strongest light do eventually pass.*

Your words hold the foresight of a seer.

Aquilus' eyes expressed a smile. *No, I am no future-gazer. I merely have the benefit of objectivity. An emotionless observer can look to history to predict the ends of present conflicts.*

What does the Queen say about the declaration of war?

The Queen is dying. She will be gone within the month. Her room reeks of death.

His candidness shocked her. Lena drew her cloak more tightly around her body with a minute, denying shake of her head.

Forgive me. I am falcon, a creature of perception, reason, and fact. I sometimes forget the sensitivity of human emotion.

You do not feel sadness?

Disappointment perhaps, if I do not catch my prey or do my job well enough. I see from a logical standpoint that the Queen's loss will be detrimental, and it worries me. Nothing more.

And love? Do you not feel love?

The bird cocked its head. *I feel connection to my mate and younglings. I have respect for my mate and take pride in the way that my children grow strong. But I do not think I feel love as you mean it.*

But what if your mate was killed by a hunter, or your children were dying of starvation and you had no means of saving them? What would you feel?

Aquilus tilted his head again, looking confused. *Do you foresee that the situation you propose will come to pass?*

No. I just wondered if you might feel a stronger emotion in that kind of circumstance.

Aquilus blinked. *I have not considered such a thing before. I do not know what I would feel. You have given me something to think about, young one.*

Lena rubbed her eyes and looked up at the moon. *It's late*, she commented, seeing that the moon had passed its zenith.

And why do you not sleep? You and your Master Jairdan are set to leave tomorrow.

I needed to clear my head, Lena replied. *I thought the night air would help.*

I was under the impression that your kind uses meditation to relax the mind.

Lena looked away and ran her fingers over the gooseflesh that had risen on her skin in the chilly air. The truth was that, try as she might, she still had not been able to meditate without falling victim to haunting memories. *I am not as skilled in that area as others of my order,* she replied guardedly.

The hawk regarded her with his dark, perspicacious eyes. Lena got the uncomfortable feeling that he was looking past her skin into the contents of her mind and soul. *You might try another method,* he suggested.

I know only what I've been taught.

The falcon stretched his wings. *Sometimes, when I am seeking prey, I drift on a current of air and let the wind take my mind where it will. I do not think I ever feel as completely at peace as when I soar over a canyon and see a sapphire ribbon of river winding through it below me.*

Lena considered this in silence, not completely sure of the hawk's meaning.

Aquilus looked up at the sky. *You should go to bed, but I am going to patrol the skies. Think about what I have said. I will certainly consider what* you *have told* me. He flapped his wings and rose into the sky, the sound of the great beat of his wings like that of sheets being shaken out in the darkness.

***

Lena lay in bed thinking about what Aquilus had said. *I drift on a current of air and let the wind take my mind where it will. I do not think I ever feel as completely at peace as when I soar over a canyon and see a sapphire ribbon of river winding through it below me.*

Lena let her eyes drift closed. She inhaled deeply, then let the air out in a gentle stream. Slowly, the touch of the sheets fell away. She no longer lie on mattress; she floated on air. Below her she saw a rust-colored canyon that contrasted brilliantly with the lapis firmament. Far, far down, deep in the canyon, she could see a curl of vibrant blue. She inhaled again and tasted the freshness of clean, autumn air. As the world passed beneath her, she looked into the horizon. The blue, autumnal sky faded slowly into panther-black with the ease of a dream. Fingers of deep blue reached out from the calm, star-speckled sky ahead. Lena stretched her wings and felt the power in them as she propelled herself forward with one, strong beat. She entered the dark calm, the world fell away, and she slept.

149

***

The next morning, the sun rose with blood red certainty over the desert dunes, paling the perfect black of Lena's sky, dying the heavens a sickly, sanguine orange.

Daimonas stepped forward out of Pioni's castle. His horse was waiting for him, still not quite opaque, not quite real, but real enough to mount, and this Daimonas did with a smile that disclosed to the dunes that all was going exactly to plan.

Chapter Sixteen
Parting Ways

Though Lena did not sleep long that night, she awoke feeling more rested than she had in weeks. A pale light outside indicated that it was still early. Lena got out of bed and took a simple, brown traveling dress from where she had left it hanging over the top of her dressing screen. She and Jairdan had to travel in disguise; they could wear nothing adorned with the Queen's insignia, certainly nothing that would single them out as warriors. She would have to hide Wolf's Bane deep in her saddlebag unless she absolutely needed it; as women typically did not travel with swords.

She stepped behind the screen and changed quickly. Sensible, calf-high boots waited on the floor next to her bed. She pulled them on and stowed a small but deadly dagger within the left one. Then, she picked her cloak up from the foot of her bed and passed through it to Hadrian's adjoining room.

He was standing out on the balcony. He turned at the sound of her footsteps and smiled. The smile she returned was tainted with a sadness she had been determined to hide, and Hadrian's own smile faded. Lena slipped her hand into Hadrian's and clung to it. Tears burned in her eyes. "I don't want to leave you," she whispered.

Hadrian squeezed her fingers. "And I don't want you to leave." He brushed away a tear that was trailing down his sister's cheek and forced a smile. "This isn't how I meant to start the morning. Here. This is for you." He pressed something cool and smooth into her hand. Lena looked down. Hadrian had pressed a necklace, a star carved from a gold-colored wood, hanging from a leather cord, into her hand. She looked back at her brother.

"I've had it for a while," he said. "I was planning on giving it to you at the Midwinter Festival, but I had to give you something before you left. The star's carved goldwood. It only grows in Aurea. Now you can take a little bit of the country with you when you go."

"It's beautiful," Lena said. "Hadrian, thank you." Her lip trembled. "Why is it," she asked, smiling through tears, "that even though we only met a few months ago I feel like we've never been apart?"

"Because we aren't meant to be," Hadrian responded,

As they stood out in the cool morning air, Aquilus rose like a tawny sun to alight on the ledge of the balcony. *Child of Light*, he said, fixing his penetrating stare on Lena's face, *our departure is near. The horses are packed and saddled. We wait for you.*

Lena gave him a forced smile and a nod, then turned back to her brother. "I'll walk with you to the courtyard," he said.

The twins walked in silence out of the room, down the winding steps that led to the courtyard, and out into the day. The sky was clear, the sun a steadily rising marble of white-light. One of the stable boys had packed and saddled Lady for Lena. Jairdan had already mounted Cougar, his chestnut stallion, and Aquilus was perched on the limb of a tree, watching Lena carefully.

Lena turned back to her brother. Hadrian gripped her fingers hard for one moment, then let her slide her hand from his. "I'll see you again soon," Hadrian promised. He was trying to convince himself as much as he was her. "Jairdan will take good care of you." Lena nodded, reluctant to tear her eyes from her brother. When she finally did, an aching lump rose in her throat and, for a moment, she was blinded by unshed tears. She managed to find the pommel of Lady's saddle through the blur, and she pulled herself onto her horse. She looked back at the Star and saw Ince's face, pale as a corpse's, in one of the windows. She forced a smile that she was not sure he could see, raised her hand in a parting wave, and then she turned Lady and followed Jairdan, who had already urged Cougar into a walk.

Be safe. Hadrian's words seared in her mind. She turned her head and nodded firmly. She continued to look over her shoulder at her brother as Lady progressed down the cobbled path that led out of the city. Just before Hadrian dropped from sight, Lena felt a pang of icy fear. Her brother disappeared from view, and the apprehension settled like a fist in her stomach.

***

Mallin had stopped to change his attire when he crossed the border into Queen Regina's territory, knowing that with the recent declaration of war by the South a Sanuulian would not be welcomed warmly by Northerners. He now wore a simple, unadorned gray tunic and nothing to mask his tanned face. Therefore, when he arrived at the gates of the Aureate City claiming to be seeking a few days' lodging at an inn the city, the guard at the gate had no reason to be suspicious of him and let him pass. Mallin had ridden hard without much rest and was glad to find an inn and rent a room for the night. The innkeeper, a stout, muscular man who introduced himself as Goffer, led Mallin upstairs and opened the door to one of the rooms with a heavy, iron key. "All yours for the night, sir," he said. "There's dinner and drinks downstairs starting around eight, and breakfast tomorrow morning. That'll cost yer extra, o'course." Goffer laughed and patted his pocket, where Mallin's money jangled comfortably. When Mallin did not respond, Goffer chuckled nervously. "Okay. Well. G'bye." He turned and went hurriedly down the stairs. Mallin closed the door, sank down onto the hard bed in the room, and was asleep within minutes.

When he awoke again, night had already fallen. The air had grown cold with the setting of the sun, and Mallin wrapped himself in a hooded cloak before he went downstairs.

The tavern of the inn was loud and bustling, filled with men in conversations or shouting matches, playing cards, dice, or whistling at the serving maids. Goffer, who had already downed a drink or two himself, was laughing uproariously behind the counter. Mallin selected his seat carefully, just behind two men who were intent on a game of cards and who, most importantly, looked sober. Mallin went unnoticed by the two, who were engrossed in a conversation they were having over their cards. One of them, who looked to be in his late thirties, had a pipe in his mouth, and the finer details his companion's features were lost to Mallin in a veil of blue-grey smoke. From what Mallin could make out, the other man appeared younger. He was thin and serious, and had a half-finished pint of ale by his left hand.

"That's what I heard," the older man with the pipe was saying. "They left this morning, from what my Ashleigh told me."

"And how does she know?" the skinnier man asked, selecting a card from his hand and lying it face down on the table.

"Got it from another maid at the castle who got it from one of Regina's handmaids."

"How many of them?"

"Two. A man and a girl."

"The girl who came here a couple of months ago? The one who's supposed to be one of their best? One of the greatest that ever lived?"

"Ashleigh's not sure of their names, but it seems to me that they'd send one of their best. Wouldn't want to mess it up, would they? We need help from the East if we have any hope in a war with the West and South."

"What are the others going to do until then?"

"The other what?"

"Golden soldiers."

"Delay the war as long as they can, I suppose." The man with the pipe picked a card from his own hand and put it on top of his opponent's on the table.

"You know, one of my friends knows one of the guards who was with the group that fought those Eastern guerrillas—what was it, seventeen, eighteen years ago?—anyway, he said they came across a group of Sanuulian elite one day—not to fight them or anything mind, just saw them as they passed close to the border. He said they were terrifying. Right terrifying. And they weren't even fighting!"

"They're evil people, those Southerners. Ten to one it's them what started the war. Their queen, Rheaa, is mad." The man turned his head and blew a jet of smoke toward the wall. "The Holy Star help us if they attack before we're ready."

The men fell silent, brooding over their card game. Mallin got up and left the table. He had heard all he needed to hear.

***

There had been no hero's send off for Lena and Jairdan, though this was by design. They slipped quickly out of the city, their hoods drawn close around their faces. The more people that knew about their journey, Jairdan had said, the more likely it was that word of their mission would reach Bruteaus.

Once out of the city, they made good time. Aquilus wheeled overhead, a black silhouette against the dismal backdrop of the clouded sky. Below him, Lena was silent, tense in the saddle. The tranquil quiet of the fields around her which had always before been peaceful now seemed to leave open endless possibilities for attack.

"Lena," Jairdan said, "you're very quiet."

Lena smiled. "Just nervous, I suppose."

Jairdan nodded. "That's natural," he said. "I was nervous when I went on my first mission as well. But look." He reached under the fabric of his cloak and tunic and tugged at something beneath it. Lena watched as a gold chain, then a pendant, came into view.

"The Charm!" Lena exclaimed.

Jairdan smiled and nodded. "Ought to give us a bit of luck, at least." He winked, and Lena relaxed in the saddle, put more at ease by the presence of the pendant.

Jairdan tucked the chain back beneath his tunic and surveyed their surroundings. "This fog has certainly set a cheery mood for our first day," he commented.

The fog thickens ahead, Golden One, Aquilus told Lena.

Lena sighed. "Excellent," she said drily.

Aquilus was right. Soon the gloomy fog completely blanketed the field, so thick that the visibility dropped to only a few feet.

Chapter Seventeen
The Hand of a Liar

"You asked to see me, Master?"

"Yes, Hadrian, please come in." Hadrian had found Scio in the meditation room. He stepped inside and took a seat on a cushion opposite the High Master. "What is it?" Hadrian asked.

"Nothing very important," Scio said placidly. "I just wondered how you were taking your sister's departure. I know it was hard on you."

Scio was taken aback by how quickly it happened. Immediately, a silent voice bit through the air between them. It took barely any concentration for Scio to hear it, though it was clearly intended only for Hadrian.

He thinks you are weak.

Scio saw the boy pale. Hadrian cleared his throat. "I miss her, but it was the will of the High Masters that she go. I accept their authority."

Scio decided against letting the boy know that he had heard the voice. "Can I offer you something to drink?" he asked. "Tea, perhaps?"

Hadrian hesitated before replying, "Ah I'm—not hungry, I'm...I just ate, actually, and I had tea, with Ince. Thank, you though."

The gratitude was forced. Scio looked deep into Hadrian's eyes and saw the sickness of paranoia. Hadrian squirmed with it; Scio's heart wrenched with sympathy for the boy. How could he force the voice from Hadrian's mind? Why was it not easy for Hadrian to expel it, as it had been for Lena?

"And how is your leg, Hadrian?"

He hopes it has not improved. He is hoping it has worsened.

Scio saw pain in the boy's eyes and was moved by Hadrian's battle to ignore it. "It—it gets better with every day, High Master."

Master—he should be addressing you as master, not the reverse! Hadrian cringed.

"I'm glad to hear it."

"Thank you, Master."

"You may go in a moment," Scio said, "but first—is there anything you wish to tell me?"

He knows...he suspects...he realizes you are beginning to see what you could be...what you are...

Hadrian's features steeled. "No. Nothing."

Disappointment was evident in Scio's voice. "Very well. You may go."

Hadrian looked at the High Master, who suddenly seemed older, wearier. "Except—" Hadrian choked.

Scio's bright eyes darted to Hadrian's face. "Yes?"

Do not tell him!

A sharp rap at the door broke the silence. Scio and Hadrian both turned as an apprentice stuck his head anxiously around the frame of the open door. "High Master Scio? Someone's here—a refugee from the West. He says more are coming. People who do not sympathize with Bruteaus, who think he's gone mad. The other High Masters are speaking to him now; would you like to see him?"

Scio looked back at Hadrian. He could see in the boy's dulled expression that all hope of breaking his silence was, for the moment, lost. Scio rose. "Yes. I'll hear what the refugee has to say. Hadrian, perhaps you would join me?"

"Yes." Hadrian rose to his feet. "Yes, of course, High Master."

Scio nodded. The two followed the apprentice out of the room.

Deep inside Hadrian, the dark voice savored its victory.

***

There are men up ahead, just beyond the crest of this hill. Aquilus dipped low in the sky. Lena and Jairdan traded looks and reined in their horses.

157

Westerners? Jairdan asked.

I cannot tell, Aquilus replied. *Stay here and I will see.*

"Here," Jairdan said softly to Lena. "We'll wait here by these trees."

Aquilus rose majestically higher. Lena and Jairdan watched in silence as he became a dark silhouette, spiraling above the dip in the landscape where he had spotted the men.

The group that Aquilus had spotted consisted of three men. They carried sheathed broadswords and large, heavy shields lie beside them. Their horses, muscular chargers, that were not, Aquilus suspected, unfamiliar with battlefields, grazed docilely a few yards from their masters. The men were obviously enjoying their first rest after a hard ride; they were sweaty and caked with mud, their hair matted, wet with droplets of moisture that had formed from exposure to the damp fog. Aquilus swooped downward and perched in a pine tree, preening innocently as he listened to their conversation.

"Damnable weather," said one of the men, emptying coffee from a tin cup out onto the ground. He carried himself with a calm, confident ease. He was the shortest and slightest of the three, but Aquilus could see a fighter's spirit in him. "Can't keep anything warm for long. And everything's wet with this dratted fog." He wiped his long, wet, brown hair out of his eyes.

"Makes the horses shifty, too," the third, a bald-headed, red-bearded, giant of a man, commented. He was propped up against a rock, picking his teeth with a long splinter of wood.

The two men that had spoken now looked expectantly at the third. Their companion was a man just barely out of adolescence, though he carried himself more maturely than some men of forty. He had blond hair that fell to his shoulders and bright, green eyes. It was evident from the way that the two other men were looking at him that he, though probably the youngest of the group, was also the leader. In response to his companions' pointed glances, he sniffed, rose, and worked his arms to stretch and warm the muscles. At last he said, "I imagine that's why we haven't seen Forrester yet. Fog's always worse out on the Fields, and as he has more men it'll be harder for him to travel."

"How long do you suppose it'll take him to reach Amensliel?" asked the brown-haired man, sticking the point of his dagger into the dirt and twisting it idly in the earth.

"Depends. If the fog lifts, we'll see him there within the week, I should imagine. If it keeps up, and if those clouds are as threatening as they look, it could take twice as long."

Aquilus turned to look the clouds the man indicated. They were swollen with moisture and charcoal gray; they looked ready to send a howling storm to earth at an moment.

"There's a singular bird and no mistake," said the big man suddenly, getting to his feet and taking a step toward the pine tree to get a closer look at Aquilus. "Well taken care of and brazen around humans. Do you suppose it's escaped from some falconer?" He took one step too many, and Aquilus shot off the branch with shriek.

The man laughed. "Probably one of those bird spies that Queen Regina's supposed to have."

"That's a load of rubbish if I've ever heard one," said the man with the dagger, still corkscrewing into the ground. "Bird spies." He snorted. "Don't you agree, Sire?" he asked.

The fair-haired man was staring the direction that Aquilus had gone. "Perhaps," he conceded softly.

***

Lena and Jairdan had sat down beneath the trees; when they saw Aquilus approaching they both got to their feet. "Well?" Jairdan asked.

They are warriors of some sort. I do not know from what country they are from; it is certainly not the South, and the accent did not sound Eastern either. They may indeed be from the West.

"Excellent," Jairdan snapped irritably. "I thought perhaps we'd be able to get through a day without running into a pack of them. How many are they?"

Three, Aquilus replied. *Well armed, young and strapping, each of them.*

159

"Perhaps we should go and talk to them," Lena said. "Say we're traveling, see what information we can get from them. We're armed if it comes to that."

"They outnumber us," Jairdan said hesitantly.

"But you're worth two," Lena said with a smile. Seeing that Jairdan remained unconvinced, she said seriously, "They're less than a day from the city. If they do mean Aurea harm, someone needs to warn the Guard to be ready."

They spoke of meeting another group at Amensliel, Aquilus put in.

"The Garrison at Amensliel?" Jairdan asked. "That's an Aurean base. If they were Wesmorian, they wouldn't seek refuge there."

"But if they're not seeking refuge," Lena ventured, "if they're meeting more men, and they mean to attack the Garrison…"

Jairdan sighed. "All right," he said. "We'll go down and speak with them. But if it comes to blows, you and Aquilus get out. The main thing is that one of us get to Marii and request help. If it goes wrong here, get yourself to Gnibri. I'll meet you there."

Lena nodded solemnly. Then, the glimmer of a smile on her face, she added, "Let's see that it doesn't go wrong, shall we?"

Jairdan nodded and remounted Cougar. "Follow me," he said.

The sound of voices startled the trio of men at the bottom of the hill. The one that had been sitting got quickly to his feet; the fair-haired leader's hand shot to the hilt of his sword. When two people, a man and a girl, both dressed in simple traveling clothes, appeared at the crest of the hill, the leader's hand slowly released his sword, a furrow of puzzlement appearing on his brow.

"Hello!" the male newcomer bellowed jovially from the hilltop. "You're a nice break from this dratted fog—we've seen no one else all day."

"It's poor traveling weather," the leader replied softly. "And," he added, more quietly still, "some would say, not the safest time to be abroad."

"My niece and I are on our way to market in a town a few miles from here. We've got wares to sell." The man patted his saddlebags proudly.

The blond man made a mental note that he had not specified what town exactly they were bound for, or what type of wares. "A few miles" could mean anything. Veiled by his cloak, his hand returned to clench the hilt of sword. "Well there's always room for a few more around our fire," he said aloud, gesturing to the smoldering heap of char that his men had built a few hours previously. "Please, come and sit. Roann, will get you something to drink."

As the brown-haired man called Roann stoked the fire, the leader drew the other man aside. "What do you suppose, Sire?" his friend asked. "Rustics?"

"I'm not sure, but I think, for now, based on the circumstances, it's best you just call me by my given name. Can't to be too careful."

"As you say, *Roarke*," Roann adjusted easily.

A tawny falcon alighted on a branch of a nearby tree, catching Roarke's eye."The bird's back," he whispered to Roann.

Eln glanced at the tree. "You don't think…" he began, but Roarke was already walking purposely toward the fire.

"You have brought us luck, friends!" he said happily, grasping a bow that lay against a rock and drawing an arrow from a quiver that lay beside it. "We have not eaten in days; falcon meat is sparse, but it will suffice." He took aim.

"I should be careful, if I were you," the male newcomer warned. "There are many falconers around here. That's a prized bird. If you kill it, and the owner finds you…"

"I'll take my chances," Roarke whispered.

Aquilus! Lena screamed within her mind, fighting to keep her face impassive. *Fly, he's going to shoot you.*

Not yet, the bird replied. *He suspects I am a spy of the queen. If I fly now, it would be too obvious that you and I have the ability to communicate.*

The bowstring groaned under the tension.

Aquilus.

Not yet.

The arrow flew.

Aquilus!

Lena could not help it, she leaped to her feet as Roarke loosed the arrow, felt a sick feeling of relief as she heard the powerful beats of Aquilus' wings carrying him out of danger.

Use caution, Golden One. I will be watching from a safer distance.

Roarke had been watching Lena's face intently. "Attached to the bird, are you?" he asked.

Lena forced a casual shrug. "I just hate to see lovely things destroyed," she said.

Roarke's eyes narrowed. "I don't believe you," he said softly, and at this signal of mistrust his men moved with catlike quickness toward Lena and Jairdan. Within seconds, the arms of both were pinned behind their backs, before their swords were halfway out of their sheaths. Lena struggled at first, hissing and kicking, but Roarke fitted a second arrow into his bow. This one he aimed at Jairdan's head.

"No!" Lena screamed, lurching against Roann's vice-like grip. Jairdan was very still. Roarke had pulled the arrow as far back as it could go; the string trembled with tension. He approached Jairdan slowly, then lowered his bow and rounded on Lena. "I want the truth," he said. He cast the bow aside and twisted something off of his middle finger. He stepped so close to Lena that she could feel his breath on her cheek. She refused to meet his eye. When he took her hand roughly and thrust something onto her middle finger, she bit her lip, expecting pain. Instead, what she felt was the cold metal of a thick-banded ring. She glanced down. The stone was midnight-black. "Black on the hand of a liar," Roarke said, "So it becomes clear that your first story was not the truth." He drew his sword and stepped toward Jairdan again, extending his arm until the tip of the blade just puckered the chest of Jairdan's tunic. "Your next words had better turn the stone white, or else be a final goodbye to your friend here."

Lena turned her gaze to Jairdan's face. He gave a minute shake of his head. Lena bit her lip in indecision.

"Tell me who you are," Roarke growled, "or say farewell."

Lena still hesitated.

"Very well." Roarke turned to Jairdan.

"Wait!" The words came the second before he thrust. "Please!" Roarke lowered his sword and approached Lena. Taking her chin in his hand, he forced her face upward, towards his own. "Who are you?" he asked. "Northerners?"

Lena's eyes flashed toward Jairdan. She nodded into Roarke's grip.

"Aureate Guard?" he pressed.

Again, a small nod.

"And the bird?"

Lena was deflated. "An avian scout," she said.

Roarke released her chin, and Lena flexed her fingers to look at the ring. It was still black.

"That was the truth!" she shouted. "I swear it was!"

"I know." Roarke stalked toward her and twisted the ring unmercifully off of her finger. "The stone is obsidian. Neither lie or truth would have changed its color." He fit it back onto his own hand and approached Jairdan. "Does the Aureate Star yet burn?" he asked.

At once, Jairdan's face changed. Instead of sober with defeat, he was suddenly elated with relief. "As long as Westmore looks to the sky," he replied.

The tension went out of Roarke's face. He nodded at Eln, who released Jairdan at once. Immediately, Roarke had Jairdan in an embrace. "Forgive me, but these are uncertain times."

"There is nothing to forgive!" Jairdan replied. He clapped Roarke smartly on the back. "I did not expect you so early! Tell us everything. How was you journey? How many more are coming?"

Lena was dazed. She was dimly aware that Roann had released her and was approaching Jairdan to shake him warmly by the hand. "What...I don't understand," she sputtered.

"These are the troops, Lena! The Western troops that pledged to join our cause. The exchange about the star is an Aurean code. When we learned there was a possibility the troops would join us, we established it so we would know friend from foe."

Roarke turned to her and gave a small, smart bow. "I am Captain Roarke, formerly of the Westmorian cavalry. Forgive the deception—" he glanced down at the obsidian ring on his finger, "but it was necessary, for security. I'm sure you understand."

Lena forced a tilted smile. "Of course. As my master says, there is nothing to forgive."

Their eyes locked. Lena's steely stare said clearly that she did not trust Roarke. The amused gaze Roarke returned replied that he knew this already, and did not really care. Lena turned away moodily.

Roann cleared his throat. "There's a stream just around that bend, if your horses need a drink. Eln got a few brace of hare this morning. We'll put them on a spit while you water your horses."

"Thank you," Jairdan said. He gathered Cougar's reins and began to lead the horse away from the camp. Lena followed suit, snatching the proffered reins from Roarke's helpful hand and hurrying after Jairdan.

*****

"You don't trust him," Jairdan commented wryly, as he and Lena made their way down to the river.

"It is not my place," Lena replied. "You trust him, and I trust your judgment."

"You are allowed to disagree," Jairdan said. "You do not think he is trustworthy?"

"No, but…" Lena sighed. "You took me in without any surety of my background or loyalty. I am in no position to question his intentions."

"Of course you are," Jairdan replied. "I value your judgment as much as my own."

Lena looked embarrassed. "Master, before, when I gave us up—"

Jairdan smiled and put his arm around her. "Lena, you kept me from being skewered. Do you expect argument?" Lena smiled, and Jairdan said, "Don't be too hard on yourself."

***

The meal was delicious. There was not much meat, but Roann had rubbed what little there was with herbs he had gathered earlier. He cooked it over the fire until it was crisp. Lena and Jairdan shared brown bread and nuts that they had with them. After everyone had eaten, Roann tossed the bones in the fire to burn them clean.

"Can't be too careful," he said, taking a swig from a flask of water. Then, he poured a little onto a rag and wiped his hands to wash away the grease and the scent of food from his fingers. He passed the skien around so the others could do the same. "If the mooncats smell food, they'll be here in droves."

After everyone had diligently cleaned their hands, Eln took another flask, this one full of ale, and offered it to Jairdan. During dinner, the conversation had been light and idle. Now, as the sky began to darken, Jairdan directed the conversation to more serious matters. "How long did it take you to get here?" he asked, accepting the flask, taking a swallow of ale, and passing it to Roarke. "I heard there was bad weather near the border."

"Thankfully we missed the brunt of it," Roarke said. "But it was hard going in the beginning, because we knew the guardsmen still loyal to Bruteaus would be out after us. We spent the first few days crossing streams and going in loops to lose them. The idea was we would get to Amensliel first and then send word back to Forrester, the other captain still loyal to the alliance, when we were sure it was safe for him to bring his men. Unfortunately, after we left some of the king's men got wind of Forrester's plans to desert, and he had to move his troops out of Westmore. Bruteaus had three of his men beheaded before Forrester could get them all out. I imagine they're about a week behind us now."

The flask had reached Roann; he offered it to Lena, but she shook her head, and it was passed back to Eln.

"Do you have any idea what suddenly angered Bruteaus? It seems so…irrational," Jairdan said.

A cloud passed over Roarke's face. "The king…is not in his right mind," he said slowly. "What put him out of it I do not know, but he is not as he was."

Roann read his captain's face intently. "The king is a good man," he said solemnly.

Eln nodded and drank a deep, silent toast to the remark.

"Can he be reasoned with?" Jairdan asked.

"Not as he is," Roarke replied. "I've never seen him so…close minded."

"It's strange," Lena said, gazing into the fire, "that it happened so suddenly…"

"I assure you, no one was more surprised than I," Roarke said, a little coldly.

"I didn't mean any offense," Lena said, trying to keep the sharpness out of her voice. "I just meant…had he been ill? Could it have been brain fever that made him…leave his right mind?"

Eln shook his head and spoke for the first time all evening. "It wasn't like that," he replied. "I've seen men go mad, from brain fever, or a wild dog bite, but this wasn't like that. There was no crossover period, he was…just…suddenly…not himself."

Lena exchanged glances with Jairdan, both thinking the same thing.

"The King raved endlessly about how the Aureans were a threat," Roann continued. "He locked his wife and daughters in their chambers. They hammered to get out, but he had guards stand outside to keep them in."

"What about his sons?" Jairdan asked. "I'd heard Bruteaus had sons."

"Prince Roarke," Roarke said suddenly. "His eldest. My namesake, actually. He's two years my senior; my father was close to the king. My brother is also named for a prince; Forrester, Roarke's younger brother. I believe it was always my mother's greatest regret that she did not have a third son to name Thorian."

"The third son?" Lena guessed.

Roann nodded.

"And what became of your namesake and his brothers?" Jairdan asked.

"He remained," Roarke replied. "As far as I know, he stays by his father still."

"A good son," Jairdan said gently, "but perhaps foolishly so."

Roarke took a deep breath. "But a good son nonetheless," he said.

"The prince was always a very good son," said Roann. "Still is."

Again, Eln nodded and tipped the flask again in toast.

There was a tension here that Lena could not decipher. She was still focused on the strange undercurrent of the conversation when she heard the beat of wings above her. Aquilus landed on the log Lena was using as a seat; she smiled, glad to see him safe.

How goes it with you, Child of Light?

How did you know it was safe to return?

I watched from above and saw you join them on friendly terms. I heard a bit of your conversation. It sounds as if the king has been taken by the same darkness that your brother battles.

Daimonas, Lena said. *He's behind all of this, I'm certain.*

"Ah. Your avian scout," Roarke said, noticing Aquilus for the first time. He touched his forehead. "Apologies for earlier, friend. For what it's worth, I did not truly mean you any harm."

I know, Aquilus replied. *Had you really meant to kill me, I would hope you would not have been so far off mark.*

Lena bit back laughter. Roarke, watching her carefully, seemed to sense he was the topic of conversation. He glanced up at the sky. "It's getting late," he said, addressing Jairdan. "You've had a long day. Perhaps we should turn in."

"Perhaps," Jairdan said, eying him carefully.

Lena shifted. There was that feeling again, that undercurrent...Jairdan suspected something, but what?

Roarke's eyes betrayed nothing.

***

It was cold that night, and it took Lena, who was unused to sleeping outside, a long while to fall asleep. When she did, it was a fitful rest, and she awoke again only a few hours later, feeling as if she had not slept at all.

The sound that had awoken her was that of Roarke getting up and slipping quietly away from the fireplace. Lena knew furtive silence; Roarke's radiated suspicion, and so she got up and followed him.

Expecting to see or hear something incriminating, she was surprised when Roarke stopped only a few yards from the camp and leaned against a tree trunk with a heavy, sorrowful sigh. Lena watched from a short distance away as he put a hand to his forehead and stretched his shoulders, as if shifting under the weight of some heavy burden. He turned and ventured further away, toward the stream where Lena and Jairdan had watered the horses only hours before. Lena followed silently, watching with confusion and interest as Roarke sat and pried off each of his boots. To Lena's mortification, he began to strip off the rest of his clothes. Lena looked away guiltily and did not look back until she heard a gentle splash of water. Roarke had slid into the river; he dunked his head and came up shaking his long, fair hair in the moonlight.

Curiosity compelled Lena to move forward; she took another step and crunched a twig underfoot.

Roarke's reaction was immediate. He plunged under the water and came up again on the very edge of the riverbank. Keeping his head mostly protected by the lip of the bank, he stretched out his hand and took his sword from the ground. "Who's there?" he called. "Be you man or beast, come closer with the risk of tasting steel."

"I'm…sorry, it's me," Lena said, glowing with embarrassment. She stepped out awkwardly from behind a thick tree.

Roarke raised his eyebrows and dropped the sword. "Lena of the Golden City," he said with a grin. He folded his arms on the bank, comfortably holding himself up, half his torso out of the water.

To Lena's surprise he seemed more amused than angry. "What are the chances that we would both be up for a midnight walk to the same banks? Or was not chance that led you to follow my footfalls?"

Lena said nothing, but looked around down, squirming with shame.

Roarke regarded her silently for a moment, letting her wriggle in discomfort. "Well?" he asked finally. "Satisfied? Or do you still think that I'm planning a meeting with enemy legions here by the stream?"

Lena blushed. "Well..." Her eyes strayed to the pile of clothes beside the bank.

Roarke's eyes narrowed. "How long have you been watching me?" he asked.

Lena was silent.

"Long enough, it seems," Roarke said. He rested his chin on his arms. "Do you have trouble sleeping?"

"I'm not used to the weather," Lena said, stepping forward tentatively. "Isn't it a little cold to be swimming?"

"Cold? Is it possible you really are from the North? The weather is mild for this time of year! Haven't you ever endured an Aurean winter?"

Lena hesitated. "No."

Roarke tilted his head. "What do you mean?" he asked. "I thought you lived in Aurea."

"I do now," Lena said. "I used to live in Sanuul."

"The desert land?" Roarke asked scathingly. "My gods, you have my sympathies. What were you doing? Charity work for the Order?"

Lena's face tightened. "No," she said quietly. "I wasn't with the Order then."

"Well what were you doing?" Roarke asked. "You weren't just *living* there?"

"What difference does it make what I was doing?" Lena asked.

"It's my business to protect my men," Roarke said harshly.

"And what does that mean?" Lena asked, drawing herself up angrily.

"Only that from what I've heard, there's a reason the crest of Sanuul is a snake!" Roarke spat.

Lena's temper flared. "You're one to be passing judgment!" Lena spat. "For all we know, you *and* your men could be Westmorian spies."

This hit a nerve. Roarke pulled himself halfway from the water, and for a moment Lena tensed for fear that he would come after her. Instead, he thrust his arm into the moonlight so that she could see a fresh and raised scarlet burn on his forearm. It was a brand of an oak leaf with the star of Aurea scorched over it. "Ask Eln and Roann to show you theirs," Roarke snapped, his voice low and soft now, with vibrating at the core with a potent anger. "They have them too. And so do all the other men that swore honor to our allegiance with Aurea. I left my own country to fight for my belief in yours. My fealty is here, burnt into my flesh. If you have any such mark, Lena of Sanuul, then show it now. If not, do not question my loyalty, or that of my companions. Eln and Roann are good men. They are willing to sacrifice their lives for your country. Whether one could expect the same of a Sanuulian, I'm not sure."

"You know nothing of sacrifice!" Lena screamed, kicking the earth in fury so that dirt flew into Roarke's face. She spun and stalked up the hill the way she had come.

Roarke roared in rage and dunked his face to clear the dirt. When he resurfaced, his expression could have boiled the river water.

***

Roarke returned to the camp not long after Lena had left him at the river; he was clothed, but his hair was still wringing wet; two drops of water landed on Lena's face as he stalked by her. She said nothing, and Roarke seemed equally determined to maintain the silence. He slept only a few feet from Lena, but on lying down he promptly turned his back to her. In response, Lena pretended to be asleep. In reality, it was over an hour before she did manage to doze off again, and she woke a few more times during the night. When she finally woke again and saw the beginnings of dawn in the east, she gave up trying and got up to stoke the fire. Her movements stirred Roann, who, used to traveling all day and sleeping on hard ground, had slept well.

"You're up early," he commented, raising his head and looking around.

"Couldn't sleep," Lena replied simply.

Roann watched her for a few more minutes, then, gleaning that she did not want to talk, he raised himself from the ground and said, "Well, you can help me catch dinner for tonight then. Have you experience with a bow?"

"Yes, but I haven't got one with me," Lena said.

"You can use Eln's," Roann said, scooping up the bow and full quiver that lay next to the sleeping man.

"He won't mind?" Lena asked hesitantly.

Roann laughed. "If you get supper, Eln won't care *what* you used."

Lena accepted the bow. Hunting could be the distraction she needed.

"I'll get the horses," she said.

Chapter Eighteen
Mallin

As Lena and Roann walked their horses slowly through the pre-dawn mist, Lena decided that she quite liked Roann; his manner was easy and light; he was content to talk or keep silent. His brown eyes were cheerful and understanding. When he stretched his hand out to point out mountains in the distance, the sleeve of his tunic rose halfway up his arm and a raw brand mark was visible a few inches above his wrist. Lena turned away, guilty nausea coiling in her stomach.

Aquilus swooped down upon them, drawing Lena's attention away from Roann's arm.

Golden One, he intoned, *if you are seeking a meal, there are several quail just ahead, stupid and fat from seeds and berries.*

Lena's eyes lit up. She urged Lady into a faster walk. "This way," she whispered to Roann. To Aquilus she said, *Lead the way.*

The pair followed the falcon a little further to where there were indeed eight fat quails flapping and squabbling stupidly in the brush. Lena felled two and Roann, three. The rest of the birds scattered.

"More than enough," Roann said, dismounting and collecting the bounty. "You're a good shot. Eln won't miss three arrows."

"I shouldn't have missed that first one," Lena said, retrieving an arrow from the trunk of a tree and rubbing her finger over the scar it had made in the bark. "I'm out of practice."

"Too hard on yourself is what you are," Roann said. He gave her a playful nudge. "Let up a bit."

***

When Lena and Roann returned to the camp, the other three were already awake. Roarke glanced darkly at Lena when she stepped past him to return Eln's bow and quiver, but his expression softened somewhat when he saw the three quail that Roann carried.

"Roann said you wouldn't mind if I borrowed this, as long as we came back with something for tonight," Lena said timidly, placing the bow and quiver next to Eln, the man-mountain.

Eln smacked Roann on the shoulder jovially. "He was right!" he bellowed, laughing. "Roann knows I value a good meal over a few arrows."

Breakfast was simple: a piece of bread, a slice of cheese, and an apple each, then a swig of water from the flask before it was refilled at the river. Roann and Eln went at this task together while Roarke readied the horses and Lena and Jairdan packed everything that the group had used that morning and the night before.

Chewing on a long, coppery blade of grass, Roarke checked the fire to make sure the flames had died. As he kicked some dirt onto the embers just to be sure, he heard Lena and Jairdan talking in murmurs a few feet away. Without looking up or going closer, he quieted his motions to listen to what they were saying.

"And now?" Jairdan asked. "Have you changed your opinion? Or do you mistrust them still?"

"No. I was wrong. Good men, all," Lena replied shortly. "I was foolish to judge." She hoisted a pack and walked toward Lady, passing Roarke without so much as a nod. He watched her stuff the pack into her saddlebag and swing into the saddle. *Foolish to judge,* he thought. *Perhaps I was, too.*

***

The day was a quiet and soggy one. Rain pattered on dead leaves; soon the whole party was soaked through. Luckily, it was still a mild enough one despite the wet. Lena chose to ride at the front of the group with Roann and Eln, both of whom she had indeed decided she liked. Eln was bigger than a bear, towering in the saddle, his muscles bulging against the cloth of his tunic, his great belly hanging over the rope belt that he wore around his waist. His horse was no fleet-footed charger, rather, Eln rode a large, black horse with thick legs and enormous hooves.

Roann was quick-witted and full of stories. As he told them, Eln added the occasional, boisterous embellishment, waving his hands wildly for effect. For Lena, the miles went by unnoticed, the chore of traveling lightened by Roann's stories and Eln's antics.

Jairdan and Roarke rode slightly behind the others. Jairdan, no stranger to the pattern of politics, expected a storm of questions from Roarke. The previous night, Jairdan had dominated the conversation; now, by rights, it was Roarke's turn. But Roarke seemed distracted, uninterested in conversation, and deep in thought. His first remark was quite unexpected.

"Your apprentice is from Sanuul," he said softly.

Jairdan turned to the young captain in surprise. "She told you that?" he asked.

"She told me she lived there before she came to Aurea," Roarke replied.

Jairdan raised his eyebrows. "Well, I'm afraid you misinterpreted her comment, captain. Lena is quite a worldly young lady. In fact, the great land of Westmore is actually the only country on this continent that she has not lived in, for some time or another."

"You're not saying she's originally from Marii?" Roarke asked.

"That is exactly what I am saying. Lena was born in a small, Eastern fishing village only weeks before it was raided. She was taken as a slave to Sanuul, where she lived a life of servitude until she was seventeen. At that age, she managed to escape, and it was her bravery that brought her to Aurea, and to our Order. In fact, she was held captive by the same man who we believe to be responsible for all of this…the war…perhaps the king's madness." He watched Roarke out of the corner of his eye to observe his reaction.

The captain turned his head sharply. "Responsible? How could he be responsible for madness?"

"He possesses the powers of an Aureate Guard," Jairdan replied, "but fled the Order and has chosen to use them against us."

"You speak of Daimonas," Roarke said. "I've heard the story of his disappearance…you believe he is responsible for all of this?"

"Yes," Jairdan said. "But he's maddeningly impossible to find. We've been trying for years, without results."

Roarke gazed ahead, to where Lena was red-faced from laughter. "And she was his prisoner, you say?"

"That's right," said Jairdan quietly.

Roarke was silent. "I'm afraid I've…made a terrible mistake," he said at last.

Jairdan surveyed the young man's concern. "Whatever it was," he said, "I have no doubt that Lena will forgive you. She is a singular girl, if you get to know her."

"I intend to do so," Roarke replied.

"Her acquaintance is an asset," Jairdan said. "As, I suspect, is yours."

"I don't know about that," Roarke said. It was not false humility; Jairdan saw true self-doubt in the young man's eyes.

"I can't help but notice the burn mark on your arm," he commented. "It looks quite painful."

Roarke sighed and rotated his forearm to examine the mark. "We all have them," he said. "Roann, Eln, all the others…we made the brands and did them ourselves the night before we left. 'True allegiances before mad suspicions', we all said."

"I imagine that's in reference to the king," Jairdan said. "It must have been hard, to leave so much behind. A home, a good position…a family?"

Roarke did not answer right away. When he spoke, he said briskly, "Roann and Eln are my family now. They always have been part of it, and now they're all I have." Roarke spurred his horse a little ahead of Jairdan's, signaling that this part of their conversation was finished.

***

The man who the High Masters received in the council room was handsome, with thundercloud-black hair and lightning-blue eyes. In keeping with his appearance, he carried himself with all the gravity of a storm; with his presence came a powerful tension.

175

Hadrian could not help being awed by the man; even weather-worn as he was, he radiated power. He was damp and muddy, his black locks swept over his forehead, his face lined with exhaustion from the journey, but he held himself tall and his gaze steady.

"You say you are a Westmorian refugee, and that more are coming?" Even Prudentior's authority seemed dimmed by this man's presence.

The dark-haired man bowed. "Yes," he replied. "I am of Westmore. I am one of a few dozen nobles who saw the insanity of King Bruteaus for what it was, and fled the country. More will come. Many have their women and children with them."

"What is your name, friend, that we may address you properly?" one of the High Masters asked.

The man swept his eyes around the room and, surprisingly, finally fixed Hadrian with his electric gaze. "My name," he said grandly, "is Lord Stoorm."

***

Roarke sat before a pile of dry leaves and kindling, striking two flint stones together, waiting for a spark. His fingers were clumsy with fatigue; what would normally have taken moments had become a painfully drawn out chore.

The captain was startled when a small, white hand closed around his and gently took the stones from his unresisting hand. Lena made a small, quick gesture and instantly flames leaped from her fingers to the kindling. Roarke smiled and shook his. "Easier than flint," he said with a smile.

"I wanted to tell you," Lena said softly, "I'm sorry, about last night. What I said was out of place. It's obvious that you and your men have made many sacrifices, and I respect you for it."

"I'm as guilty of misjudgment as you," Roarke said. "I made assumptions about you that I shouldn't have...I've been raised to think of Sanuul as a land of sand and traitors and little else, but I should be more open-minded."

"These are dark times," Lena said, "when we all must be suspicious of everyone else. Let's put it down to that."

"Agreed." Roarke nodded.

Lena gave him a small, grateful smile. She hugged her arms around herself and shivered.

"Are you cold?" Roarke asked. He swept his cloak off and draped it around Lena's thin frame. "Thank you," Lena said, gathering the cloak around her.

Roarke unpacked the quail that Roann and Lena had caught earlier that morning and began to prepare it for the fire. Jairdan took the horses down to the stream, and Eln accompanied him to fill the water flasks.

"What is Westmore like?" Lena asked Roarke, taking up a small knife to cut slices of bread and cheese for their dinner.

Roarke considered for a moment, and then said decidedly, "Green. All the time, even in winter, there is green in Westmore. The winter pines stand out against the snow like emeralds. In the summer, everything is lush and beautiful. The forests are deep and cool, with beds of moss like goose-feather cushions and blue-black streams rich with silver fish."

"It sounds beautiful," said Lena, smiling.

"It is," Roarke said. He looked down and murmured, "It nearly broke my heart to leave it."

Lena busied herself with the bread, and Roarke eventually broke the uncomfortable silence by asking, "May I ask you the same of Sanuul? What was it like there?"

"Much as you would imagine," Lena said. "Dry, sparse, hot. Sometimes windstorms would whip across the dunes and it would be impossible to see for the sand."

"And did you ever see a black viper?" Roarke asked. "They're creatures of legend."

Lena laughed. "Not as awe-inspiring when you find one coiled under or beside a rock just before you step on it."

"You nearly stepped on one?"

"I was inches away from it," Lena said. "And the fangs go right through leather soles." She tapped the bottom of her boot. "These wouldn't have been much help."

Roarke looked awed, and Lena laughed again. "It's not that impressive. You must have some terrible beast in Westmore—what about the Oak Bears?"

Roarke snorted. "So named because they only eat Copper Oak leaves. The only damage they could do would be if they crept out too far on a limb and dropped on you. Great lazy things."

Lena laughed again and held out a piece of bread to Roarke. "Well, you'll just have to hope we meet a pack of mooncats, so you'll have an impressive story like I do."

"Just one mooncat will do," Roarke said, accepting the bread and taking a bite. "No need for excess."

Laughing, Lena stood to return the leftover bread to her saddlebag. Roarke paused in his supper preparations to watch her pat Lady gently on the neck and comb her fingers through the horse's mane.

Roarke had a talent for preparing food; from the quail, a few wild mushrooms, and the bread and cheese, he produced a delicious meal that warmed everyone to the bone and put them in good spirits. When they went to sleep that night, it was with full stomachs and lighter hearts, and Lena felt happier than she had since leaving Aurea.

***

That night, as they all lay sleeping by the dying fire, someone stole silently across the camp. Eln was keeping careful watch, but the intruder approached from behind and was so careful, so silent, that there were no sounds, not even the snapping of twigs or crunching of leaves to alert Eln to the danger.

When he was close enough, the intruder hurled a small, glass sphere into the midst of the camp. The glass smashed and a crimson vapor was released into the air. The sound of breaking glass caught Roann's attention and roused the rest of the camp, but the intruder kept to the shadows and remained unseen.

Roarke's hand was on his sword, but already he could feel the vapor burning his lungs as he breathed it in. He felt sluggish, his body weighed down. He struggled to overcome it, but he could feel himself succumbing.

Jairdan was holding his breath, struggling to his feet to try to get clear of the campsite before he had to breathe again. Still, the vapor was in his eyes, making them sting and water. Unable to see, he tripped over a log and fell onto his stomach. The fall knocked the wind out of him and he took an automatic breath. He felt the vapor enter his mouth and nose and immediately felt the effects. He managed to crawl a few steps more before he too fell unconscious.

Roann and Eln had already passed out. Lena could not see Roarke or Jairdan. She got to her feet, dazed, and cried her companions' names, not realizing the danger of opening her mouth. The vapor curled inside her mouth and into her lungs. Lena dropped to her knees, her eyes closing gently. Coughing, she fell to all fours.

Their assailant watched Lena finally lose consciousness. He drew a deep breath, approached, lifted Lena from the ground, and retreated quickly from the camp, his eyes watering.

He lifted Lena onto his horse, mounted, and rode away like a shot, leaving the rest of the companions unconscious and unaware of Lena's danger.

***

When Lena woke again it was cold and dark; the only sound was made by the occasional dripping of water and a busy shuffling somewhere behind her.

Lena's arms, bound behind her, ached with stiffness. Her mouth was dry, and her entire body felt bruised.

A man stepped into her view; he was tall, dark-skinned, and familiar; the mere sight of him froze Lena's insides with an icy fear.

"You!" she choked, her voice raspy and tight.

If Mallin had heard her, he did not respond. He was starting a fire; flint struck and a spark leaped. Mallin glanced over his shoulder to examine Lena by the light of the flame. He picked up a flask from the ground and approached Lena with it.

"Drink," he ordered, holding it to her mouth.

Lena clamped her lips together, eying him with angry suspicion.

Mallin rolled his eyes and took a deep draught of the liquid himself. "See?" he said. "Not poisoned."

Lena tentatively opened her mouth and let him tip a cool, sweet fluid down her throat.

"It'll clear the headache," he said coldly, and turned his back to her.

Lena saw now that she was in a cave. The fire had lit it well, but the blue-black of night still clung to the edges at the entrance. A pile of furs and blankets were spread out in one corner; a loaf of bread rested by the fire.

Lena twisted her wrists in frustration. The tough ropes that bound her grated against her skin, rubbing her wrists raw. Without turning back to look at her, Mallin asked, "And what do you intend to do if you do get those ropes loose? Run across the cave without my noticing?"

Lena gave the ropes one last, frustrated tug. "You don't realize what you're doing," she said. "A city is depending on me—you're putting the entire country of Aurea in danger! If the mission fails and no help comes from Marii, the City and all its inhabitants will be damned."

"There is hope still. Perhaps your teacher will make it to Marii," Mallin said apathetically.

"And if not?" Lena asked.

She received no reply.

Hot, bitter tears burned in Lena's eyes. "For every coin you will get for my capture, there is a life, maybe two, that you are endangering. Don't you understand that what is underway is bigger than you and me?"

Still, Mallin did not respond.

Lena set her jaw. "I suppose it was naïve to expect to be able to appeal to the honor of a man of your moral stature."

Mallin whirled and raised the back of his hand as if to strike Lena. She did not flinch. Breathing hard, Mallin spat, "My moral character is shaped by this world. There has been no honorable cause to pledge my allegiance to for more than a decade. The heroes of old are dead. Now, men are motivated only by lust and greed."

Lena shook her head. "There are good men left, that you don't follow. Your allegiance is to gold, your alliance with your benefactors only. Pretend to be a tortured soul hunting for an honorable cause if you wish, but in truth you are no better than the men you serve."

There was a storm in Mallin's eyes. After a moment of tense silence, he said, "I am under no obligation to discuss my views of the world with you." He turned away.

Lena leaned her head against the wall of rock behind her. "The blood of Aurea will be on your hands."

***

Hadrian pushed open the wooden door and inclined his head. Lord Stoorm stepped grandly into the room and swept it with his gaze. Hadrian followed behind him.

"There is an excellent view from the balcony," Hadrian offered eagerly. "I can have food and drink brought to your room, if you wish it."

"Thank you, my son, but I am not hungry." Stoorm bestowed upon Hadrian a smile that made him glow with pleasure. The air of power that clung to this man fascinated Hadrian. He was loathe to leave, even though his task had simply been to show the Westmorian noble to an unoccupied room.

Stoorm seemed to notice this, and accommodated for it. "Sit down, my boy," he said kindly, gesturing to one of the chairs. Already, it was as if he owned the room and everything in it. His manner in merely offering the seat made Hadrian grateful, and he took the seat carefully.

Rather than sit, Stoorm wandered to one of the windows and gazed out at the City. "This is a beautiful city," he said. "I fear for the safety of it, now that Bruteaus has lost his mind. He is merciless in war."

181

"A mission has been sent to request aid from Marii." Hadrian knew that he should not reveal this to Stoorm, that it was a secret of the Order, but, strangely, he felt no guilt or even sense of wrongdoing, drunk on Stoorm's aura of power, eager to impress.

"Let us pray that it succeeds," Stoorm said. He furrowed his brow and said, "I would have thought the Order would have sent their best on such an important mission. Why did they not select you?"

Pride and embarrassment clashed within Hadrian, thrilled that Stoorm thought he was one of the best, ashamed that he had not been chosen. "I am injured," he said, gesturing to his wounded leg.

"Ah," Stoorm said. "But no doubt the healing powers of the Aureate Guard could remedy that quickly enough?"

"Unfortunately not," Hadrian said bitterly. "I have been lame for over a month."

"Strange," Stoorm said. "I wonder if I might see the wound? I have some slight experience with healing; perhaps I could suggest something."

Had anyone else suggested this, Hadrian would have been skeptical, doubting the power of any man over that of the Aureate Guard, but it was with breathless anticipation and desperate hope that he unwound the bandages around his calf to reveal the brutal, open wound on his leg.

Stoorm squinted appraisingly at the gash. "If I may?" he asked, holding out his white hands. With a nod from Hadrian, he rested his cool fingers on the warm, infected flesh of the boy's leg. "But surely not," he murmured to himself. "It seems impossible that…" He pushed his cloak aside and pulled a glass bottle from its folds. He uncorked it and poured a blood-red liquid into the wound. For a moment, a searing pain nearly blinded Hadrian. He felt Stoorm's hands on his shoulders, supporting him. Steam hissed and rose from the wound in a gray thread. The red liquid ran in a thin stream around Hadrian's leg, pooling on the floor.

Hadrian opened his eyes. He had a white-knuckled grip on the bedpost; his jaw was set against the pain. Slowly, the burning faded, and Hadrian was left with a strange, tingling sensation. He looked down and was shocked to see fresh, pink skin where the bloody wound had been. It no longer throbbed with pain; the lack of it was unfamiliar. Hadrian touched the new skin as if afraid that it would disappear beneath his fingertips. "I don't understand," he breathed. "The wound...it's closed."

Stoorm watched as Hadrian took a tentative step forward, leaving the wooden cane abandoned on the bed behind him. He went forward without a limp. He turned back to Stoorm, his eyes glittering with disbelief and gratitude. "How?" he whispered.

Stoorm shook his head. "It is a simple cure," he said. "The first I would have tried. How your healers failed to employ it I do not know. I only wish I had come sooner, to spare you a month of pain."

"I...I don't understand," Hadrian murmured. "Why? Why did they not try it sooner?"

Stoorm was silent.

Hadrian slammed his fist against the wall. "For weeks I've been limping around like a cripple, and they had not the skill to heal me; what they were unable to do you achieved in minutes..." his voice dropped again to a broken whisper. "I don't understand."

***

Roarke was the first to wake, his head pounding, mouth dry and throat sore. He heard Jairdan coughing beside him, and saw Roann and Eln stirring in pre-dawn light.

Roarke sat up slowly. "Where's Lena?" he rasped.

Jairdan looked around wildly. "No," he said hoarsely, struggling to his feet. "No!" He staggered dizzily around the campground, rasping Lena's name.

"Water," Eln croaked, finding the flask and giving it to Roarke. Quickly, Roarke took a swig, swished it around in his mouth, and spit. Then, he took a gulp of it to drink and passed it back to Eln, who did the same.

Roann was crouched, examining a shard of glass he had found.

183

He took some of the water Roarke offered, then said, "I've heard of this. It's magic from the black monks of the Cristuk Isles. Glass balls that break and emit poison."

Roarke's mind was racing. He brought the flask to Jairdan, who was still searching furiously for Lena.

"This is the work of the enemy," Jairdan said finally. "A human hunter. One of Daimonas', I'm sure."

Eln and Roann traded glances, and Jairdan could tell from their looks that Roarke had shared with them the information about Lena's life in Sanuul that Jairdan had disclosed the previous day.

"Well then we must get her back!" Roarke said. "There must be a way to track him, to…to…do something!"

Jairdan shook his head. "He was silent enough not to alert us; no doubt he is careful enough to avoid being tracked. We can't avoid to deviate from our course. We must continue to Amensliel."

"But," said Roarke, "anything could happen to her…it could mean—"

"I know what it could mean!" Jairdan snapped suddenly, rounding on Roarke. He stopped and sagged suddenly, as if under a great weight. "I know what it could mean," he repeated, more softly. "But the men at Amensliel await a leader. They await the prince of Westmore."

Roarke froze. "You know," he rasped.

Jairdan inclined his head and put his hand on Roarke's shoulder. "We must get you to Amensliel. The men need you."

"But Lena," Roarke said.

The pain was evident on Jairdan's face. "We must leave Lena to fight for herself now," he said. "There is nothing we can do for her now. She has been taken from our protection."

Roarke nodded slowly. "Then we ride," he said.

***

Lena woke again later to a stifling darkness so complete that she could barely distinguish the cave walls from the opening that served as a door. Unsure at first of what had woken her, Lena quickly became eerily aware of breathing beside her. In the darkness, she just made out the glint of Mallin's dark eyes and the flash of errant moonlight against the blade of a dagger. She bit back the urge to gasp; instead she waited for the blow to fall.

The blade swept nearer; in the darkness it made contact and cut through something with a swift deadliness.

Lena fell forward. The ropes that had bound her arms a moment ago dropped to the dusty ground beside her.

Mallin hauled her to her feet and shoved something into her arms. "There's a compass, food, and a flask of water, half full, all I have," he said. "Your saddlebags I left untouched. All you had before you will find still there. Your horse is fed and watered; she'll bear you back the way we came; before daybreak you will have made progress. If you ride hard, you may be able to catch up with your companions."

"I don't understand." Lena's eyes searched Mallin's face.

"You were right," Mallin whispered. "It has been too long since I have dedicated myself to an honorable cause. Perhaps I have been greedy, but at least at the start I had lost faith in men. I think, at last, in you, I have found a cause to which I could pledge myself with pride."

Lena was speechless.

"You represent more than yourself, Lena of Aurea. I know that now, though I did not see it before. You cradle lives in your arms and echo the voice of the world with your words. Even if I had tried, I could not have held you long. Shadows cannot for long grasp light."

"But what if Daimonas discovers that you have—"

"You have enough to occupy your thoughts without worrying on my account. Go now, quickly. The Garrison at Amensliel is due east from here, barely fifteen miles."

Lena's eyes glittered. "Thank you," she whispered.

Mallin nodded.

Lena's boots crunched over the grit on the cave floor as she stepped slowly toward the cave entrance. She pulled the satchel onto her shoulder, and almost reluctantly turned her back on the bounty hunter. She shot him one last glance over her shoulder, then whisked out of the cave and was gone.

***

Within the guard tower of the Garrison at Amensliel, two guards sat playing dice by candlelight. It was well past midnight, and the guards, their eyes itchy with sleep, had stopped paying attention to noises outside a long time since. Soon though, one echoed throughout the black night which the guards could not ignore.

"Hello! Hello!" The voice was urgent, and the guards stood up from the table so quickly that one of their chairs tipped over and crashed to the floor. Both went to the window and looked down. At the gates were four men. One, the largest, was bent with exhaustion and looked even pale by firelight. The other three looked haggard, their horses frothing with sweat from a hard ride.

"Who goes there?" one of the guards called.

"We three are the first of the Westmorian men sent to ally with Aurea in the coming war," Roarke replied.

"And I am a messenger of Her Majesty the Queen Regina of Aurea, who sends her greetings, and an entreaty for aid." Jairdan straightened in the saddle.

"We seek food and shelter for the night."

The guards exchanged glances. "How are we to know you speak the truth?" one asked.

Roarke threw a harsh glance at the guard. "I am Roarke of Eglionan, Son of His Majesty Bruteaus and the Lady Elixa, Captain of the Westmorian Army, Prince of the Western Lands, Heir to the Throne of the Country of Westmore. This should be proof enough of that." He held something up in the night, and with a screech a tawny hawk swooped down, swept it from his hand, and rose to the tower window to deposit it into the hand of one of the guards. It was a ring, obsidian, set in rich, white gold, with a raised imprint of an oak leaf.

"It is the signet ring of the royal family of Westmore!" the guard exclaimed. "Open the gates! Open them!"

Creaking with the hesitation of age, the gates were drawn open. The four riders proceeded into the garrison.

Chapter Nineteen
Field of the Dead

"It defies logic, Master!" Hadrian railed. "Tell me how it is, that what the brightest of our city could not achieve in weeks this man completes without strain! How?"

Scio had listened in quiet thought while Hadrian related the events of the night before. It was true, the boy now walked without a limp, without, in fact, any sign of his former injury. Rather than joy, however, Hadrian was irritated to read suspicion in Scio's eyes.

"Tell me again what the substance looked like, that he applied to your wound."

"It doesn't matter what it looks like, I want to know why it wasn't used before!" Hadrian snapped.

Within an instant he regretted the words. "High Master, forgive me," he said. "I don't—I don't know what came over me."

Scio's face was grave. "Recall yourself, Hadrian," he advised. "Such outbursts go against the respect you have been taught to show."

Hadrian bowed. "High Master, again, please forgive me."

Scio sighed. "Why our healers could not resolve your injury more quickly I cannot say. But I must advise you, Hadrian, to be careful of the man who calls himself Lord Stoorm."

"Calls himself?" Hadrian asked. "That is his name."

"That is what he says is his name," Scio said. "But so far, no part of his story has been corroborated by events. The refugees he said were coming have not arrived. Also be aware that though he claims he is from Westmore, he bears no emblem of the country. I merely recommend caution. It is the way of Aureate Guard to be wary."

"I see," said Hadrian tautly, setting his jaw. "Tell me, High Master, is it also the way of the Aureate Guard to lay suspicion on the name of any man who may be superior in skill to members of the Order?"

This time, Hadrian did not apologize.

Scio's eyes hardened. "That was out of place, Hadrian."

The boy's eyes glittered strangely. "Can you forgive me?"

"You will address me as High Master, with the respect I deserve, Hadrian. And you would find that my forgiveness would be granted readily if you truly desired it."

"But I do desire it, *High Master*," Hadrian grinned.

"You will spend tomorrow in contemplative silence. This time tomorrow evening, I expect a full and a sincere apology."

It was a common punishment for insolence, one that most apprentices had served at some point. The order of silence from a master was considered absolute. Many, once realizing their error, were more than willing to accept the ensuing punishment.

Hadrian broke Scio's order within moments of awakening the next morning, and he did not return that night to apologize.

***

Lena rode hard, hoping to reach Amensliel by sunup or soon after. The night was still suffocatingly dark, and Lena had to strain to see the ground in front of her. When Lady pulled up and reared suddenly, Lena was caught off guard and tumbled to the ground. Dazed, she reached out blindly in the darkness. To her horror, her hand brushed what was unmistakably human flesh. Lena gasped and scrambled backward, only to bump into another cold, fleshy mound. Lena pushed herself to her feet and staggered to Lady's side. Her fingers trembled as she pulled a candle from the saddlebag and lit it with a sweep of her hand. Guarding the candle from the wind with her hand, turned to survey the field before her.

Corpses. There were corpses before and beside her, perhaps twenty, maybe more. They were bloodied and battered, their limbs stretched out at odd angles, their heads flung back and their eyes wide with terror. Most still clutched bloodstained weapons. They all wore the same tunic, flaxen colored, with an amber oak leaf emblazoned on the front.

Motion to her right caught her attention; she held up the candle to see a mooncat, white and luminescent by the moonlight, with its muzzle buried in the innards of one of the dead men. It lifted its head and showed Lena its bloodstained, ivory tusks and crimson muzzle. It regarded her for a moment with predatory interest, but, with such a feast surrounding it, and unprotesting one at that, it decided against pursuing her and returned to its meal.

Lena fell to her knees and was violently sick. Coughing and wiping her mouth with the sleeve of her tunic, she crawled to the side of one of the corpses. She crouched beside the dead man, whose hand was cast out beside him, apparently seeking the sword that lay only inches from his side. Tears ran down her cheek as Lena reached out and placed the weapon in his cold hand. She swept her fingertips over his eyelids to close those frightened, staring eyes. She gently pushed up the sleeve of his tunic and saw, branded into his flesh, a star imposed on an oak leaf. Lena shut her eyes in horror. She rose slowly, trembling. She returned to Lady and guided her cautiously and reverently away from the bodies. When they had passed out of the corpse-littered fields, Lena swung onto Lady's back and rode harder than she had all night.

***

A sanguine sun was just coming up behind the garrison when Lena reached it. She was hunched in the saddle, spent with both emotional and physical fatigue. Lady, too was tired; each step was laborious; they approached Amensliel at a walk. Lena's riding dress was splotched with dark bloodstains; whether it was her own or had been transferred from one of the corpses, she did not know. All she knew was the exhaustion that clustered at the corners of her eyes, the soreness of tired muscles, and the sustenance of a single, driving, ambition; to reach the garrison. She must, at all costs…because…because…

She struggled to recall why. Her head nodded. Her eyes drooped. The vision of a pair of dead and staring eyes seared across her memory. Her eyes bolted open again, and she shook herself, looked at the silhouette of the garrison again. Not long now…

***

"How? *How* could he have known the cure immediately, when we have struggled futilely with it for months?" Prudentior was at a loss to explain what Scio was telling him.

"He could be a disciple of Daimonas," Chista said.

"We will look into this together," Scio said. "I suggest we go now to question this Lord Stoorm."

"Agreed," said the other two in unison. Together, the three High Masters left the room and went looking for Lord Stoorm.

***

Hadrian had no intention of keeping the silence that Scio had ordered him to observe. When he met Lord Stoorm in the hallway the morning after his conversation with Scio, Hadrian greeted him loudly and without qualm.

"My friend," said Stoorm coolly. "I meant to speak to you earlier; I hope that I caused no disagreement between yourself and the High Master by my healing of your wound. My only intention was to help you; if I was the source of any tension, I do apologize."

Hadrian's insides twisted with guilt. This man, who had with one swift motion cured the wound that had plagued Hadrian for months was apologizing—apologizing! How insightful he was, Hadrian thought, and how intent to please!

"I assure you, you caused nothing but joy and deserve nothing but my gratitude," Hadrian replied. "If there is anything I can do for you—consider me in your debt."

Stoorm inclined his head. "You could honor me with your company for a walk in the gardens," he replied. "I am a stranger here, and feel lonely without the company of friends."

"It would be my pleasure," Hadrian said eagerly, and together the two men descended the stairs that let to the gardens.

Stoorm surprised Hadrian by remarking, "I hear that you have a sister. I would be honored to meet her."

A dark scowl appeared on Hadrian's face. "I am afraid that you cannot. She was forced into a mission for the crown. As I was injured, she was required to take my place."

"Against her will?" Stoorm inquired.

"Certainly against mine," Hadrian replied angrily. "I was really quite fit enough for the mission, and Lena...she was not ready for the task. She has not seen as much training as I have...she was not ready for something so dangerous."

"That must have angered you, as an older brother," Stoorm sympathized.

Hadrian smiled. "Actually, I'm not any older than she is. We're twins."

"Ah." Stoorm smiled. "Excuse my mistake. It is just...when one encounters a young man with such a healthy sense of responsibility and honor, one assumes..."

Hadrian glowed.

"You say that your sister has not trained as long as you have, and yet the masters sent her in your place; was this not unwise? Could no one else go?"

"I felt that it was poor judgment," Hadrian replied. A small sense of guilt crept over him. "But one does not like to question the High Masters."

"And why not?" Stoorm asked. "The opinion of a young man of your standing surely must hold sway with even the highest members of your order."

Hadrian grinned bitterly. "Not in this case," he replied. "I was reprimanded for disobedience."

"Out of the desire to protect your sister!" Stoorm hissed violently. Hadrian looked startled. Stoorm smiled ruefully. "You must forgive my vehemence, Hadrian. I am a foreigner, and as yet unused to the ways of the Aureate Guard. But it seems to me that your masters should have praised your motives in questioning their decision. They are not, perhaps..." he hesitated. "Well, it is not for me to say."

"Please, go on," Hadrian asked, thirsty for more praise. Everything that Stoorm said made such sense!

"My opinions, those of an outsider, and a cynic, may sound most egregious to a disciple of your admirable craft. I do not wish to offend."

"Please, I will take no offense. I value your insight."

Stoorm seemed to hesitate, but went on. "I am a man, Hadrian, with little patience for unyielding pillars. I admit that I do not—cannot condone the brainwashing of the promising youth of a city with ridiculous dogmas. It allows no room for internal improvement; the same ideas, recycled again and again, drilled into the best and brightest...it comes to control them, to discourage independent thought."

Hadrian's brow furrowed in conflict.

"It is men like you, Hadrian, who hold promise, who could be great...but within the confines of your order...too many remain merely mediocre."

Something in Hadrian was stung and enraged by the comment. Mediocre, he?

"It is not a fate that should be forced upon you, Hadrian," Stoorm went on, as if reading Hadrian's inner emotion. "Because...I think...though I have not known you very long at all, something tells me...you could be great...the greatest, perhaps."

Hadrian managed to shake his head. "This...this is everything the order warns against...I...modesty...humility...these are the great sacrifices, the only way to true greatness..." but his voice warbled, unsure of the words it spoke.

"Modesty, humility, yes, but what about honesty? Hadrian, it is a disservice to yourself, to your instructors, to deny the true nature of your potential in the name of humility."

Hadrian's eyes burned with painful, opposing emotions.

Stoorm clapped his shoulder. "Hadrian, forgive me. It was too much...it was out of place. You are dedicated...I should have said nothing." He led his hand slide from Hadrian's shoulder and strode from the gardens.

Hadrian remained, and sank slowly onto a stone bench. For the first time he noticed the chill, the drizzle, the general dismal quality of the day, and he shivered. His conscience was in agony, and writhed with protest and dismay.

But deeper, something vicious and unapologetic in its ferocity, something raw and hungry, had awoken.

***

Glodin, the guard that had replaced the night duty, yawned widely and rubbed his face with a large, calloused hand. He leaned out of the window of the watchtower and looked out without much hope over the field and its rolling hills, with the tall grass that rippled in the wind.

And then, suddenly, over the crest of one of these hills, came a white horse, effulgent with the sunlight bursting from behind it. For a moment, Glodin was fascinated and breath-taken by its splendor.

However, as it came close, it soon became obvious that the horse was exhausted, and that its rider in equally worn. When the horse got near enough that Glodin could make its rider's features, he saw that the figure on the mare's back was a girl, slender, with tousled, golden curls that were lifted on the wind. She was slumped in the saddle, her head nodding. Her steed approached along a veering course; it was drunk with fatigue, and staggered over the field. As Glodin watched, the girl's head drooped to rest on her chest. She slipped sideways from he saddle and fell to the ground, raising a cloud of dust from the dry earth. Her horse continued a few paces more, then tossed its head and whinnied in concern.

It took Glodin only a few moments at a run to cross the field to where the girl had fallen. She was stirring on the ground, her eyelids batting. He bent and helped her to her feet; she clutched his arm dependently. A sword hung from a belt that looped around her waist, but Glodin knew that in her current state she was no threat. Still, there was something sharp about the girl, even as she grasped him for support, something that kept Glodin from sweeping her from her feet altogether and carrying her into the garrison. She had a quality like steel about her, as if on lifting her he might cut himself.

"Lena...of Aurea..." she breathed. "I seek four men who journeyed here not a day ago...I must...tell them..."

"They are here," Glodin said quickly, for he had seen four men accompanied into an inn on his way to duty at dawn.

"Safe?" she asked.

"Safe," he nodded. "Safe, as you are, Lena of Aurea."

Relief relaxed her face, and she wilted into his arms.

His hesitation gone, Glodin lifted her and carried her bodily back toward the garrison. The ivory mare followed.

Chapter Twenty
Amensliel

Jairdan stood at a window by Lena's bedside, gazing out at the bustling interior of the garrison to distract himself from his anxiety, tapping his foot with an impatience he was loathe to acknowledge. He glanced at the girl sleeping on the bed, nestled beneath the starched, white sheets. Though her dress was stained with blood, a search for wounds had been fruitless. Then—whose blood? Who had taken her from their camp? And what else, in the name of the Star, had she been through?

Roarke came into the room, holding two steaming mugs of coffee. He handed one to Jairdan and took a deep draught of the other. "Anything?" he asked.

Jairdan raised his mug in thanks before taking a sip. He shook his head. "She hasn't stirred."

Roarke put his hand on Jairdan's shoulder. "She would have been exhausted," he said gently. "We have no notion how far she was taken, or what happened afterward. We were some miles from the garrison already. She must have ridden hard, to get here by this morning."

Jairdan shook his head. "But why? She wasn't being pursued. If she escaped, why ride herself and Lady to exhaustion? What sense is there in that?"

Roarke sighed. "I suppose we shall have to wait," he said.

Jairdan shook his head. "I hate waiting," he muttered.

***

Hadrian made his way back into the temple, his head bent low in thought, his cloak drawn tightly around him. A sound behind him made him turn.

Ince was coming down the corridor at a run, pale, his eyes wilder than ever, his usual cheerfulness washed away by shock. "Hadrian, I—I've been looking all over you…the queen…she…she… Hadrian…oh, Star save us, she's dead!"

Hadrian's face tightened. "Dead?" The word sounded strange on his lips.

Ince nodded. "This morning…she…she's gone. There's a funeral procession…the whole city's turned out for it."

The word seemed suddenly gray and bare. The connotations of the queen's death were horrifyingly clear. Without the queen, and with no heir to take her place, there was no one to head the campaign against Westmore and Sannul.

***

"Dead?" the word stopped the three High Masters where they stood.

"Yes, High Masters. The messenger just arrived with the news."

The High Masters exchanged glances.

"We must go out into the city," Chista said. "If we don't, we will appear indifferent."

"We will complete our intended task the instant we return," Scio said. "I have reservations about leaving, even for a moment."

"Lord Stoorm can do nothing when the entire Star has emptied for the funeral," Prudentior reasoned. "We must go out."

Scio nodded, and the High Masters moved out toward the grieving City.

Hadrian was vaguely aware of following Ince to the entrance of the Star, where the entire Aureate Guard had assembled. Hadrian and Ince joined the stoic ranks, the lines of gray-cloaked men and women who watched, with hands clasped behind their backs, their faces emotionless, as the procession mounted the hill that led to the temple.

The queen's casket was proceded and followed by her advisors and personal servants, guards and handmaidens, all cloaked in black.

197

In the middle of the inky procession, her body was borne in coffin with a glass covering. She wore a flowing, white gown, and a net of pearls had been placed on her head. Her coverings matched her lily-white complexion. She looked, to Hadrian, like one asleep, floating amidst her mourners. The only change in her appearance was her hair, which had, in the final stages of her sickness, turned to a strangely luminescent ivory, sapped of its copper color as her body had been drained of health.

The procession came to a halt just outside the temple, in the central square of the city. The men carrying the coffin laid it on the cobbled ground and stepped back, forming a loose circle around the casket.

The queen's subjects had come forth from their homes in droves to pay their last respects to their beloved monarch; Hadrian watched a tiny child walk solemnly past the mourners and drop a fistful of white flowers onto the queen's casket. The air was heavy with muffled sobs.

The sky opened; rain fell in sheets from the gray clouds. As one, the members of the Aureate Guard turned the hoods of their cloaks up against the elements.

Beyond that, no one moved.

***

Lena's eyelids quivered. She felt that a cool cloth had been placed on her head, and thought dazedly that it felt like a cold, dead fish had been slapped across her brow. Cold and dead, like the hand of a corpse…

…like the hand of a corpse reaching up from death, staring, staring at her with wide, sightless eyes.

The spark of a memory flashed across Lena's mind; she sat up with a gasp and the cloth on her forehead fell into her lap.

A wiry, elderly woman was sitting in a chair in the corner of the room. She smiled at Lena, crossed to the bed and patted her gently on the arm. "There now," she said kindly. "No need to worry, you're safe here."

Lena stared blankly up at her. A sense of urgency nagged at her; she had to do something, she had to tell…to tell…

"Jairdan!" she said, her eyes wild. "I have to tell him! I have to tell him what I saw!"

"Easy now," the old woman said. She turned her back to Lena. "What you need, my dear, is a nice hot cup of tea and some soup, maybe. You can't be getting yourself all excited, not after such a hard ride…all night, Heavenly Star, what were you thinking? When that young soldier carried you in here, I thought to myself, goodness, the girl's ridden herself to exhaustion. Just right to exhaustion."

Lena was not listening. She swung her legs over the side of the bed and got to her feet. The old woman turned and made a move to stop her, but Lena shook her off. "You don't understand, I have to tell him—"

"You have to *rest*," the old healer said firmly, trying again to push Lena back into bed. Instead, Lena stumbled into a small nightstand and upset a porcelain vase on its surface. The vase careened to the floor and smashed.

The sound drew Roarke and Jairdan into the room. The healer tried ferociously to force them back out, hissing about indecency and the need for rest, but Jairdan did not listen to her this time. Without worrying about the heaviness of his tread, the volume of his breath, or the appalling indecency of seeing Lena in an ankle-length nightgown, he quickly put one arm around her for support; she looked pale and close to fainting.

He was surprised, therefore, when she caught his forearm in an iron grip and met his eyes. She was trembling, and close to tears, but she set her jaw and whispered, "Master…dead men…there are dead men in the Copper Fields."

"Dead men?" asked Jairdan. He glanced at Roarke, whose grip on the healer's arm had prevented her from throwing herself at Jairdan in fury. When the healer heard Lena's words, she fell back, stunned into silence. Roarke released her and gazed gravely at Lena.

She let Jairdan direct her gently back to the bed, and sat without protest, but she would not loosen her grasp on his arm; she clutched him like a frightened child.

199

"What men, Lena?" Jairdan asked. "What men did you see in the fields?"

"Twenty or more," Lena whispered. "All Westmorian...all... dead."

"Westmorian?" Roarke choked.

Lena nodded. "All with tunics bearing the oak leaf crest...and the brand...Roarke...the brand," she said. "I'm so sorry."

Lena fell silent, white with the horror of memory. Roarke got up and left the small and suffocating room, inwardly paralyzed by the awful connotations of her words. Jairdan tightened his grip on Lena's shoulders.

***

Roarke, Jairdan thought, handled well the horror of seeing the corpses of former comrades at arms strewn across a expansive field, some of them gnawed by wild beasts, all wide eyed with final terror.

Roarke went from one body to the next, pausing in silence beside each one, sometimes closing eyes with the sweep of his fingers, sometimes putting into an open palm a weapon that, at the final moment, had been just out of reach.

He reached one body, however, and lost his composure. He dropped to his knees and pulled the man's head into his lap. He bowed his head and touched it to the dead man's, and Jairdan saw Roarke's body shake with grief. "My brother!" Roarke shouted, turning to glare at Jairdan, his face ravaged by sorrow. "My younger brother!"

Jairdan bowed his head, letting his eyes drop away from Roarke's. The still air was punctuated only by the sounds of the grief that Roarke could not contain.

When he rejoined Jairdan, Roarke was silent, with bitter anger burning in his green eyes.

"This, then, is the work of Daimonas," he said darkly.

"Yes. He must have somehow discovered their location, and warned the Sanuulians, or your father."

"That was my brother," Roarke said, his voice taut with anger and grief. "My father could not..."

Jairdan put his hand on Roarke's arm, and the young man composed himself.

"These men deserved a proper send off to the next world," Roarke said. "I know a burial would take too much time; we should get back to the garrison quickly. But...something. I cannot just leave them."

"Perhaps...fire..." Jairdan suggested softly.

Roarke nodded jerkily. "Yes. Yes."

Somberly, the pair piled the bodies. When they were done, Roarke knelt and closed his eyes in prayer. Jairdan stepped forward and, with a sweep of his fingers, sent a flame dancing onto the pile. It caught quickly on cloaks and tunics, and soon the pile was a broad column of flame.

***

There were whispers, when they returned to the garrison. Roarke saw the men staring at him, knew that their murmuring was about him. He had known his secret would not last long, not here in the garrison. With so many soldiers, someone would have been bound to recognize him eventually. But Roarke had sacrificed the secret of his identity the night they had reached the garrison; he had cried out his name so that they would be allowed entrance, thrown off the cloak of his feigned identity. Now everyone knew that he was Prince Roarke, the son of a deranged monarch, a son, no less, who had betrayed and abandoned his father.

Chapter Twenty-One
The Realization

"I assure you, my lords, that I did not mean to cause such strife when I helped to heal the boy—what is his name—Hadrian?"

"Not at all," Scio replied. "We were merely interested in what power you used to cure him; we have been at a loss to do it ourselves."

"I studied with the monks of the Cristuk Isles as a lad," said Stoorm. "It is from them that I learned the cure. It is a basic formula—you say you had not thought of it yourselves?"

Scio ignored the needling. "The monks of the Cristuk Isles have been known to use the powers to create their medicines."

"Well, it worked, didn't it?" Stoorm said evenly, with an infuriating smile. "Or is your apprentice complaining of the cure?"

***

Roarke offered to stable the horses, both Jairdan's and his own, just for something to do, something to distract him from the vision of his dead comrades. When he entered the stables, Lena was seated on a stool in Lady's stall, gently grooming the dirt from her horse's flanks. The sight of her was immediately soothing to Roarke. She rose when she saw him, and when he had stabled the horses, approached him with grim and understanding eyes.

"I'm so sorry," she whispered, putting her hand on his shoulder.

Roarke nodded, and the two fell silent. Lena slipped her hand from Roarke's shoulder, but to her surprise, he caught and held it. Lena looked up at him, and met his steady eyes, with her own frightened ones. Roarke leaned in and kissed her gently on the cheek. She trembled.

Roarke pressed his lips to hers, and for a moment she returned the kiss, her eyes closed. Then, to his surprise, she pulled away. "I—I can't..." she whispered. "I'm sorry...but I can't." She turned away and walked quickly from the stables, Roarke too puzzled and hurt to stop her.

***

"High Masters." The young messenger entered the room with a sharp bow.

Scio nodded in return. "What news?"

"High Master, Queen Rhea has mobilized her troops in the desert. They march northward as we speak. Whether they intend to attack Aurea alone or to join with Bruteaus we cannot discern."

Prudentior sighed. "And no news from Amensliel? From Marii?"

"None, Master."

Chista shook his head grimly. "Thank you."

The messenger bowed again and left the room.

Scio put his hand to his head. No word from Lena or Jairdan...the queen's troops mobilized...and Scio was even beginning to question the safety within the Order. Hadrian had not come to apologize, and his insolence the night before was unusual enough in itself...the presence of Lord Stoorm, whoever he was, had seemed to add tension to everything. Scio doubted that the High Masters' order for Stoorm to remain in his quarters and not speak to any member of the Order would do anything to help. The damage, Scio feared, had already been done.

"Hadrian no longer trusts the Order," he said. "He has become a danger."

"A danger? Hadrian is disturbed, yes, but he would never harm a member of the Order," Prudentior said. "He will recover from what has happened and be as good an Aureate Guard as he ever was."

"Still," said Chista, "we cannot risk his paranoia deepening. He must be watched."

Scio nodded. "Yes. We must survey his movements."

"I will do it," Prudentior said. "I will find him and speak to him and see to it that he does no harm."

"Very well," Scio said. "Be careful of him, Prudentior. He is not in his right mind."

"I will be careful," Prudentior said. "But what I might be more worried about, Scio, is that Jairdan and the girl have sent no word. You know that I questioned the delegation of that task to the girl—"

"Lena and Jairdan will send a message soon," Scio said. "We will receive word from them before the week is out."

Prudentior raised his eyebrows. "I hope you are right," he said.

***

Hadrian was in the training room, his sword drawn. He was swinging viciously at an intangible foe.

This city, this order, is my life, he argued vehemently, lunging his blade forward.

Parrying an imaginary blow, he countered, *More's the pity, if it's been holding me back.*

But I know it hasn't been. This *is what's good, what's true.* He swung again.

But, —he parried and lunged—*am I willing to gamble my potential on that? If Stoorm's right...if the Aureate Guard squander skill, hinder talent...*

*But they don't. I know they don't. They've never...they've only encouraged...*Desperately, he scrambled backward, raising his blade to defend himself from a flurry of blows, almost more than he could keep up with...

...And when they did not heal my leg? When they didn't listen to me, allow me to go myself to Marii? I am the more experienced, the more capable...how could they be so blind as to send Lena in my place? They're threatened by my power, they know the prophecy, know that I'm supposed to be the best...know that I will be...they want me to fail, they don't want me to reach my

potential! His blade flashed like lightning, raining a more powerful series of attacks than his opponent could handle. He almost heard the slicing of flesh, the last, gasping breath.

Then there was silence.

Hadrian sheathed his sword with a terrible grin.

He had won.

***

When Roarke caught up to Lena, she was doubled over, clutching her waist, gasping in pain. His other emotions forgotten, Roarke dropped to his knees in front of her. "Lena? Lena what's wrong? Lena!"

She could not answer. She clutched his shoulder for support, gritting her teeth.

"Jairdan! Jairdan!" Roarke screamed. People stared. "Get Master Jairdan!" Roarke roared. "The girl's ill—get Master Jairdan!"

Jairdan was already streaking across the grounds. "What is it?" he asked. He crouched beside Roarke, cupped his hand under Lena's chin and raised her head. "Lena?"

She was shaking, red-faced, as if it were hard to breathe. "H-hadrian…something's wrong…very wrong…" Her eyes rolled back in her head. Roarke and Jairdan caught her as she fell forward into unconsciousness. It had begun to rain.

***

Lord Stoorm stood on the balcony of his room in the Aureate Temple. The rain had started lightly, but quickly begun to pour. Thunder purred in the distance; the inky sky was blue and white-veined with lightning. Stoorm raised his hands and turned his face upward to the elements. The wind whipped his cloak around him, and Stoorm began to laugh. He was vibrant, the source and power of the storm itself, and he threw his head back, laughing.

***

"Something's happening, something terrible's happening at the Star…Hadrian's in danger and I must go to him! He needs me!" Lena had woken now and was railing against the grips of Roarke and Jairdan.

"You must let me go; Hadrian needs me! He needs me!"

"Lena, please, just sit one moment and talk to us!" Jairdan begged.

Panting, Lena fell back. Tears streaked her face; she was clutching her stomach to rid it of painful cramps; every part of her vibrated with the terrible knowledge that something was very wrong. The rain pouring steadily down now; Lena's hair was matted against her head; her tunic was soaked.

"I can't explain how I know, but Hadrian needs me. I'm sure of it. I need to go back, to go back to the Star, back to him."

"But Lena, *I* need you. This was your mission. This!" Jairdan stabbed his forefinger into the ground. "You cannot forget what the High Masters would want. You were given this task in good faith, Lena. You cannot turn your back on that."

"My brother needs me," Lena whispered. "He could be in danger. The Star could be in danger, or the City! Master, please believe that I know the seriousness of this matter. Nothing but a feeling of the greatest importance could draw me back now."

Jairdan shook his head. "We have yet to cross the Crispin and get to Gnibri."

"Dodging a blockade is a task best undertaken by one. You'll slip through more easily without me. You are good at diplomacy; you can convince Gnibri that we need Marii's help."

"I don't know," Jairdan shook his head.

"Aquilus could fly ahead of me and get news of the city, then fly back and report it to you."

"And if there is no news?"

"Then he can report that to me. I will turn Lady around and accept whatever consequences come of my deserting the mission."

"Those consequences could determine the fate of Aurea!"

"What is happening to Hadrian right now will define our history," Lena said.

Her face was so grave, so serious and absolutely convincing, that Jairdan relented. "Go as quickly as possible," he said. "Send Aquilus ahead for news, and I warn you Lena, that this action, this decision, could decide what happens in Aurea, in this war, not to mention your future as an Aureate Guard."

Lena nodded.

"Go."

She got to her feet and sprinted to the stables. Lady was ready, stamping and snorting when Lena entered. Lena saddled and bridled her; Lady's saddlebags still held flask of water and half a loaf of bread. Lena pulled herself into the saddle and spurred Lady out of the stables, toward the entrance of the garrison.

Aquilus! Lena shouted for him, though there was no need. The bird was already streaking through the sky above.

As soon as I can make it so, you will know what is happening in Aurea.

Thank you, Aquilus.

I trust you, Child of Light. Now it is you who must trust yourself. Make great haste. If you sense that something is wrong, then it is. The bird darted further ahead and rose in the skies, into the clouds, out of sight.

Roarke stood at the garrison entrance, blocking Lena's way. Lena pulled up and Lady reared; Lena struggled to keep her seat in the saddle.

"What are you doing?" she cried.

"I cannot come with you; I am the one who must lead these men into battle. They need me."

"I didn't ask you to come!" Lena replied desperately. "Please, I must go, move aside."

Roarke touched her arm. "Before, in the stables…"

"I don't have time!" Lena cried, trying to wrench herself from his grasp.

"I may not see you again," Roarke said. "Or if we do meet, it may be in battle, and we will be lucky to both come out of that unharmed."

Lena fell silent.

"So, I pray that we do meet again, Lena of Aurea, and I pray that our reunion be in favored circumstances. If it be so—" he took her now unprotesting hand and kissed it delicately— "until then, my lady."

Lena blinked. "Until then," she breathed. She flicked her heels, and Lady lunged forward. Lena gripped the reins, determined not to look back. She succeeded for almost a minute, and when she did finally look over her shoulder, the young captain stood there still, staring after her.

Chapter Twenty-Two
The Attack

Hadrian descended the steps to Lord Stoorm's chamber with a fire burning in his eyes that was foreign to his countenance. No one who had ever known him would have recognized it. He reached the top of the stairs and saw, through the door to Stoorm's room, that the man was standing out in the tumultuous night, his back to his door. Hadrian stepped forward into the doorway.

Without turning, Stoorm greeted him. "Hello Hadrian."

***

Lena was breathing wildly, crouched low over Lady's lunging neck. "Not fast enough," Lena whispered desperately. "Faster…it's not fast enough."

Hadrian! Hadrian!

She concentrated all her efforts on reaching him. The distance was her obstacle; she had never communicated with Hadrian from so far away. Beads of sweat formed at her temples. Her heart raced. Lady tossed her head in the rain, her mane tangled in the wind. Lena knew it was a two day's ride to Aurea.

She would make it in one.

***

Prudentior searched for Hadrian in vain; the training room was empty, the dining hall vacant. The Star was grieving the loss of the Queen. Most people had withdrawn to their rooms. Prudentior had looked in Hadrian's chambers, and asked the young man in the adjoining room if he had seen him. No one seemed to know where he was. Prudentior was trying to suppress a growing sense of concern. He did not know where else to look.

***

Hadrian took the greeting as an invitation and entered Stoorm's chamber. Stoorm stepped in from outside. His eyes met Hadrian's. He saw the fire there, and he knew it for what it was.

"You are changed, my son," he said. "You have seen the light."

"I have seen the truth," Hadrian said. "You have shown it to me."

Stoorm smiled. "So you see now that I was right. The Aureate Guard are much too inebriated with their own power, much too dogmatic in their views. You understand."

"I do."

"And so the question is, Hadrian, what is to be done about it?"

Hadrian fixed his gaze on Stoorm's face, but he remained silent.

"They must be ousted from power, Hadrian. For the good of the city."

Hadrian inclined his head. "For the good of the city."

***

Aquilus shot like an arrow toward the City of the Aureate Star, but he need not have gone much further than the boundaries of the country itself. Within moments of entering it, he felt it.

The country was sick and dry, as if with queen's death it had sucked it of its lifeblood. But there was a worse sickness than death here; there was something terrible and alive, some malignant presence feeding on the country. This presence was at the heart of the Aurea, at its capitol, at the City of the Aureate Star.

It would take Aquilus half a day less to reach the city than it would Lena, though he had not her desperation. Before sunup, he was soaring over the city gates. He spiraled down to alight on a branch in the main gardens. He preened his feathers innocently while eavesdropping on a conversation that was happening below, between two men, High Masters, cloaked in the pre-dawn shadows.

"—grows more and more desperate. Sanuul has mobilized and still there is no word from Jairdan, or the girl. Scio, we are running out of time." This High Master was squat and bald. Aquilus struggled to recall his human name.

"I know that, Chista, that we can do nothing to affect their speed or communications. We must act here, as best we can." This came from the tiny, hunched old man, Scio. His name was one of few human names that Aquilus respected enough to commit to memory.

"And what is our best course of action, Master? Do we alert the citizens to the approaching danger from Sanuul? Fortify the city and risk terrifying them? We do not even know Rhea's plan. Will she meet Bruteaus at Gosriti and cross the Steadmark there, joined with his men? Or will she march due north, across the Shintu, over the Copper Plains? Will we fight a double-fronted war, with Westmore attacking from the west and Sanuul from the South? Or will we simply fight a single, joined enemy that is double our size and strength?"

Scio sighed. "These questions are unanswerable. Only time can tell. But we must secure the city, at the risk of frightening the citizens. Wherever we are attacked, I want us to be ready. And we will need to prepare to provision the farmers and their families on the outer plains; when the attack comes, they will seek shelter in the city, and we must be ready to provide it."

Aquilus considered revealing his presence, freeing the men at least from the yoke of uncertainty, revealing that Lena and Jairdan had reached Amensliel. But before he became mired down in a report, he would find out more information for the Golden One. She was his primary concern.

He had not yet found the source of the evil that he sensed resided in the Temple; something drew him to the upper levels, to the well-rounded bellies of the balconies that jutted out into the growing dawn. Around one of these the air hung like an icy shroud, poisoned from within by something in the inner chamber.

211

Aquilus was more furtive here; now he could take no risk of being seen. He huddled into a small alcove formed where the balcony met the wall of the temple and closed his eyes, his sharp hearing barely straining to overhear the conversation that was transpiring within the room.

"We are two against many. We will need allies, ones that can help us, if we are to overtake the city." This voice Aquilus recognized; it belonged the boy, the brother of the Golden One, but it had changed since he had last heard it. It sounded hollow, strange, void of all the care and kindness it ever had possessed. It even chilled Aquilus, whose animal senses knew fear but had never before encountered dread, this sick horror that Aquilus found welling within him. He had known animals to go mad and had heard the last thoughts of some, before they collapsed, frothing and twitching, into the arms of death. This voice possessed that angry fear, that recklessness.

"They are already here, my son." This voice, cold, hollow, was even more terrifying than the boy's, worse not because it was maddened but because it was not. It was deliberate, calm, with all the calculation of viper in the grass, waiting for its unsuspecting prey, waiting for the chance to strike.

No, Aquilus decided, this was a viper that had found its chance. This was the voice of one who was ready, who had finally achieved a terrible goal.

"Men? You have men here?" the boy sounded uncertain.

"Not men, my son. Allies."

There was a momentary silence, the rustling of cloth. Then, Daimonas extended his summons, and a wave electrifying power sent Aquilus reeling from the window.

***

She had never pushed Lady so hard, not even the night that they fled the dead corpses in the Copper Fields. Lady's coat was slick with sweat, the saddle sliding, chafing her back. Lena's grip on the reins was white-knuckled, her eyes fixed on the horizon.

A screech overhead made her look to the sky. Aquilus circled overhead. His voice sounded in her head, more urgent than it ever had. *You must hurry. Your city, your country, are in danger.*

What did you see?

You must hurry!

I cannot push Lady any harder. She won't make it before sunset.

That will be too late!

His desperation terrified her and made her seize with hopelessness.

Fly with me!

What?

Fly with me!

How?

Meditate, as you did the first night that I met you. See yourself flying and you will.

That's impossible!

Try.

Barely believing that she was attempting it, sure that it would not work, Lena closed her eyes and tried to see the landscape as it would appear from Aquilus' view. But now, as usually happened when she tried to meditate, darkness encompassed her. Panicked, she opened her eyes again. *I can't!* she cried.

You must! Everything depends on it! Aquilus beat his wings furiously in frustration and desperation.

Lena closed her eyes again. The darkness crept in, framing the vision of her mind's eye, but she beat it back...*beat it back with wings, and saw the ground beneath her. Saw it from thirty feet above.*

In the saddle, Lena spread her arms, releasing the reins, and began to slide sideways. Unconscious of the movement, she made no attempt to hold herself in the saddle. Lady whinnied as Lena slipped off her back accipitrine

...and was caught in an updraft that carried her skywards, to where Aquilus waited.

This is impossible, she whispered.

No child, Aquilus responded, *if it were impossible, you could not be doing it.*

***

The indoor shelters at Amensliel were crowded, full of people eager to avoid the rain. Men were packed shoulder to shoulder into the huts where Jairdan and Roarke had chosen to take shelter.

A slow sense of dread had begun to grip Jairdan. As the storm raged on, the emotion slithered into the room like a serpent, coiled itself around Jairdan and constricted slowly. Doing his best to shake the feeling from himself, Jairdan tried to engage Roarke in discussion.

"When do you—" he cut his attempt at conversation short when he saw Roarke's face. The young captain did not looked seized by dread, as Jairdan was; he looked like a spring, taut, trembling to release its energy. He looked like his veins had been injected with lightning. When he rose his eyes to meet Jairdan's, his gaze burned.

***

Hadrian went to the balcony and looked out over the City. He could see the dark mass that was approaching the City. A slow, sickening grin spread across his face.

"They are powerful," he said.

"Their presence will create chaos, and their strength with crush our lesser foes. It is to the greater ones that we must turn our attentions."

Hadrian nodded and faced Daimonas, looking away from the enormous pack of black wolves that was making its way toward the city.

***

Hadrian! Hadrian! Lena thought she would die of frustration. Why does he not answer? she begged of Aquilus.

The hawk flying beside her looked troubled. It was an emotion Lena had never seen before in Aquilus, and it frightened her. *There is something you have not told me,* she ventured. *Something about my brother. Is he all right?*

Aquilus himself was surprised to discover that it pained him to tell her. *He is sick,* he replied hesitantly.

Sick? With what? What's wrong with him?

Something has happened in our absence. The country, the city, has been deceived by a lord of evil. He has latched on to your city like a tumor. He has poisoned your brother's mind against the order.

Lena was silent. Then, she shook her head, beat her wings so she was a stroke ahead of Aquilus. *That's wrong. I do not believe you.*

You will see soon enough.

They neared the City now, and Lena felt it, suddenly and deeply. It was a presence, terrifying not because it was foreign but because it was familiar. Lena tumbled from the air, as if blown back by a sudden wind gust. She fell to the earth with a cry, and Aquilus watched her body change as it fell, from the body of a bird to that of a human.

Aquilus circled down to her sprawled body. Luckily, she had not been far from the ground when she had returned completely to her human form; the fall had not been injurious. Therefore, when she raised her head, Aquilus was surprised to see tears in her eyes.

What is it, Golden One? What did you see?

"Daimonas," Lena whispered aloud. "He is here."

Aquilus did not know the name, but the horror in her voice told him that it was the same man whose voice he had overheard. He understood now what had made her plummet from the sky; her terror at recognizing the presence of that evil in her beloved city had broken the extreme concentration that she needed to preserve flight.

Lena sat up. Her body trembled, but her eyes burned with grim purpose. The city gates were in view; not a hundred yards from where she had fallen. She got to her feet, unsheathed her sword, and began to run.

***

The wolves moved like an ocean, leaping and sprinting, one overtaking the other, then falling back; they came in black waves toward the City; they were a hundred minds of a single purpose, maddened with Daimonas' poison. They snapped their jaws and yipped as they ran, wild and frenzied.

Lena did not see them approaching.

Aquilus turned, his senses screaming that predators approached. He screeched his warning to Lena, who had just made the last strides to the City gates. Now, she spun, saw the wolves, and took one step backward, her spine grazing the tall, wooden gates. She could not now call to the guard to open it and admit her, for in doing so, he would also open the gates to the wolves.

To the beasts it was a game; they, danced, snarled, snapped around her. Given no other choice, Lena unsheathed her sword, knowing it was useless, knowing that one blade against a hundred wolves afforded her only moments.

But the night that Lena had named her blade, something had happened to it. Blades in the hands of Aureate Soldiers became different, malleable. The night that Lena had christened her blade "Wolf's Bane," she had molded it to a specific task.

The wolves shied away from the blade, none wanting to test its strength, or the girl's desperation. The pack knew what ferocity cornered prey was capable of; they were unwilling to feel the sting of steel.

You know this blade! Aquilus screeched from above. *And you should know its wielder! This is the Golden One, the savior of the land! You have allowed yourself to be poisoned, to be fooled, by the one who would defy this girl! But you are beasts of the earth! You know the consequences, for all, should this girl be killed. You know!*

Breathless with fear, Lena watched for a reaction, brandishing the blade. Then she saw him. The alpha, the scarred, one-eyed male, was swaggering to the forefront.

Are you all fools, to be tricked by a creature of the air? the alpha asked scathingly. *This is not the chosen one. The boy is the Chosen One. Our master has told us.*

Our master has told us, the wolves repeated. *Our master has told us.*

You are wild beasts, not domestics! Aquilus screeched. *You sound like cattle, dulled by the whip. Master? You have no master!*

This feathered one is irksome. Kill him, before we kill the girl.

Some of the wolves hesitated, but one, deranged with anticipation, leaped and snapped at Aquilus, catching some of the bird's feathers in his teeth. Aquilus spiraled upward, shrieking.

Lena crouched, ready for the attack that she knew would now come. One wolf jumped at her and met its death on her blade. But then two more leaped, and Lena was knocked to the ground. She tucked her chin, refusing to expose her throat. She rocked back against the city gates, and felt them give way. She risked a glance behind her and saw them opening to release the Aureate Guard, blades drawn, glorious in multitude. A hand grasped her upper arm, hauled her to her feet. A voice whispered, "Go to the Star. It is your brother. Few remain, and they are doomed without you." The warrior who had paused to pull Lena to her feet was pounced on by a snarling wolf. He fell to the ground, the wolf on his chest. Lena hesitated.

The man stabbed the wolf and yelled, "Go, or it will have been for nothing!"

Lena ran.

Chapter Twenty-Three
Within the Star

Lena reached the Temple, stepped through the door that had yielded to the gusts of wind, and met a scene of complete chaos. No knowledge of what had happened in her absence could have prepared her for what she saw. Bodies lay strewn across the scorched, marble floors, some still writhing in the last, agonizing grip of death. Daimonas stood at the top of the stairs in his true form, his arms raised. Lena took a step toward the staircase, but he brought his arms together, and one of the pillars in the entrance hall cracked in the middle. Lena dove to the floor as the top half tumbled from the ceiling and landed on the marble floor and smashed, sending pieces flying.

Lena rose from the plaster dust, still gripping Wolf's Bane. The pillar had fallen across the first steps of the staircase; Daimonas had gone. Lena scrambled over the pillar, and hesitated on the steps. She closed her eyes, breathed deeply.

Show me the way to Hadrian.

***

In another room of the Star, Hadrian stabbed a former comrade through the abdomen and threw her aside, leaving her for dead. He smiled and turned to Daimonas, who now stood calmly by the window, watching the Aureate Guard fight the wolves below.

"My sister is here," Hadrian told him.

"Go and meet her."

Hadrian nodded, stepped over the pile of bodies that he had dispatched, and hurried down the hall.

***

Humans who house opposing forces will be inseparable, even in their hatred of each other, the Eternal Paradox reads. *They may be as one for but a moment in time, and then the natural order of things will interject. They are either side of the scales which must always remain balanced; the prevalence of one over the other will determine the fate of the world. One will fall, the other will prevail. Their story will be the great tragedy of the world. Only one can be good; one will be evil, though mankind will try to intervene, and risk damning itself in the process.*

There was momentary silence in the room, when Lena and Hadrian finally met. The clashing of swords, crumbling of stone, the screams and curses, faded to the background.

Lena's eyes had rid themselves of tears, but the paths these tears had taken were left as streaks in the plaster and grime that dirtied her face.

Hadrian had not wept, had not known remorse that day. He met his sister's gaze with defiance in his eyes, though the simplicity and apathy of her question caught him off guard.

Why? she asked, her voice as cold and frozen as ice.

Because it is right, Lena. I see now, that you, Jairdan, Scio, all the others, were trying all this time to overcome me. But I have found a power now that is incomparable to any other. Your own pales in comparison.

Lena snorted. "You have found no truth. You have simply seen temptation, and you have let it corrupt you." In her scorn she abandoned the intimacy of thought-speak for the spoken word, dull in comparison. "Look at what you have done," she commanded. "Look at the bodies of your companions, dead on your sword!"

Hadrian shook his head. "No. No. I do not need to look. It was the right thing. It was," he muttered, nodding.

"And you will kill your own sister, in pursuance of the object of your greed."

This seemed too much. Hadrian glanced fervently aside. "No. I mean not to kill you, Lena. If you will only join us…I feel certain I can convince my partner in this that you are good, that you will help us to undermine the Guard."

"Your partner? Hadrian, are you so naive? Your partner is Daimonas, my former master, and he does not share power. He will kill you when you are no longer useful to him."

"That's not true," Hadrian said. "Lena, it's not. Lord Stoorm, Lord Stoorm is my partner. He is from Westmore, not Sanuul."

"He has tricked you, Hadrian. He has made you believe that, but soon, you will see the truth."

"I have seen the truth!" Hadrian snapped. "And I was wrong to sway from it. Stoorm said you were conniving, and I see now that it is true. You are my enemy, Lena. You, and your Order."

Lena nodded. "My Order," she said. "You certainly have no claim to it now."

"And I want none!" Hadrian snarled. "My only goal here is to destroy it."

"Then you have met your adversary," Lena said, tightening her grip on the hilt of her blade. "I would rather die than see the ruin of this Order."

"Well then, as you were my sister, I'll oblige you!" Hadrian snapped, wielding his own sword.

The twins clashed at the center of the room, their blades ringing as they met. Lena spun, Hadrian blocked; their swords locked. Neither was strong enough; finally they each took a step back. Lena brandished her blade, but waited for Hadrian's attack.

It came with ferocity. He swung his sword in an uppercut that would have cut Lena belly to breast if she had not stepped back just in time. Before she could recover, Hadrian swung again, this time knocking her blade from her hand. It skittered away across the floor. Hadrian looked after it, granting Lena the opportunity to roll behind an overturned table, out of his sight. She glanced at her blade and reached out a hand to call it to her. The hilt trembled, but was subdued by Hadrian's boot. He pressed it to the floor, grinning, and looked up, eager to see Lena's expression. She was gone.

She leaped on him from behind, knocking him to floor, and heard the air go from his lungs. Still atop him, she grabbed her sword.

Hadrian uncurled and rose with such force that Lena, while still gripping her sword, was flung to her back on the floor. She scrambled to her feet, lunged at Hadrian with her blade. He blocked it and knocked her blow easily aside. Lena tried again, and again was parried. Once more their blades locked; still they were at an impasse.

Lena narrowed her eyes at her brother, sweat streaming as she focused. To his shock, Hadrian was lifted from his feet and thrown the length of the room. Lena approached her dazed brother at a sprint, but Hadrian jerked his head up and caught his sister in his gaze. He raised his stare, and she rose with it, her feet leaving the floor.

You thought you could outdo me? You thought I could not learn this power?

He threw his gaze to the ground and Lena slammed against the marble tile. He had not blinked; she was still a prisoner of his stare. She writhed, burning in his gaze. Her fingers unclenched spasmodically; her blade fell from her hand. Her back arched, her neck twisted, her legs and arms turned out at odd angles.

Hadrian blinked.

Her limbs untangled, she lie free from the physical pain but not the torment of his betrayal. She sobbed when he kicked her blade out of reach, wielded his own high above her head. She glanced up into his face, his terrible, thunderous face, for what she believed would be the last time.

Hadrian took a deep breath and brought down his blade.

He turned it in mid-swoop so that it was the hilt, not the blade that cracked against Lena's forehead. Then, he spit on her unconscious form and stalked out of the room.

Twenty-Four
Safety by the Sea

Scio was running. He had lost track of Chista; they had each gone to a separate part of the Star in desperate attempts to secure it. The attack had blindsided them. It had come shortly after the funeral procession; he and Chista had been speaking in the gardens, and someone within the Star had screamed. More cries rose, and upon charging into the Star, Scio had seen something that made him freeze with dread.

The worst had happened. Hadrian was furiously fighting his own companions, attacking them without hesitation or remorse. He felled three before Scio had even mounted the stairs. There was a new and terrible fury in Hadrian. Scio called to him in an attempt to distract him; the boy turned, but seemed infuriated at hearing his own name. He spun and cut down two more of his former friends as Scio raced up the stairs, unable to stop him. Then, just before Scio reached the top, Hadrian turned and disappeared down a corridor, away from him.

Scio had started to follow, but noticed a thick, crimson smog rising from the stone floor. He backed away, motioning for the Guardsmen charging up the stairs behind him to get back. "It's poison fog!" Scio said. "Get back. We'll have to use another stair. Get back!"

He knew that Hadrian's knowledge did not extend to conjuring poisonous smoke. His darkest suspicions about Stoorm confirmed, Scio was now hastening to the chamber they had given him.

The noxious fog filled the entire corridor. Scio raised his hands and made a swift gesture. The smoke rolled back as if blown away by a sudden gust of wind. Scio stepped in front of Stoorm's door, the smoke already billowing back up around him. With a hand motion from Scio, the door burst open.

Scio stepped into the room. The orchestrator of this terror was sitting calmly within the room, looking as Scio had always seen him.

"Scio. I suspected you would come."

"You are Daimonas," Scio said.

The man rose. "That is correct," he said.

Scio moved first. The blast that Daimonas had sent toward him with a small motion of his fingers swept over the place where Scio had been standing, catching instead a small table and smashing it to splinters against the wall.

Scio hit the ground and rolled. He jumped to his feet and sent a net of power toward Daimonas, who leaped into the air and swooped toward Scio like a bat. Scio put his hands up and Daimonas hit an invisible wall; he crumpled in the air and landed in a heap on the floor.

He was up again in a second, snarling at Scio, changing form as he lunged. His skin turned black, lightning veins visible. His hair lengthened and turned silver, and his eyes were silver slits. Scio moved his hands in a series of complicated patterns; a golden net appeared in the air. Daimonas had misjudged his leap; Scio moved the net into his path and Daimonas fell, shrieking, seized in its folds. Scio moved his hands in the air, twisting the netting around his captured opponent. Daimonas fixed his glare on Scio, and suddenly Scio's body burned in pain. He lost concentration and fell back, skin searing.

Daimonas snarled and the net disintegrated. When Daimonas rose, golden scars shone on his black skin. Hissing with rage, he charged again at Scio. The High Master tried to put up a shield, but he was not in time. Daimonas tackled him, knocking him to the ground and mauling him like an animal with his claws. Scio focused through the pain and managed to send Daimonas flying backward with a surge of power. Bloody and exhausted, Scio made one last attempt; he netted Daimonas again in the golden ropes, trying to wrap them around his opponent's throat. Daimonas hissed and whined in the clutches of the burning net. He struggled to stand and staggered to the balcony, Scio trying to pull him back but instead being dragged along behind him. Daimonas reached the balcony and leaped; Scio had to release his hold or else be dragged over with him. As he watched, Daimonas released himself from the golden bonds in midair and suddenly, in an explosion of black, sprouted enormous, bat-like wings that guided him safely through a window on another level. Scio, bloodied and worn, hurried back down the stairs, searching desperately for Daimonas, or at least the boy.

He was overwhelmed by the scene in the atrium of the Star. In the time that Scio had taken to duel Daimonas, Hadrian had been merciless. Bodies were strewn across the floor, many dead by Hadrian's sword. Some, Scio could tell, had asphyxiated from the poison gas.

He heard the swoop of wings from outside the Star and ran through the door. He was just in time to see Daimonas alight on the steps of the Star and transform back into a human. Hadrian ran to him from the gardens. Scio lunged, but Daimonas grabbed Hadrian's arm, and the two of them disappeared. Scio fell to the ground, clutching at the empty air, and shaking with grief.

The buildings outside the Star were on fire. The wolves were devouring the dead in the streets. The City was ruined.

***

Lena awoke with a blinding headache. She put a hand to her forehead and felt a large lump.

Something moved in the shadows of an adjoining room. Lena sat bolt upright, her hand scrabbling for her sword.

"Mistress Lena?"

It was a whisper that nearly broke her heart. She let the blade slip from her fingertips. "Elissa!"

The little girl was running, her skin streaked with grime and blood, her dress stained with sweat. She fell into Lena's embrace, sobbing, shuddering, inconsolate.

"The others?" Lena asked. "Elissa, the others?"

Elissa pulled her face from Lena's shoulder. Her features crumpled with horror, sorrow, exhaustion; she shook her head.

"Crispin? Roland?"

Elissa sobbed harder and buried her face in Lena's shoulder. "We all hid," she said, her voice broken by tears. "We hid, because Lady Magistra came and told us to. I was hiding with Roland behind the curtains. And then Hadrian came, and he found Lady Magistra and she screamed and Roland jumped out to help her and he...Hadrian found everyone but me and now they're gone and gone and I'm the only...the only one..." she broke down, her hysterical voice falling to grief.

Lena gasped and clutched the little girl close to her, her eyes wide with disbelief.

***

Scio waded through the rubble of what had been the home of the Aureate Guard. Broken glass clinked against crumbled stone. Scio surveyed the dead, the countless dead, who lie among the carnage.

One still had breath. His chest rose and fell sharply. Scio hurried to the side of the dying Prudentior, who had been run through by Hadrian's blade.

"I found him at the last," Prudentior said, "and felt his blade. It seems I mistrusted the wrong twin," he said, laughing apprehensively through his pain. "Will you...will you tell the girl for me...that I apologize?" he gasped, near death.

Scio nodded, put his hand on the man's shoulder. "I will," he said.

Prudentior gasped again, nodded. "Thank you," he said, and death took him.

***

Lena led Elissa through the ruined building by the hand. The little girl had inserted one sooty thumb into her mouth. Her tears and sweat had nearly washed her face clean.

Lena saw one still alive, and rushed to his side. Her eyes welled at the sight of him, her fallen friend, Ince...it was too much to bear.

"Ince..." she whispered, dropping to her knees, not caring that bits of broken glass scratched and cut her when she did. She pulled his head onto her lap, stroked his pale face, took his clammy hand in hers. "Hadrian?" she asked.

Ince nodded, his face wrinkled with confusion. "I don't... understand..." he said.

"He was possessed," Lena said. "Corrupted. Not himself."

"Aah." This seemed to give Ince some inner peace. "Not himself. When I saw him, I almost didn't recognize him. He was different...changed. I went to find him because there was trouble...I thought he would help."

Lena was weeping.

Ince seemed intent to tell her one more thing before his time ran out. "Lena, before you left for Marii, there was something I wanted to tell you, but I had not the courage." He smiled. "Strange now, that I find it in death."

"No. Not death." Lena shook her head desperately, looking at his wounds.

"Lena." He squeezed her hand. "I am dying. Before I do, I wanted to tell you. I love you, Lena. You were the first one. The only one."

Lena gasped, her lips trembling, her eyes streaming.

Ince smiled. The smile became frozen on his face as it was paralyzed by death. His lungs emptied in a final sigh, and he, too, was gone.

***

Jairdan was making his way across green fields, to the banks of the Crysalin River. A strange, sudden pain in his side caught him off guard. He had to sit, closing his eyes, pained at what it meant.

Lena had been right. Something was wrong.

***

Hadrian looked back over his shoulder, at the wreckage that had been the capitol city of Aurea. They had left the city razed to the

226

ground, every building torched, every protester murdered. Men, women, children, strangers, friends…he had not distinguished.

"I hope I do no detect…regret, Hadrian?" The icy cold voice of Lord Stoorm pulled Hadrian from his thoughts.

"No," he said quickly. "No, of course not."

***

The girl emerged from the smoke and dust like a vision. For a moment, she was lighted by the sun, its rays filtering in through the broken windows, every one of her features thrown into sharp relief, so that she looked classically heroic. Then, she came forward into the reality of shadows and meager light, bloodied, weeping, leading a small child by the hand, and it was somehow more impressive.

Scio stepped forward, his arm outstretched, for the girl looked close to collapse.

"It's gone!" she cried. "Everything is gone, gone beyond recall!"

A screech from outside the window made Scio turn and shade his eyes to see a huge bird sail through the broken window. As Lena swayed, the bird landed in front of her and spread its wings. She fell and was supported by its massive wingspan, sobbing, bleeding, sweating into its feathers.

You *remain, Child of Light. And so hope has not gone yet.*

***

The rain stopped. Roarke took a deep breath, and plunged through the crowd, the way Jairdan had gone. Roarke wished now that he could have gone with him. He would have traded any lot for his, done anything to avoid stepping forward and declaring himself the betrayer son of a mad king. What reason had the people to believe in him?

But Lena had known, and had believed in him. Roarke found great comfort in this knowledge. He stepped out into the rain.

"Soldiers! Warriors! Join me now, if you hold true to the alliance, for I am Roarke of Eglionan, Son of His Majesty Bruteaus and the

Queen Lady Elixa, Captain of the Westmorian Army, Prince of the Western Lands, Heir to the Throne of the Country of Westmore, and our time has come!"

***

After five days, Hadrian had the courage to ask.

"Forgive me, but I thought that Westmore had much more greenery than this. Is this sand, this desolation because we are so near the desert?"

"No," Stoorm replied coldly. "It is because we are *in* the desert."

"What?"

Stoorm smiled. "I'm afraid I lied to you Hadrian. My name is not Lord Stoorm, and I am not a refugee from Westmore. My name is Lord Daimonas."

"No!" Hadrian gasped. He tugged at his horse's reins, pulling away from his companion. "I—I thought…"

"What you thought was a lie."

"But you—you tortured my sister! You took the first seventeen years of her life! You tried to corrupt her as…as you have me."

Daimonas sighed, pulled his horse to a stop. "This is very tiresome, Hadrian. Do you intend to continue this strain of madness?"

"Madness…madness I must have been mad to follow a murderer, a snake like you, Star above, what have I done?"

"I see." Daimonas rose his hands, shook back his sleeves, and swooped his hands downward.

The boy fell, unconscious, from the saddle. Daimonas raised his hands and the boy rose, levitated by Daimonas' power. When Daimonas nudged his horse forward, the boy moved forward as well, still suspended in the air, still unconscious.

When he awoke again, he was lying on the stone floor of a dungeon. He sat up, slowly recalling the events of the past hours. Shaking with horror, he closed his eyes and saw the events of the massacre in the city, and was violently sick on the floor.

When the door opened to admit Daimonas, Hadrian did not know how much time had passed. Hadrian moved to lunge at the man, but Daimonas extended a hand and froze him where he was.

"I was disturbed by that outburst in the desert, Hadrian," he said. "I think, perhaps, you need a reminder, of who you serve, and why."

Daimonas turned his hand slowly, and the boy rotated with it, so that his back faced Daimonas. The dark master took a dagger from the folds of his cloak and sliced through the cloth of Hadrian's tunic, so that the boy's left shoulder was exposed. He pressed his fingers into the boy's skin at the shoulder blade, until a white-hot pain blossomed there. Hadrian's muscles tensed; he screamed. He could not see the ebony stone that had grown where Daimonas's fingers had been, but he could feel it, the pain radiating from the fresh Keeping Stone, filling his body, wracking it with spasms, as Daimonas released him from his paralysis.

Hadrian's screams filled the lower level of palace. Daimonas walked slowly, delaying the ascension of the staircase, so he could hear.

***

It took Scio, Lena, and the little Elissa a week on horseback to reach their destination. Lena felt hollow inside. The only spark that she had left was the little girl, bobbing in front of her in the saddle, one hand clutching the Lady's mane, the other clinging to Lena's sleeve.

Scio led the way to the safe haven. It was in the northeast of Aurea, too far from the capital, frequented by too few warriors, to be worth a blockade by enemy troops. Scio led them to a cave in the wall of rocks by the sea. The floor was damp, but Lena and Elissa were hopelessly exhausted. They lay down together on the floor of the cave and entered a deep and dreamless sleep.

Scio watched, then went to the sea and stared for a long while at the crashing waves. When he returned to the cave, the sun was setting. He looked in at Lena's sleeping figure, curled comfortingly around that of the child

As the day faded, the last scarlet and orange rays of the sun highlighted the slumbering form of the world's last hope.

Printed in the United States
129666LV00001B/1-48/P